Decrescendo

by Gerry Brennan

Decrescendo

ISBN-13: 978-0-9978706-9-5
ISBN-10: 0997870699

for more books, visit Pski's Porch:
www.pskisporch.com

Printed in U.S.A.

To John Brown for helping me fight the good fight.

Decrescendo

Decrescendo

CHAPTER 1: TRAVELLING ON A GUSMAOBILE

The precision built mechanical marvel that is an aircraft started its slow, inevitable, interminable wind up towards take off. She sat petrified, if indeed that was the correct word - in the midst of her terror, she paused to wonder if it was the right word and also, if indeed there always was a right word. The week before, her father had drummed into her head all the relevant statistics which conclusively proved just what a safe mode of travel flying actually was but the initial whirr of the gigantic engines had shredded those statistics to the meaningless confetti of worthless data she had known them to be in the first place. Up here in the clouds-if we ever even get that far - there is no reassurance in the fact that road travel is ten times more dangerous. Oh for the hum of a combustion engine... one attached to an ancient bus with rusting body and loose chassis and struggling gearbox. The ascent was worse, the clouds were worse, the descent was worse... even the smell of the airport waiting area, which had no discernible smell, was worse. Blame it all or at least some of it on that crazy Portuguese speaking padre, Bartolomeu de Gusmão wanting to imitate the birds.

Caged at thirty thousand feet, profane, inane, insane and my fear of flying is not a phobia nor is it irrational - perhaps I have a fear of water and therefore don't like to be too near the clouds. Camels cost too much to feed assuming you can master the humps and boats hit icebergs except for the Titanic, which hit an iceberg - singular. All around her people were smiling, apparently enjoying the experience, pointing out the serene æsthetics of cloud formation to each other as if each one had some kind of unique personality. Fools. Didn't they realise how even the failure of a single strand of wire or the unloosening of a mere metal nut could spell disaster? Not to say the human side of the equation - some jubilant aircraft mechanic quaffing the champagne the night before, possibly celebrating the fact that some girl with mousey hair had done them the honour of consenting to become their betrothed or worse still what if mousey hair had spurned his attentions - felt too good to hitch her wagon to a man whose hands tightened nuts for a living and so there was no uncorked bottles of bubbly, merely a depressed, suicidal aircraft mechanic turning up for his utterly pointless, meaningless 5 A.M shift-his world in pieces - shattered - sundered beyond all repair - what did he care if the big metal bird with the intricate parts were to suffer a similar fate to his heart. Mousey hair has probably had a lie in this morning - no 7 A.M. flight for her.

Recovering no doubt from the fatigue of the dinner date the previous evening when Roger the mechanic had the audacity to propose to her - the cheek of him. She may have mousey hair and a face to match but that dœsn't mean she hasn't got an exalted picture of herself. Dear old Roger's not a bad catch but I'm sure I could do a trifle better. What dœs it matter anyway that I've got mousey hair as he only runs his fingers through it in the

dark and even if it were blonde or black or brunette, he'd
barely notice. Hardly my fault that he dœsn't reach that
distant part of me - the one full of mystique and enchant-
ment. No, but it was your fault for encouraging poor old
Roger that the girl next door could possibly be his soul
mate - I mean even you must have known the statistical
unlikelihood of that one - what were the chances? The
other side of town perhaps or even half a dozen streets
away or at a push the other side of the street perhaps...
but the house next door?

Billions of people, countless dialects, five continents not
to mention all those thousands of scattered little islands
dotting the entire planet and yet you didn't slap him
down when he thought he was in love with you and your
mousey hair all the way from next door? Perhaps it was
the travel sickness en route.

And to make matters worse you're the only female in
a family of five children - at least if you'd been one of
three or four sisters, you could have deluded yourself with
the notion that he'd fallen in love with you despite the
fact that your older sister had a mane of lustrous blonde
hair or that your youngest sister had a deeper cleavage
or at the very least dear Roger had had to wrestle with
his emotions to finally decide which of the charming
sisters had won his heart. But no - you didn't so much
invent a statistically improbable fairy tale - more that
you chopped down the tree yourself to get the lumber to
make the paper that it was to be written on and now I'm
left with the consequences of sitting close to the wing that
carries the engine that his nervous, hapless, despairing

fingers oversaw as fit to fly... I may never forgive you.

Touchdown (is it one or two words), is it the most beautiful word in the English language and if it is it's the most beautiful word in any language because English is the most beautiful language. All languages are religious in nature... protecting what they have... consolidating... conserving... avoiding awkward truths about the purpose of language, that indeed its raison d'être has to be communication, all other facets and considerations are subsidiary. Languages proud and noble and defiant. Verbal genealogy to let us know we can do more than grunt and squawk. Each language a temple to its past. Sacred past. Sacred cow. Altar of the unchanging. English - Kings English, Queens English too, a gift to the great unwashed to do with it what you will... expand it at random but never let it contract nor remain static. In the temples of language English has no Cathedral. No high priest. Seeks solely to be unburdened from the idea of language as deific sound... evolution its spur. English, embracer of all it seeks to comprehend. Expansive and expanding. Growing and living. Breathing and breathless. Being both match and fuse. Discontented to remain as fixed and immutable. For why be silent when you can be speechless or muted or quiet or noiseless or taciturn or reticent or reserved or laconic or saturnine... why not just be dumb.

Kate greeted the soft warm September air with the relief of a condemned woman whose trapdoor had just jammed. Praise be the lord for rusting hinges.

Lisbon - city of ghosts proudly standing in majesty's elegant decay. Lisboa, untouched by Achilles heel. Discoveries - but of what. Brazil could have remained Brazil and India's dust need not have been exported. Mind you gold too has its majesty and is slow to decay but it encourages decadence - save the natives from its mesmerising pull - protect them from the lure - leave them free to seek liberation from worldly goods and all illusion contained within.

The love of evil is the root of all money. The love of money is the route of all discoverers. She stepped down from the aircraft - not yet sixteen years old - and she wondered if she looked as lost as she felt.

A human package deported, departed, to foreign lands. Belfast to Lisbon. Too much trouble in that city better off in a city whose troubles lie in other distant lands. The Irish don't understand colonization - may not have had enough experience - eight hundred years is but a flash in an eternity and eternity itself is but a flash in all eternity - all debates on this subject fell into but two categories - one side which was told by the victims (real or imaginary) and a second one which was told by the revisionists/apologists/explainers, yet you couldn't but feel that if the 'explainers', no matter how erudite, had to swap the comfortable leather chairs in their studies at Cambridge for repeated belts of a rifle butt on a dusty trail in Goa or had their face spat upon for daring to speak their native tongue by the edge of some derelict bog in Tipperary, that they just might have a slightly different appraisal of why any time or age necessitated empire.

She found that she was lost and this in itself can be progress of a sort. Going to start a new life with some

Decrescendo

old lady of forty two - mind you forty two sounds less
than forty and a lot more interesting too. Charity begins
in faraway places it seems. Some woman whose floors
her mother scrubbed in some big house kindly offered to
arrange for her to live with her friend who also has a big
house which has floors that need scrubbing but as Kate
had refused to ever scrub anyone else's floors - they had
instead arranged simply for her to be companion to some
very old lady or other, the mother of forty two. After all
who'd live in a big house if they had to scrub the floors
themselves... If the floor scrub test was applied, Kings
and Queens and the odd Prince or two would live in
rooms the size of postage stamps-very cramped but easy
to clean. Better to forsake the swinging of cats if it means
kneeling on hard floors oneself. Still, I suppose one could
always give the paid help a thick satin cushion to kneel
upon whilst scrubbing but that in itself would be halfway
toward an admission that all was not well with such a
scheme - what if the scrubber was sixty with poor old arthritic knees and the scrubbee or homeowner was young
and healthy. And further to this scenario, what if they ate
well, swallowed vitamin pills, slept on a feather bed and
used silk sheets to rest their wearyless limbs upon. It's a
ball of string not to unwind as each unwound strand only
rebounds to tie you in knots as it were - that's all you get
for your immense humanity and wanting to provide a
cushion for that bony kneed oul scrubber.

No sign of the old woman of forty two supposed to pick
her up. Sit down at the café bar and throw your money
about, the money that your mother scrubbed big floors

in big houses for. Have some água in a glass - it's a dirty glass by the looks of it but you've been reared to interpret unclean things as a source of silver - pay dirt. Money gained from scrubbing dirty floors can't really demand a clean glass - too unironic. The Portuguese refuse to call água by its real name of water. I bet all those Portuguese sailors toiling through the heat and dust of faraway lands wouldn't have said no to a glass of cool water - two glasses of water or one glass of água... choose.

Still no sign of forty two - perhaps she has a phobia of scrubber's daughters.

Her father too refused to scrub floors - told her mother that it belittled a pœt to serve others. She in turn told him that the money scrubbers earned bought the same things as the money neurosurgeons earned and beside they both dirtied their hands. She didn't bother saying that they were paid a trifle less as she assumed he knew this much at least. Once she had asked him to define what exactly this thing called pœtry was and he as always, able to think in that sly way pœts do, spouted out something about any collection of words that almost made sense and she had asked in return as to whether making sense excluded it from being considered pœtic - he just muttered 'possibly'. He reminded her that pœts understood better than anyone else the pain suffered by all floor scrubbers and that even a second rate pœt could describe the trauma of scrubbing better than a veteran scrubber herself could. She thought it somewhat unfair that a pœt could describe her pain better than she herself could. One night when they had argued over his inability to embrace

reality she had cried and he had told her that reality was
more unreal than. Sometimes he told her that he loved
her and was unworthy to touch the hem of the silk gown
that he couldn't afford to ever buy her and this made her
cry but with happiness. They use Greenwich Mean Time
in Lisboa which means they have clocks that look like
the ones in Greenwich. If you're a scrubber from either
place chances are that the clock was made in Taiwan and
if you're a scrubbee you probably use a clock made in
Switzerland - maybe even a cuckoo one if your grandfather looked after his possessions or was lucky enough to
have a servant who remembered to wind the mechanism
methodically and carefully. Hard to know if Einstein
would have even visited Switzerland if he had of been
born in Belfast but if he'd been born in Belfast, especially
on the Falls road, he may have been tempted to build an
atomic bomb for the Provos and not those petty booby
trap bombs that kill maybe four or five British soldiers at
a time and sometimes even leave no casualties - after all
what's four soldiers when you've got tens of millions of
people to choose from. She wondered if the same soldiers
would do the same things on the streets of London if they
were ordered to and wondered if in fact they were all the
one 'united' kingdom - like the British government endlessly insisted - why the British army were only sent onto
her streets as the 'rest' of the United Kingdom had more
common murders than the north of Ireland had - why not
send troops onto the streets of Scunthorpe or the lane-
ways of Cornwall - for after all, murder is murder and by
what right is a political murder deemed to be less tolera-

ble than some wretched person cutting the throat of some hapless victim for the sheer sport of it.

Oh... you think that a stupid question... I agree, it is... but of course it was meant to be stupid. Too many intelligent people asking too many intelligent questions - why are stupid people not allowed to ask stupid questions. It's meant to be a democracy and as by definition it's difficult for stupid people to ask intelligent questions - we either have to permit and also encourage them to ask stupid questions or else disenfranchise them from all input into any matters concerning society - I know what you're thinking... this'll only be the start... if we urge stupid people to ask their stupid questions then the same stupid people will want us to listen to their stupid ideas and before we know it we'll have a society where stupid people feel entitled to espouse their opinions on every subject under the sun and perhaps even on subjects relating to other solar systems...

It's not that I'm entirely unsympathetic to their plight it's just that I find this leather chair in my Cambridge study so very, very comfortable and frankly I don't see why I should share it with people who don't understand the complex mechanics and profound nuances of an Empire and how and why it was necessary and how the trickle down effect from it actually benefitted the great majority of people and even more importantly how if WE hadn't done it to THEM... they'd have done it to us and I strongly resent applying twentieth century wisdom to a bygone age - it's just not cricket and on the subject of cricket - only the pigheadedness of the Irish prevented them from enjoying what is a perfectly good game - their loss.

You definitely have a point there about cricket - a wonderfully weird mix of meditation and action - no disagreement from me - I've often thought that Don Quixote himself would have been far better off playing cricket - if ever a game was created with someone in mind - but on the subject of stupid people being entitled to ask stupid questions... may I please continue - and by the way I don't wish to be seen to advocate stupidity per se - I'm more of a lobbyist for a society that blends intelligence and stupidity which I feel may in some bizarre almost esoteric way accidentally lead us to the perfect balance of all things or at least some things or at the very least, not too big an imbalance - anyway my point being this - in all probability the society which we call human will be around for quite some time yet - don't bore me with the nuclear/meteorite proviso - so as we have quite a bit of time to explore, rearrange, plan our world - why not let the stupid people have some say on some things and if and when they derail your intellectual blueprint - I'll apologise - and considering that the Utopia which you seek to build may take the best part of eternity - what's a little slice of time stolen by the stupids. I take it that you are intent on building a Utopia, because if you're not, then your desire to disbar stupidity is even more petty and vindictive than even I had imagined - it could even mean that you're doing so only because you personally can't stand stupidity and not because you necessarily believe it would hinder and harm progress.

I see what you're up to... you're using intelligent language in a stupid way in order to make an intelligible point about the necessity of stupidity.

Am I?

Yes of course you are.

Perhaps I'm too cunning for my own good.

You're using a paradoxical approach to show the irony of even measuring such subjective terms as stupidity and intelligence.

I am?

Yes... don't you see - the very fact that you've dressed your ideas re stupidity up in intelligent attire means that I'm able to relate to them and in fact can even begin to find merit in them.

So... if I'm clever enough to mask my stupidity up in a sumptuous banquet - you'll dine at my table?

Absolutely - nothing I like better than an intellectual cul-de-sac... an empty box with an intricate wrapping.

Decrescendo

And a fancy tied silk ribbon?

The more intricate the knot's weave the easier I can untie it.

You must enjoy the odd game or two of chess?

Ah, you know me so well - who dœsn't enjoy the opening flourish of a queens pawn gambit?

Or even the anticipation of a Sicilian defense?

Indeed - straight to the mattresses.

Don't you find chess just a little bit limited after all there are but a finite amount number of moves to be made and most of the really clever ones have already been discovered?

Now that you mention it... I have been finding it a trifle routine lately - found my mind wandering at my Tuesday night game.

That's exactly what I was alluding to - chess is a decent enough game for the average man but for a mind like yours... it's positively stagnant.

Go on, please continue.

Well the way I see it is that for a man of your fathomless depth chess is merely interesting rather than stimulating - why after you'd mastered all the textbook openings and devoted sufficient study to your endgame... there'd be almost no point in you continuing to play the game.

You make a strangely solid argument my friend.

Or if I may put it in terms more agreeable to a creative spirit like yourself - you've seen Michelangelo's DAVID?

But of course - who hasn't?

Well would I be correct in saying that even though it is technically perfect there's just something about it that dœsn't quite excite you?

Well, he's not especially well endowed.

Besides that.

Yes - as you say almost something fishy about its aura.

I bet you find it too complacent?

Complacent - yes that's it - that describes my feeling entirely.

I'll further wager that a lesser known Michelangelo... one say like THE REBELLIOUS SLAVE would be far more to your complicated æsthetic taste?

Decrescendo

Yes - I am indeed quite complicated and I think I know the one you mean.

Of course you do - its unfinished emptiness fills you up - you marvel at how the master overcame all those technical difficulties presented by the inert block of stone and then simply left the remaining figure to wander motionlessly through all eternity - the very idea of a rebellious slave being confined to stone for the rest of all time fascinates you even as it appalls your profound sense of justice - it haunts you and it intrigues you all at the same time.

May I commend you on your remarkable insights.

Not for you the near parody of male beauty presented by DAVID - its brilliant yet finite representation of apparent perfect manhood leaves you almost unmoved.

I couldn't have put it better myself.

Hurry up forty two or else I'll have to have another água and why pay for water just because it's in a bottle - I mean who'd pay for rain.

Forty two was upon her. She found her as she thought she would - older, adult, other. Whatever forty two thought of her she kept to herself - always a sign of good breeding and/or emotional repression.

Forty two kissed her on both cheeks in that functional, socially conditioned, soulless way. She in turn squirmed and muttered. She spoke English in a reasonably good way - fairly distinctively - typical Belfast accent but forty two was an educated Portuguese woman with an English mother as a bonus - so she spoke it quite beautifully - it would be petty to mention the odd aspirated h.

The road bumped - bumpy roads in a car with a smoothly purring engine, which is not entirely dissimilar to riding smooth roads in a bumpy car with its dodgy suspension.

The sea shimmered the way it sometimes did in her father's poems and the sun again made light of the gap of miles and millions. She thought the city beautiful. She had thought of seeking out other more poetic word to use for its description but in a sense the use of the word beautiful eclipsed them all. The beauty of words, the beauty of a word like beautiful. She wondered could a word describing beauty be in itself ugly.

Forty two was polite, well mannered and even kind. She pointed out things here and there. Strangely enough she kept mentioning how small Portugal was - perhaps she'd never heard of Ireland - God knows such ignorance wasn't due to our neglecting to talk about it - sometimes to the point of thinking all colours are green.

CHAPTER 2: *FURTHER DISCUSSIONS ON THE SUBJECT OF FLOORS*

A rrival. Welcome. Two totally separate words. Often used in tandem but not necessarily interconnected. Arrival was inevitable - a logical outcome of all and any travel. Welcome was different. It put a burden on the arrived and also on the one who welcomed. It had a protocol. Protocols were artificial and unnatural but sometimes helped build bridges to awkward out of the way places. I live here in this big house my mother lives here too. My mother dœsn't scrub floors and neither do I scrub floors. It's not that I wouldn't, you understand, it's just that... forty two didn't say any of these things and may not even have implied them but sometimes the children of pœts must also consult with a muse or a chorus or failing that, with the silence.

'Oh my God!!! I'm terribly sorry... I've forgotten your name... please forgive me.'

'Kate'

'So sorry Kate, I can't apologise enough.'

At least she didn't say that she wouldn't forget a name like Araminta or Elizabeth or Hermione.

Decrescendo

No, and I wouldn't forget a name like forty three.

Kate surveyed the house in silence. Big and huge and enormous and not small either. Floors, lots of.

If the house had say thirteen large floors and each floor had to be cleaned at least once a fortnight that would be thirteen multiplied by twenty six which is approximately three hundred and thirty eight times per year and it's also exactly the same number. Further to this if the house was one hundred years old, that would mean that the floors had been scrubbed thirty three thousand and eight hundred times exactly or approximately depending on how accurate or inaccurate we choose to be.

It's a lot of scrub a dub dub. Where dœs the scrub fault line lie. All those tired aching bony knees bereft of that hypothetical cushion. Knees grazed with imposed humility. Knees calloused with the early onset of tumours. Knees without the means to walk back home to rest their head on a pillow next to an unpublished pœt, who had the ability to describe their drudgery in heroic terms or at least to possibly soothe them with contrived symbolism. And compounding the problem was that if the house was to stand for say at least another hundred years then we'd have to double the amount of floors to be scrubbed - and this is a best case scenario - where is all this scrubbing blood - because that is what it is - to come from?

Is the ability or the passion or the necessity to scrub genetically programmed? Can it successfully pass through from mother to daughter?

Put up any defense that you wish except this particular one...

Decrescendo

'Of course the scrubber's daughter may not have to scrub floors as she will have the chance to better herself in the social firmament', for that simply transfers the problem and as it's the soul of the problem which we're solely concerned with here - that's of no use. In fact that could be even worse because some other scrubber's daughters may not have even have the consolation of having an unpublished pœt for a husband or a father - because that's what pœtry is - a consolation - it begins as a consolation for the limitations of human thought, then moves on to console us for the isolation of existence and then finally it's coup de grace is that it consoles us by its courage in always attempting to pick the perfect word to describe all those embryonic thoughts that tease the recesses that we only partly dwell in. The point is really very simple. Unless we think that some are born to scrub like say a scrubber or some odd, cuckoo, crazy, old witch who likes to rub a dub dub - we must limit each person to one floor.

The one floor theory is this - each human being must clean one floor each - apologies for the lack of complication in this theory - did you expect floor theory to be complex? Nuanced? Layered? Abstract? If it was in fact considered to be so then some bastard somewhere would do his/her Phd on the subject which would lead to much academic discourse and eventually achieve a place on the college syllabus for it - countless books on every aspect of the subject.

I say Thaddeus old chap I'm reading a marvelously

engaging essay by a former colleague of mine on FLOOR THEORY... absolutely fascinating... I hadn't remotely realised quite how multi faceted the whole thing was.

Actually Dorothy, I have indeed read it but I have to admit I'm a COUNTER FLOOR THEORY woman myself - in fact I'm in the middle of writing a nine hundred odd page book on the subject...

Are you indeed - by Jove it sounds really intriguing stuff - counter floor theory -who'd have guessed?

Take it from me, that's how it'd go down - floor theory and counter floor theory - learned people each attempting to outdo the other in the race to be the one who cracked floor theory - the one who resolved its baffling, perplexing enigmas - mind you none of the theoreticians would ever have so much as kneeled before the soiled altar of a stained floor - but back in the real world floor theory is quite simple. All rules require exceptions - (Kate wondered why the Japanese army seemed to need to torture it's WW2 prisoners just for the sheer fun of it) - and there could of course be many exemptions to the seemingly draconian rule of CLEAN YOUR OWN BLOODY FLOOR - the obvious ones first... the dead (practical reasons here)... the aged (infirm bones and besides even the healthy ones are unable to scrub too hard)... anyone with wings (as they could credibly say that they'd never walked upon the floor)... a case could easily be made for exempting babies and it's certainly tempting to but this is out-

weighed somewhat by the fact that they often contribute
more to the state of dirty floors than any other sub section of the populace... also it's tempting to exempt ladies
with perfectly manicured fingernails, but here again it
would be self defeating... really, really lazy bastards could
get a partial exemption on the basis that they spend the
entire day in bed or lounging on the couch which necessarily means that they don't travel the floors as often as
others... no exception would be made for geniuses with
the single exception of Michelangelo who although he
surely messed the floor of the Sistine, had no real alternative other than to do so, I mean he could scarcely have
kept hopping up and down that scaffold - could he.

'My mother, Elizabeth will be out shortly - she's a little
slow these days - seventy nine years old you understand.
In the meantime I can show you to your room'.

The room was square and soft and had a lovely window and best of all it had a door that locks. Only a door
lock truly makes a room a private space.

Elizabeth arrived. She was so old that Kate could not
have guessed her age. She seemed a type to her - English,
proud, confident, strong, deep eyes and the obligatory
walking stick. This summation of Elizabeth took seventeen seconds but a lifetime of prejudice helped it reach
such a rapid conclusion.

'I am so pleased to meet you - I hope you don't mind
cats?'

'Well I don't exactly like them.'

'That's okay - no one really likes them but they have to live somewhere.'

The cat question was good because it allowed Kate to further class Elizabeth as eccentric.

'Good-good girl - but I wonder why do so many people pretend to like them, some fools invariably think that they do. They start comparing them favorably over dogs - so do they mean that if every bloody dog on the planet died tonight they'd reconsider their so called love of cats?'

'I see what you mean.'

'I hope that you do because one thing too many people lack is the ability to name stupid, stupid.'

'I don't eat meat...'

She interrupted Kate's confessional... 'well be that as it may and I can't say that I approve but what's that got to do with cats unless of course you eat cats?'

Kate laughed nervously-the old lady could certainly talk - 'No of course I don't, what I meant was that sometimes when I go to the shops and try to find things which I want to eat, it can be difficult and I'm often a little bit jealous of how well pets, especially cats, are catered for - that's all'

'Oh... I see... you're not one of those crank vegetarians... are you?'

'Well I can be a crank and I am a vegetarian... so...'

'So you'd think a chicken more important than a human being'

'Well...'

But Elizabeth interrupted her response -

'I'm sorry, I meant to say AS important as a human being.'

'That's quite alright - and I can answer both questions simultaneously', 'I don't think chickens are as important as most human beings - nor ducks either and yes I do think chickens are more important than SOME human beings'

'I knew that the Irish tended to be a bit metaphysical but...'

'Well, when I think of a cute yellow fluffy baby chick and say I think of someone like chairman Mao, well then of course a chicken is worth more than someone like him - how could it be any other way - and a pig would be more important than someone like Adolf Eichmann.'

'It's a little extreme to put it mildly but I take your point.'

'And I haven't even mentioned a serial rapist killer on death row yet.'

'No you haven't - I've a feeling that I'm going to need my jockeys code book very shortly - how much?'

'Sorry?'

'Nothing - it's a reference to an old film that's way before your time, I'm afraid.'

'So - no - I don't think an animal is as important as most human beings.'

'This time I really do get your point.'

CHAPTER 3: HISTORY

In the days that followed Kate had nothing much to do but be a companion to the old lady. Forty two went off to work each day, as an investment banker and Kate and Elizabeth spent their afternoons in the garden - surrogate grandmother - all this talk of motherless children but no songs about a grandmotherless child. Bridge of ages. Old and young - two extreme states both arrived at by an accident or whim of time. Chronology explained and exchanged.

Britannia, ruler of the waves. Storm bringers. Riders of the sea. Birthplace of Newton and Shakespeare and Shelley and refuge to all those anarchists who didn't know how to light a fuse...

England - great giver as well as great taker. Land of Robin Hood. He of Sherwood green. Proud. Noble. Green. Socialist ideals long before Marx or Engels drew breath. Robin and his bow precursor to England's Agincourt. Robin - man before his time. His men each one merry. But chosen for their stoutness of heart. Little John, brave too - could have played basketball in another age. The band lacking perfection - too many absentees - too many should have and could have been includees if only Well's time machine had been ready - Joanne of Arc for starters - though Marian's position on ménage à trois is undocumented - Mandela of course - in his way a real Robben Hood - perhaps even Garibaldi for his flash and again our

Decrescendo

friend Don Quixote who could have found the ultimate focal point for all that romantic energy... unfortunately there are no windmills in Sherwood. Basil Rathbone too as he knew the soul of the wondrous Mr. S. Holmes as well as the sheriff of Nottingham. Mary Reilly, victim of Whitechapel's Jack - as much as anyone in history, she deserves to live again. This list like all indulgences is open to much amendment.

Seven hundred years of broken history to fix, mend, repair, patch up, renovate, redeem - no revision please.

My name is Elizabeth.

I'm called Kate.

Born in 1894, next birthday I'll be eighty.

This year I'll be sixteen.

I never met Cromwell.

You never compared him to Genghis Khan.

I never approved of plantation or colonization.

You never trumpeted it as land thievery.

Decrescendo

I hate Rudyard Kipling.

Me too, though not for his imperialistic claptrap, more for his mind numbing, sanctimonious words.

I have never taken the Queen's shilling.

Me neither but my grandfather Jack was moved sideways in Guinness's in 1915 for declining the King's shilling.

I hadn't been born during your great hunger - famine.

No but I've never heard you criticise Marie Antoinette and her alleged cake theory.

I like Shakespeare.

I love Shakespeare.

We never perpetrated actual genocide in your land.

The individual man whose head you've severed dœsn't care that statistically speaking another million haven't joined him - for he cannot speak of statistics.

I didn't realise that you believed that the sins of the fathers...

I don't... but even as we speak your troops still walk our streets.

Decrescendo

That's just to keep order.

Whose order?

To keep the tribes apart.

Isn't a tribe allowed to hunt in their own village?

Yes... but...

You use the same methodology to keep order in our society as you used to defeat history's greatest tyrant.

Sorry.

So you should be.

No, I mean I don't understand the reference.

At Normandy you used tens of thousands of armed soldiers... like in Belfast - how could our threat be as great as his?

Since we're speaking of that man - someone told me that your leader actually sent condolences to the German Embassy upon his death but I know that couldn't be so - it would be too unthinkable.

Anymore unthinkable than stealing soil that people use to grow food to feed themselves?

Decrescendo

We are playing games now... name calling.

Yes, I know, but sometimes it's necessary to call names... to return to the playground... primitivism like civilised society has its minuses but it also has its plusses.

You Irish seem a spirited, fighting people.

So they say.

Did you ever wonder how such a spirited people were overcome by invaders?

We were outnumbered.

Millions of people on a secure island in a time before guns and bullets and bombs and when invaders could only have come hundreds at a time and you were outnumbered? And when they arrived they'd have been tired and disorganised and had no local knowledge whatsœver and yet still this spirited people were outnumbered?

Perhaps the truth is that you were a bitterly divided, tribal people who took great delight in the invasions as it meant that some other tribe on the island was put to the sword?

Surely with any semblance of togetherness or cohesion whatsœver you'd have easily repelled them... surely there are some rousing ballads detailing your heroics from that period?

Decrescendo

My brother is rotting away in a prison cell right now.

Your brother - what did he do?

He planted a bomb.

What a terrible thing to do.

Yes, killing is always terrible.

Bombs do other things than just kill - they sever limbs - leave people brain dead. Did they bomb the man from Germany?

It wasn't their fight.

Babies being put into ovens and it wasn't their fight - whose fight was it then?

Yours for one - you invented concentration camps - you invented deportation of people from their native soil - you invented apartheid and your late nineteenth century continued land theft in faraway places ensured that the Kaiser would want a bit of the action - so it's even possible that without all this British empire thievery, there may well have been no battle in 1914, in which case it's certain that there'd be no treaties or entreaties at Versailles, ergo a very different chancellor in 1933 - go on, I dare you-dispute all or any of this? And just for good measure I find it ironic that your most admired statesman, Churchill, had some of the same qualities as the Nazis that he defeated, he believed in superior ethnicities and that somewhat bizarrely the white faced English man was of superior intellect to the Irish, the Indians, the native Americans and so on - how many men have been imprisoned or killed for far less repugnant behavior?

In history all hands are dipped in blood - those who could take did - those who couldn't didn't.

Strangely that's what the pœt says.

The pœt?

My father - rarely takes sides in history.

He's a wise man - it's easy to be judgmental with hindsight.

No, I didn't say he wasn't judgmental - I said that he dœsn't take sides the way that I usually do - he's the most judgmental man I know.

Oh... I see.

He says he forgives all historical atrocities once they are acknowledged and atoned for.

How do we atone for the ghosts of past generations?

On that point he's less specific, though he once suggested that reinventing language would help.

Decrescendo

Such as?

Well... like taking a name like CROMWELL and using it
as derogatory term only.

Could we use the word IRA only as a derivative too?

You already do.

That's because they plant bombs.

As we've already agreed, bombs are a terrible thing
but you could say maybe IRA scum and add a caveat or
a context 'second class citizens in their own land'... this
would give some framework to the barbarity of their acts.

I'm confused - what exactly are we saying here?

It's okay to be confused - we're acknowledging a paradox - life is full of contradictions - the pœt says paradoxes
are necessary to make sense of life's chaotic conundrums.

So you definitely condemn all bomb makers?

Unreservedly - I would never plant a bomb.

Would you break bread with those who do?

Would you spit at Cromwell's statue every time you
walk by it?

Decrescendo

Probably not... most unlikely - a lady shouldn't spit.

Same difference - things are not linear - the poet says history is never black and white - it's full of grey areas.

Except for 1939 - there were really no grey areas there.

Who can disagree with that one, I agree and so does the poet - he visited Auschwitz to write some poems about the place.

Understandable for a poet - they must have been dark?

If you can call a blank white page dark.

Explain.

He didn't write a single word - he just cried - said sometimes words break down and fall away under the futility of language.

At least we can learn from history - it'll never happen again.

The poet says that it will - simply a matter of time - when and where.

Why would it happen again?

The poet says why would it not?

Decrescendo

It won't - it was a collection of extreme social circum-
stances that converged in order to permit it to happen
- without all those pieces there could have been no holocaust.

The pœt says that such historical analyses of it are
probably wrong...

Herr Leerkopf, I understand that you were an active
member of the SS during the last war?

Yes, I had the privilege to serve the fatherland faithfully.

May I dare ask you if after all these years you have any
regrets?

I suppose I have... it was a difficult time for all involved.

Yes I'm sure it was.

I was young of course and wanted to do my bit.

Of course - it's easily understood.

And besides those uniforms... something about them
just grabbed me.

Indeed... I totally get it... Hugo Boss never designed

anything more æsthetically beautiful than that particular creation and the world was its catwalk.

Thank you for your empathy - people nowadays have no clue what we were up against.

That's why I'm here... to lend a supporting shoulder... I'll understand too if some of the subject is a little too raw for you to talk about.

No... it's okay... I have nothing to hide... I've done nothing of which I'm ashamed... war calls on men to do things that they would never otherwise even contemplate.

Like putting strong healthy men into gas chambers - like burying beautiful young girls in pits - like sending world weary aged to eternity without a shroud?

That makes it sound so cold, so calculated.

Did I forget to mention precious innocent babies roasting in ovens?

You're just like all the rest... you don't understand at all. Do you think that I'm such a monster that I'd kill sweet, fat, happy gurgling babies?

Profoundest apologies - I have perhaps been misinformed.

Decrescendo

We didn't see them as people - we simply saw them as subhuman.

Ah... I see... the old subhuman defense... mmmm may I elaborate for just a moment.

By all means, do.

Who on earth coined this 'subhuman' angle?

I'm afraid that I don't quite follow you...

What is a subhuman?
Tell me exactly what do you mean when you say that you saw flesh and blood as subhuman? What does subhuman mean?
Did you believe that they were a different species?
Would you have made love to a beautiful Jewish woman?

Yes... I suppose so.

Would that same woman have potentially been capable of physically bearing a child of yours?

Yes... of course.

Would that baby have been only fifty percent human?

Well...

Decrescendo

I suppose the Jews were close to taking over Germany in those days - even near to taking over the whole world?

Yes - they were.

How is it possible that these sub humans had the ability, the intellect, the resourcefulness to achieve such a goal?

Well...

So you considered yourself and all of your comrades intellectually superior to a Jew like Einstein?

Well...

But he was simply a subhuman - he too would have ended up on a lampshade.

But don't you see...

You must be mute now... contrition can only begin with the guilt of silence... there are no sub humans - there are only humans - the only difference between you and the primal hunter in the darkest forest on the edge of creation is that you may have discovered fire a fraction of a moment faster than him on the evolutionary scale of things - and probably not even you but one in your tribe. No intellect or Holmesian deduction is called for here. Only the merest glimmer, the tiniest discernible iota of visceral strings is necessary in order to know that a being that walks and talks and breathes and cries - feels grief and sorrow - joy and happiness - laughs and dances - loves and is in return, loved - thinks and ponders and wonders too as to the purpose of the stars, is as worthy as any of life, full life.

The squeals and unimaginable sounds as the children were ripped and torn from their parent's arms may indeed have sounded subhuman but it was but the echo of your own inhumanity reverberating back at you as its echo informed you through each and ever decibel - nothing, absolutely nothing about these actions can ever radiate the right shade let alone lead to some alleged rainbow Utopia.

No cloak, nor creed, nor semantics could ever begin to weave the semblance of the fig leaf of justification necessary to even bear witness to, let alone participate, profit or prosper from even one such single action. We have counted their quantity in measurements which we call millions but in truth the zerœs have no meaning – yet are perhaps tragically fitting in some perverse way that they deliver the only equation to a question that has no answer.

'So the pœt is a historian then?'

'How can a pœt not be a historian? - the pœt wonders how would a poor economy or social circumstance encourage university educated medical doctors with well

fed bellies to perform experiments on live babies - and
to ban jazz music and to outlaw Einstein's intellect - for
renowned philosophers to actively support such utter
inanities, history is full of vile revisionists but we'll refrain
from it here as we should have no personal agenda.'

'You seem to simply parrot the pœt's thoughts'

'That's not because he's my father but more that he's
the only one whom I've ever met who has no real hint
of absolutism - he dœsn't mind skin colour or lack of
intellect or strange names or worshippers or atheists
or gender orientation or poor people or rich people or
academics or socialists or conservatives or classical art or
abstract art - he's even in love with a floor scrubber '

'I must say he dœs sound somewhat interesting.'

'It's not so much that he's interesting - more that he's
interested'

'What did he do when his son planted bombs?'

'Told him that destruction was easy and that creativity
was difficult and railed against the republic of Ireland - he
called it 'that place down south' how it eventually threw
out the British monarchy to replace it with the monarchy
of Rome - it makes him very angry. He said that the most
screwed up English rule was no more oppressive than
allowing a man in Rome to dictate every moral aspect of

the lives of millions of people - said that nobody was that capable or that smart and that was even assuming that their heart was in the right place to begin with. He said that it was ironic too that men who liked to wear dresses refused to treat women as equals. He said that nothing on earth was further removed from what a potential God might be than the structure of religion. Said religion should deal with philosophy and all those unanswered questions - the fact that these men from Rome had a black and white answer for every question showed that they were dishonest as well as stupid and sometimes even evil.'

'I can take it then that he's not a true believer?'

'Like many atheists and agnostics he's a little bit obsessed by it... religion confuses him more than a little – he appears to respect each man and each woman's right to believe what they need to - says children are different - they have it imposed upon them - perhaps children should learn to think and divine and wonder and all those amazing things associated with curiosity - also he says that it took courage in the past to question clerics but now that every Tom, Dick and Harry can do it. Says it makes him feel the way communism dœs... he can accept aspects of communism but can't stand communists...'

CHAPTER 4: ACHILLES HEAL

Elizabeth's other child, a son, occasionally showed up. His face appeared with a permanently fixed grin which remained constant no matter what topic he discussed. Kate longed to tell Elizabeth that she thought him an idiot but was aware that children are the most sacred of all the cows. Her own mother too kept a well tended herd of those same beasts but as always Kate found that Elizabeth was nothing if not different...

'My son is a doctor - a psychiatrist - as a child he examined and analysed the behaviour of animals yet didn't seem to be particularly affectionate towards them, so we thought that psychiatry was probably an appropriate profession...'

My name is Doctor Adolph Ponsonby Gonzales - I was given that forename because my father, an eternal optimist, hadn't read the small print on the document that Chamberlain held aloft in his hand on his return to England, which is strange in itself as one of his favourite sayings was about how the devil lurks in the detail. Almost a war baby - born 1938 - I became a psychiatrist because I had not the talent to be a baker. How I love cakes. My mother Elizabeth is an institution - should be in an Institution. My work is complex and financially rewarding. I work in a code which is bombproof - the

Decrescendo

IRA will never get me - we are indestructible - we call
the shots - we invent new language as we need it - I
love labels - once attached, the residue of the glue remains - we invent illnesses as we go along - no one can
challenge us for if they do we will invent an illness that
we'll allege they suffer from - our baseless discipline was
invented largely to control spirited females - in those days
we called them hysterics - you know the type - girls who
thought that they knew better than their fathers - women
who challenged their husband's authority - what were we
to do. We're not idiots by the way - we knew they were
sane and normal but the bitches insisted on challenging
male orthodoxy - something had to be done to maintain
the status quo - they were literally on the rampage, with
all sorts of demands. Should we have conceded that patriarchy was a tool to repress them? Tell them that they were
entitled to feel and think unencumbered by male wisdom
and affirmation? You see our problem.

Recent times are easier - our orthodoxy gœs unchal-
lenged - we have permeated every aspect of twentieth
century society - all fear us - our opinion once spoken
becomes fact - we never have to empirically prove anything - two of us can have the sanest person on the planet
committed to a strait jacket for all eternity - power - a
beautiful thing - only the odd crazy religious nut chal-
lenges us - they believe in a quaint notion of good and
evil - we dispute this - we like to give parity to the rapist and the rape victim - we recognise that the rapist's
mother may have bathed him with a sponge in such a way
as to disturb his wires for life. Church folks believe in the

absurdity of freewill - the ludicrous idea that a human
being can make his or her own choices regardless of what
tunnels they may have had to crawl through. See that boy
running endlessly around the schoolyard - we can stop
that - call him hyper - say it's not normal - we'll drug the
little bastard... put a halt to his gallop... call it a disorder
and bask in a society that refuses to challenge our prescription. How I love this job - it's impossible to be wrong
- if my patient jumps from the tenth floor on a Thursday
- I'll claim that 'without me, he would have jumped on
a Wednesday ' - How I love Freud -which is amazing as
I'm wary of Jews - Wonderful that a cocaine user's rants
on sex became the foundation for the twentieth century's
most potent tool - The whole idea of a subconscious
was a masterstroke - a license to always be right - such
a beautiful thing - no good or evil - In those early years
it was hard - hard to peddle our unprovable sales pitch
- especially amongst the great unwashed - but the more
cultured types were far easier purchasers of our wares
- how they loved our clever levers - we made jigsaws
and we decided where exactly the pieces fitted - Darwin
would have hated us with his pedantic proofs - The few
things we did say which were accurate we stole from what
already existed, for example, everyone knew that some
people were more reserved than others - they didn't need
Jung to invent the label INTROVERT - cavemen knew
that some cavemen were more socially adept than others
but once we put a ribbon on it the educated types said ,
wow!, what insight! Those boorish workingmen were of
course much more sceptical but we could attribute it to

their lack of culture - If they didn't get Picasso or Joyce - how could they get us.

Though even I must confess that I still find it hard to believe that psychiatric findings are considered 'scientific' by so many people - I mean surely the entire point of a thing being scientific is that whatever it's conclusions are... that they can be exactly replicated under laboratory conditions anywhere in the world? Surely accurate data gathered by a specific methodology would be almost identical every single time UNLESS the compilers/analysts had no objectivity...

I don't like too much heat.

You suffer from solar aversion syndrome.

I don't look forward to dying.

A clear case of AU REVOIR AVERSION syndrome.

I worry about the state of the planet.

We call that INABILITY TO KEEP YOUR SNOUT OUT OF THINGS WHICH DON'T CONCERN YOU syndrome.

My twenty two year old daughter is undergoing open heart surgery and the surgeon is blind and drunk... and it has me worried.

Decrescendo

CUT THAT UMBILICAL CORD.

I'm worried by my desire to enter a profession that is obsessed with amassing money on the back of human suffering and usually only offers help to well heeled people.

That's not an illness - not at all - that's quite healthy and normal - why, you sound particularly well adjusted to me.

Once I had a patient - such a normal woman - in many ways - but she had this belief that existence was futile which pissed off her ambitious, superficial, upbeat, fiance. So he sent her to me for reorientation - I still have the transcript of the session.

Me: So, why do you think that life is pointless ?

She: Because existence is full of pain and uncertainty and injustice.

Me: The reason you say this is because you're afraid to experience life.

She: I'm not.

Me: You are.

She: No, I'm not.

Me: Yes you are.

She: Life makes no sense.

Me: That's because you're depressed.

She: No, I'm not.

Me: You're in denial.

She: No, I'm not.

Me: Those in denial always say that.

She: You're an arrogant bastard to think that you know my thoughts better than I do.

Me: Subconsciously, you hate me because I see right through you.

She: I don't hate you subconsciously - I hate you consciously - I think that you're a bastard.

Me: You're transferring your aggression - its not me that you really hate.

She: Why could I not hate you?

Me: You don't know me.

She: Nor you me.

Decrescendo

Me: Therapy dœsn't work that way - my words are irrefutable - if I say that you feel something unconsciously - you have no way of disproving that - play the game please.

She: I think that I'm in love with you.

Me: No need to apologise... it's common and natural... within this relationship you see me as wise, aware, empathetic, human - warm, distant yet close - close yet aloof - dangerously safe.

She: I was joking - it's called sarcasm.

Me: Yes... of course you were... believe that if you must. I understand. I undoubtedly embody your absent father.

She: My father was ever present.

Me: Your insensitive husband?

She: I'm not yet married.

Me: I've replaced the lover who spurned you.

She: I left him.

Me: That dark, strong, silent type you possess unrequited love for.

Decrescendo

She: I prefer blond men.

Me: Your maternal instincts inform you that I'd make a wonderful father for your babies.

She: I don't want children.

Me: Your barren womb is a manifestation of your inability to embrace masculinity.

She I fuck who, where and when I choose.

Me: You seek solace in meaningless connection.

She: I enjoy casual sex.

Me: You're afraid of real intimacy.

She: All human connection is to some degree real.

Me: Your hour is up.

CHAPTER 5: *SOME CHILDREN THEMSELVES*
BECOME MOTHERS TOO...

The house next door is big as well. In Belfast all the houses are squashed together. Poor Catholics and poor Protestants, the sardines of that particular world.

The little boy, Jose, plays in the garden. He is in childhood - he is of childhood. Yet he knows not of the concept of childhood. He can never be considered an expert on childhood. The volumes which 'childhood' take up on the bookshelf will never be reached by his tiny hands. He is innocent and he is ignorant. He is bi-lingual which at his age means that he mispronounces words in two languages. He likes cowboys. He dœsn't know the history of the native American Indian. He never saw the buried hearts at Wounded Knee. Geronimo scares him - all that paint and so many feathers. He dœsn't believe that they ride bareback - he thinks that even cowboys can't do that but he dœsn't realise that saddles are necessary to hold Winchesters. Indians have no sheriffs - maybe they don't believe in justice.

But he has to admit he likes the sound of their names - the pœtry of which he cannot explain yet can feel - their echo not unlike the very canyons which they roam... Comanche... Sioux... Blackfoot... Cheyenne... Choctaw... Cherokee... Apache... such beautiful sounds even if they're injun names.

Decrescendo

Babies... beautiful... perfect - but in reverse. Wise - elegant - unbridled - emotive - cool - imperturbable - in the moment - this is now. Sleeping. Sleeping like logs, long since cut cleanly from the limbs of great oak Motionless. Blissful. Empty - empty of artifice - agendaless - Blue or pink. Teddy bears, only acquiring cuteness from proximity to baby. Baby - waiting for perfection to end. Chysalis. Butterfly. Abandoner of the womb. Rejecter of umbilicality. Fat. Fat and happy. Heavy with light. Light with heavy. Skin. Skin soft. Skin new. It's all downhill from here.

Mother - such a vague job description. Bundle. New precious bundle. Used to be inside you - don't you remember.

Parasite. Never you. You shared a placenta... until. Blank white page - fill him up. Beware - each word you write is carved in stone. No erasers. Had it easy, lying on your back whilst he had to source good quality cigars for all his friends. How hard could it have been. Peasant women have done it in fields for Millenia. No obstreticians in those damp fields. One woman had twenty seven - you only had one. Shame. Just one. Weighed less than six pounds - barely a push involved. Wanted a boy, wanted a girl. Maybe next time you'll get lucky. Chance. Labour. Love's labour. Carried him in your belly for nine months - now carry him on your back for ever. Can't remember the moment of conception. Didn't think that you could have been pregnant... even the word itself sounds heavy - a burden. It came from sex but the word itself is sexless. No rubbing of lotions will erase the stretch marks in your mind. Living... growing... being. Breasts filling up with substance better off in bottles. Cow. Human cow. Mood for moo.

Mother and smother - such semantic proximity - don't blame it on another - blame it on the mother. We entrust you with society's most sacred role, primary caregiver, sculptress of clay, unmoulded thing, don't destroy it with too much this or too little that. Don't caress him in excess, don't hug him too little. Give him freedom but teach him discipline. Only the exact amounts of each ingredient please. Sacred role... entrusted to no man. Highest honour we can bestow. Our eternal respect is yours for this extraordinary vocation. We cannot salary you for the task for that would demean it - a job beyond the snare of filthy lucre. We cannot apportion equal blame to the father for that would fail to recognise your unique association with the child. Each manchild and each womanchild needs an outlet, a fuse, a touchstone with which to trace the root of all their problems - for this you have been chosen.

You were there at the fall of Adam and we feel it only fitting to keep you to the fore at the fall of his descendants.

Here we wish to speak, off the record, if we may, in song and verse we eulogise your role, the soul of maternity we toast, the beauty of that bond we hail. We celebrate your identity in painting and prose... but let's be brutally honest here - still off the record - in private we feel our elevation of this motherhood thing to be a joke - we use these words to smooth feathers - we call it vocation as it saves on expense - how hard can it be to hug a tiny, tiny bundle. To cook a meal and plaster a cut knee. To

encourage knife and fork. To tell 'avoid the road'. To
say this right, that wrong... No mountains to climb... No
rocket to fly... No bridge to build... No war to fight... No
Sistine to carve... No world to run. Perversely you make
us overstress the import of what is but a basic task - we
supply you with expert advice and healthy babe - at birth
unblemished by worlds sway - perfection - unspoiled and
in return all we ask is not to add tarnish and warp but
even such simple remit seems so often beyond your scope.
Mothers ruin.

Your grandmother dropped one a year for twelve and
never a gripe, they were real women in those days.

Real men too.

The women didn't need silk, poetry nor perfume.

The men either.

Women certainly knew their place.

Yes, as you said, in the field dropping one.

They were proud and privileged to serve their men.

You forgot obey.

Well that goes without saying, almost as though they
instinctively knew their own best interests.

Decrescendo

As you said we knew our place.

Was that really such a bad thing?

Depends I suppose from where you're standing.

I mean we dug the land from dawn till dusk.

We made your breakfast before the dawn.

Don't think we didn't appreciate it.

Funny way of showing it.

We sincerely tried to compensate.

We just wanted a little more.

Sometimes less is more.

That's too Zen for our simple female minds.

We'd buy you a pretty dress whenever we could.

That's so sweet - can I have a red one please?

I was thinking more along the lines of white.

Too virginal, what about red?

Decrescendo

But red's a little too out there.

Sorry, I thought you liked a girl to flirt.

We do but you're not a girl, you're my wife.

So?

A wife is special.

That's so touching, you looking out for my modesty.

There are so many wolves out there.

Other men?

Yes but...

You were about to say the role of mother is special.

You took the words right out of my mouth.

Sacred?

Yes.

Beyond a soiled thing like sexy.

Yes - you know my thoughts so well.

Decrescendo

Of course - after all that's what a wife is for.

To please?

But of course.

To fit in as we see best?

Why not... you are my master.

You're such an amazing lady.

You're absolutely sure of that?

Of course I'm sure, it's my core belief.

But sometimes I dream of fucking the man next door.

Then you wouldn't be a lady - a lady would never do that.

So what exactly does a lady do?

A lady tries to do any reasonable thing that a man tells her to do.

And a woman?

Women tend to please themselves more.

Decrescendo

So - ladies are well behaved and act in the way a man approves of?

You ability to comprehend is most impressive.

If you were at a ball and you met a female out on the balcony...

Would there be music?

Yes - may I please continue?

Pardon my bad manners.

And if I wasn't there - would you prefer her to be a lady or a woman?

If I say woman, will she be sexy?

Yes.

Sensuous?

Yes.

Independent?

Yes.

No apron on?

Most unlikely, I'd imagine.

Spirited?

Very.

Impulsive?

Possibly.

Liberated?

Very likely as she'd have no gang of children or possessive other to chain her.

So, she'd be a force of nature?

Why wouldn't she be?

My God, I could really go for that.

So you definitely don't want her to be a lady then?

no.

I can't hear you - can you please speak up.

No!

You're absolutely, positively sure?

Decrescendo

Yes.

I mean I thought that a lady is a most desirable thing.

It is but in a different way.

Surely a lady is the ultimate male compliment?

It is... but...

But what?

It dœsn't mean that a lady possesses raw femininity.

On the one hand you're telling me that the term LADY is the most praiseworthy thing a female can be?

Yes, of course, totally.

But on the other hand you say you think a woman is more feminine.

Sort of.

Speak up - what dœs sort of mean?

Well, there's different feminine.

Different feminine! What on earth dœs that mean?
... Well... they're feminine in very different ways.

Decrescendo

You're confusing me - two different types of feminine...
what could that possibly mean?

Well... the Lady/mother/wife is sacred feminine and the
woman is wild/pœtry/natural feminine.

If I said that you were being disingenuous, that would
be kind.

You're entirely missing my point.

Two different versions of feminine?????

Yes... it can be rather complicated.

The world's going to end in twenty four hours and you
have to choose the most feminine company you know to
spend time with -woman or lady?

Woman.

Not lady?

No.

So lady isn't the ultimate male compliment then?

Probably not.

Lady is as lady dœs.

Decrescendo

Yes.

Lady is a female organ that responds to male programming?

You perhaps put it a trifle harshly.

Forgive the obvious, but why not just go for woman every time and bypass the charade of lady?

Female sexuality is too complicated.

I thought you welcomed complexity... crosswords... chess... cryptograms... black holes... parallel universes... Finnegan's wake... Archæology... casuistry... Kant...

We do but female is a step beyond.

Is that a back handed compliment?

No - and even if it were... the game of seduction permits the usage of compliment to flatter... to appeal to your ego. Ladies love compliments but women are slightly more wary of them.

Women too like compliment but we don't seek affirmation from you. We are what we are - like all flesh we are riddled with fault and flaw - but these are independent of your censure or approval. Why should you hold domain over us?

Decrescendo

As it was in the beginning... We use patriarchy because we are patriarchs. It's rooted in our history and besides most females don't seem to complain too much about it.

Happy slave. Blissful in her ignorance.

You make it sound worse - we too were slaves of history - we too were cast out of Eden.

We object to our role as slave - but even more so to being slave of the slave. Why should a slave have a slave?

You don't fully understand philosophy... the only revolution is the inner one.

Says who?

All the great thinkers.

Surely you mean all the great male thinkers?

Yes and unapologetically so.

Like Plato?

Yes.

Aristotle?

Yes.

Decrescendo

Rousseau?

Yes.

Hegel?

Yes.

What if I simply think of them as women haters?

That's utterly ludicrous.

Why?

Because it just is.

Thousands of years of privileged learning and that's the best you can offer?

There is a natural order to things - this even you must know. This order has served humankind well. It gives male and female different roles - each according to their talent.

That's what Pharaoh said when you resented breaking your back lugging heavy chunks of useless stone through the desert to assuage his ego.

Pharaoh was wrong.

Decrescendo

That's what monarch said when you objected to living in mud huts.

Monarch was wrong.

That's what Lord and master said when you didn't wish to wait at table any longer.

Lord and master were wrong.

That's what industrialist said when you looked for fair wage.

Industrialist was wrong.

That's what plantation owner said when black man didn't wish to pick more cotton.

Plantation owner was wrong.

You said we didn't ken to know medicine.

Academia was wrong.

You said the political process was too complicated for our tiny confused minds.

Government was wrong.

Philosopher, Pharaoh, Monarch, Lord, Master, Industrialist, Planter, Academic, Government... and you... what say you?

Decrescendo

You look so passionate when you're angry.

Every step along the way... you were wrong... totally wrong... nothing given without fight.

I find your lips exquisite, especially with lipstick.

And still you persist... the good ship MANSUPREME lies rotting and rusting at the bottom of a deep ocean - even some of the idiots have at last jumped ship and yet still you cling to the wreck?

Go on... give us a kiss.

Kate and the little boy played. Connected and accepted. He a baby and she a different kind of baby. Worlds apart together.

His minder an old lady called Margarida who spent more time with the cats than with Jose - naturally Kate named her cat woman.

She didn't think originality important in renaming someone - only accuracy on the subject. His mother and father were rarely home. Important people doing important things. The boy liked her presence in ways beyond his articulation. He liked that she was loose and that she was a girl and sometimes smart and always funny. He spoke English as his mother too was originally from that place and often spoke it back to cat woman to confuse her when he found her too bossy. Cat woman was okay.

Decrescendo

Not too fussy, not too nosey. She was relaxed about Kate whenever they met in the garden with the low fence. Forty two worked from early till late. Came in tired and disinterested in things - spoke a few words to Elizabeth, greeted Kate and then went to bed. Life. Every second day a black woman came for a few hours to clean things and make soup which she then left in the fridge in a big green container. Who eats soup?

The woman was downcast - Kate didn't know her name as she was just referred to as the cleaning lady. The woman's face was almost always pained. Maybe she had a pœt for a husband or maybe her first born planted bombs that blew people's eyeballs out of their sockets or fused their limbs together as plastic.

More than once Kate attempted to say something to the woman - some gesture - but the black woman didn't seem to notice or to care.

I'm not really white inside and you're not really black. Soul is colourless. Probably odourless too. I never went to Angola or Mozambique or wherever - nor did my ancestors. My hands are clean. No blood stains nor marks of rusty chains used to enslave you. We too were slaves... for far longer than you and we were the right colour. I feel your pain. We are black in our own land. We are the uppity nigger of our world. We too yearn to be free. We too are denied civil rights. White men with guns shoot us too when we protest. We too had a Queen and King which we never voted for. I like your skin colour. I too cannot comprehend this obsession with skin pigmentation - why

would one colour be superior to another - artists use
colour... all colour - short of strangling every new born
baby you bear, I don't know what they want from you - I
think black and white compliment each other... you know
Yin and Yang and stuff like that. Chiarascuro. Balance.
Harmony. Mind you I don't really like grey, which is what
you get if you mix black and white but I think that I
could learn to like it if it made you feel a little bit better,
a little bit freer. I apologise even though my hands are
clean. They cracked no whip. We planted no bombs in
Africa - at least I think we didn't. I support liberty for all
living things. I don't eat animals. I don't even swat flies.
Sometimes I even hate to crunch the autumn leaves in
case they have some remote, vague hint of being sen-
tient. I only blame the white man for all your problems. I
exculpate all your savage tribal warlords. I'll wash the red
blood off their black hands. I forgive them for doing to
their people what white men did for centuries. But don't
do what we did - don't replace a foreign tyrant with a
tyrant of your own.

Every warlord should wear a tee shirt saying I LOVE
POST COLONISATION POLITICAL VACUUMS (ok,
that's probably a tad unwieldly for a motif and the onlookers still wouldn't know your favourite band) - for
more than any other single thing it helps them do what
they do. Warlord's swish swagger semi-silent machete
does the exact same end job as ugly white man's noise
shattering bullet. Same difference. All flesh falls asunder
when enough aggression is applied, whatever its design
or origin. But the cleaning lady didn't hear her say these

things and if she had it may not have made the slightest difference to her. Even the clumsy attempt to play loud jazz music didn't mean anything to her.

In our mud hut we don't really compare the relative merits of Ella Fitzgerald and Billy Holliday. You cannot touch me or reach me in that way. I am not a stereotype or even an archetype. Like everyone on this planet I have a tribe, a class, a gender, a root. I think too but I think in silence. My words have no sound. They live and die within the enclosed space that is my consciousness. My thoughts are no purer than yours. My soul no nobler. I too am flawed. I too am of mother, am mother, am mother of mother. I didn't scrub marble floors in Africa. We had no marble floors in Africa but if we did I would no doubt have scrubbed them. And I am aware that although I would have scrubbed the marble floors for some white man or other - without colonisation, I would simply have scrubbed them for the black man who would have taken his place. My man is not a pœt. But he is touched by the abandonment of pœtry. The fatalism of pœtry weighs heavily on his shoulders. Maybe he is post pœtry, sensing the futility of words, the pointlessness of fragmented thought as a balm for wounds without end. He likes the wind and he likes the rains. His hands fit me as though carved by a blind sculptor but nonetheless they fit me. Perfect.

I clean your floors but perhaps if I too was rich, I would have someone like you clean my floors - this has occurred to me. It makes me feel uncomfortable so I tell myself

that I'd tread softly on them, leaving no footprint. I imagine too that I'd sit and have coffee with you, say 'forget
the floors today'. Ask how you were and how the kids
were and ask if you had a pœt for a husband and if his
hands fitted you with clumsy perfection. I'd pay you twice
the going rate and at Christmas time I'd buy you some
beautiful thing - anything at all once it was beautiful and
you'd be overcome by my kindness and my humanity. You
could not be black - I could never ask a black woman to
clean my floors not because I'm so noble and pure but
because I'd be too embarrassed to. I'd hire a woman from
the east of Europe - know how she might hate scrubbing
black floors and I'd try and change her hate. It's only skin
I'd say. Within the skin is what counts. I'd show her that
deep beyond my dark pigmentation I was Eastern European. Each gesture which I'd make would say 'I apologise
for Stalin and Ceaucescu and Honecker - I'm sorry you
were used as a social experiment. I'm sorry that so many
European intellectuals continue to be apologists for one
of the most failed political ideologies in human history.
I'm sorry that totalitarianism sees you simply as an object
by which to prove its jaded, inane, ludicrous social theory.
I'm sorry too that you have to scrub floors. I'm sorry that
you think me savage. You'd be tempted to remind me of
witch - doctors dancing around crazily in their uncomfortable grass skirts but I'd simply remind you of how you
burned women at the stake for being left-handed - I'm
sorry that I'm not white but I accept white as a credible
colour and even though it suggests sterility, I wouldn't
continually use it as a negative adjective - I'm sorry that

Decrescendo

my ancestors weren't there to defend Stalingrad. I too
would play you the complex notation of Jazz music to
show you we have more than primal rhythm in our root.

CHAPTER 6 : EVEN REVOLUTIONARIES
NEED A DAY TIME JOB.

Today we went downtown - Chiado - baixa chiado. Streets. Fine streets. Elizabeth likes Chiado, forty two likes Chiado. I like Chiado. Such unique shops. Finery. Lace and finery. Old charming cafes and rambling bookshops that somehow enhance the twisted, winding streets with their endlessly beautiful shiny stony tiles. Chocolates too. No waitresses. Only waiters. The waitresses must be off scrubbing floors somewhere. The pœt would have made a fine waiter.

How about ya sir and what can I get ya - excuse my Belfast accent it wont hinder my ability to say sir and it wont make me any more likely to drop trays. I can show the requisite humility. I wear an apron so you'd never know that I love Browning or Shelley for if you did you might tip me less. This might upset you as it would bring disorder to the order. In mitigation, you'll be pleased to note that my wife scrubs floors back home in Ireland. We know our place. Really. I come from a bardic tradition which is why I write pœtry, its not subterfuge nor an attempt to dodge the waitering draft - I swear.

Your son plants bombs, I hear?

He dœs, foolish boy but he'll see the error of his ways.

Decrescendo

He must think that colonisation is a bad thing then?

Oh he dœs sir but it's simply the misplaced ignorance of youth.

His mother must have failed in her nurturing role then?

I can't possibly say as it's outside my domain of expertise.

Ah you're sublimating your desire to blame women for their many sins - I like that -excellent survival skills, if I may say so.

I knew you'd respect the tokenism sir.

I hear that you read Shelley.

Not really sir, its more that I look at the pictures.

You should read Kipling.

Not quite to my taste sir.

That's a shame - damned fine writer - well travelled too.

Yes he surely was sir.

You're obviously not Portuguese?

Decrescendo

No indeed but in mitigation I've read Camões.

Now there's a proper pœt.

Yes indeed sir and a fine swimmer by all accounts.

A man's man.

I do agree - I always think that Camões lived as Shakespeare wrote.

That's so terribly true.

Too busy mirroring all those human frailties and vanities back to us to waste trivial thoughts of how his furniture should be dispersed with upon his death.

And do you write yourself in your spare time?

After Shakespeare and Camões... dœs anyone really write?

You're so right there my good man.

I mean what would the point be - and if I did I'd never seek to have it published, it would be much too arrogant.

Did you say your wife was a homemaker?

Indeed I did sir - doing her own wee bit to keep some

order on the chaos.

That's why I always dine in Chiado - so many colourful characters - you certainly deserve a tip.

You're too kind sir - to serve one's social betters is tip enough in itself.

I must concede that I like your attitude.

Chiado - home of claustrophobic crooked streets and men without legs to walk them. Shops old and shops new. From father to son - no daughters need apply. Quality maintained. Politeness in the best sense of that word. Commerce built without gold. Nooks and turns and more crooked streets. Majesty and decay walking hand in hand.

Elizabeth bought me a book today THE LISBON VAMPIRE - first and only edition - can't think why it didn't run to a second print.

If you only read one more book, let it be this one. Says that vampires are really of the city and not of the hills. She knows a lot about blood by the sound of it. Wanted to be a doctor. Her father was killed at some battle of the Somme or other - seems there was more than one. He'd encouraged her to study medicine. But she says that the battle of the Somme showed the futility of saving lives. Even vampires blush when the Somme is mentioned. So much blood. Blood seeping deep into the soil of France. English blood. Bet Napoleon would have loved that. Napoleon perhaps unconsciously dreamed of being German-

ic. No ships at the Somme. Napoleon was a real man. All
those plans for world domination. Can't imagine though
that basketball would have been his forte.

That hat can't have helped, should have gotten himself
a good leather belt too. Didn't want to be a king. Didn't
sound quite grand enough by all accounts. Maybe the
shops in Chiado wouldn't quite have suited his elegant
taste. Never asked the pœt about Napoleon though, for
he'd simply say something about 'just another wee tyrant
bastard' - sometimes pœts miss the obvious - I mean what
was he to do? No television to watch - cocaine wasn't yet
in fashion - a nymphomaniac for a wife - the English trying to cover the globe with empire - and a mediocre chess
player by all accounts and with a name like Bonaparte
he could hardly have scrubbed floors - mind you even
in those days high class waiting staff were in short supply and his French accent would have put him in line
to be sommelier - not sure if he knew too much about
wine but blood and wine are both frequently used by the
romantic pœts and after all that was his age. And speaking of pœts, many revolutionaries put pen to paper long
before they even dream of lighting a fuse. Stalin may have
been more successful in his quest to create havoc but his
pœtry is certainly readable - perhaps he may have been
a somewhat different man if only he had the life learning
task of waiting table for just a few years - all that measured, learned humility couldn't but have helped - but
somewhere along that walk which we all take he chose
other diversions - wanted people rather than words to do
his bidding - the urge to programme people far stronger

than the one to control imagery - late on some summer's evening as the sun went down and all was calm with the world and its way, if on that particular night of all nights, what if a young vibrant teenage Joseph Djugvallashi climbed over the wall of the orchard at the far end of town and tied a rope to a sturdy branch and threw it round his young neck and swung in the soft breeze till all life passed away from his youthful body, all and everyone who surveyed the grim aftermath could only have lamented bitterly the tragedy of such a promising young life force extinguished - and the peasant women who would have gathered around would have sobbed and wailed and sobbed some more and the peasant farmer who owned the orchard would have used fine, comforting words as consolation to those standing by and perhaps someone would also have been tempted to suggest that the world had lost an embryonic Shakespeare... how little we all truly know.

But the orchard graveside oration never quite took place - nor possibly did his brief stint as a Parisian waiter.

Yet even in that brief theoretical stint in I can so easily imagine him as a waiter. I can see his restless, repressed ruthlessness, concealed ability to scheme in quantum leaps, unimaginable to most who entered his orbit - the one even bereft of the glorious beauty of dying stars. A man not content to simply be from hell but one wired to ensure most everyone would join him on his return excursion.

Eyeing up the diners. Making plans. Picking favourite and least favourite diner. If the restaurant was one of fine French cuisine, Trotsky would have been a typical customer as he had those sophisticated notions of taste you know. And as he waited for service he'd be likely to drum his bony fingers on the table. It's doubtful if Jœ would have appreciated this though. Trotsky would probably have ordered from the menu in perfect French - which Stalin might just about have tolerated. Even if this went okay - the wine list would be bound to cause problems. Leon likely to select some rare chateau this or that - consoling himself no doubt with the belief that as a true smoked salmon socialist he advocated champagne for all, so why shouldn't he too indulge a little. Uncle Jœ meanwhile would be seething. This Jew with his cultured ways aping the bourgeoisie and all the while pretending to liberate the peasantry -fucking kulak - At this stage of his waiting career uncle Jœ would have a whole range of conflicting emotions re the customers and re his fellow waiters - mind you he wouldn't yet be a mass killer let alone tyrant of great note as working a double shift at la maison something or other dœsn't leave one with much spare time to plan the downfall of a czarist regime - I can hear you say - well let's try and be fair here - as a firm believer in PERMANENT REVOLUTION, Trotsky would realise that no matter what the outcome of 1917, there'd still be a revoultion in 1918, 1919, 1929 and so on -so what would be the point of skipping meals until the revolution was over... you'd starve. Meanwhile back in maison something or other Stalin is being an impeccable table servant... suave, precise, attentive to the curly headed ones every whim but all the while furtively awaiting an opening

Decrescendo

- a single moment to carve and dissect this parvenu.

Waiter was that the '87 or the '88 which you brought me?

As we've run out of '87, I took the liberty of bringing you the '88 - I trust that it was okay?

Oh yes - the '88 is fine - in fact there's a small school of thought that even suggests that the '88 is superior.

Is there indeed sir - that's incredibly hard to believe.

Yes it is hard to believe - by the way, do I detect a feint Georgian accent underneath your passable French?

Indeed you do sir, indeed you do - I spent some years there - and do I also hear the merest soupcon of mother Russia behind your impeccable French?

You're sharp as a rapier and thank you for the very kind compliment.

That's my raison d'être sir.

Mind you this seems like a jolly nice place to work.

And do I also detect from sir's vocabulary that he's been to Oxford?

You're making me blush now - no, in fact I haven't

Decrescendo

I'm merely a student of English writers - so many great English writers like Yeats and Shaw and Wilde and Le Fanu and Swift and so on.

Yes indeed - all great Englishmen.

You seem quite familiar with their literature?

I don't have sir's in depth knowledge but I am partial.

Bram Stoker's another favourite of mine.

A little too sanguine for my taste I'm afraid.

Blood flowing not quite your thing then?

No - I can't stand the sight of it.

Poor sensitive soul - you've a touch of the pœt in you.

Thank you - I write the odd bit of verse in my spare time.

Must be hard with all those double shifts?

Yes it is but one always hopes for a better future.

Can you bring me a little more veal please?

Right away sir. There we are, another thick slice of veal.

Decrescendo

Thank you - oh I'm so sorry for my manners - you'd been telling me about your plans for a better future.

Sir, you're too kind to give breath to my superficial whims.

No, no - we're all equal beings - can you please bring the dessert menu and perhaps I should wash down that veal with a second bottle of '88.

I must say sir that it's a privilege to serve such a cultured guest and one who has such empathy with the common working man.

No, it's my privilege - perhaps I too shall go somewhere peaceful and write down of my life.

Perhaps sir would enjoy the solitude and tranquility of Siberia.

Perhaps - they say that it's an oasis of calm and treacherous beauty.

Sir's never been then?

No - but perhaps one day.

Yes, indeed I can even picture you there in a fine log cabin, contemplating, philosophising, bringing that immense, razor sharp intellect to bear upon the telling problems faced by the downtrodden masses.

Can you really?

Oh yes - the winter sunshine - soft gentle snowflakes - hot red fire - toasted croissants

And soft cream cheeses?

Oh yes - lots of different cheeses - you could have them sent up from a big fancy store in St. Petersburg.

That would be absolutely ideal, but mind you the temperature might play havoc with them.

Be that as it may but the temperature of that isolated place would only enhance the champagne and the hand made chocolates from Geneva.

I could cope with the cheese in fact I often think that privation and hardship is good for the soul.

Perhaps one day sir will get the chance to test his theories - one never can quite tell.

How true - indeed one never can even half guess the future, why only last night I had a dream of a funny little man with a moustache sleeping in a doorway in some city like Paris or Vienna who eventually ruled the whole world.

That's so very interesting... - you say that he had a moustache ?

Yes - not totally unlike your own.

Ha! ha! ha!... perhaps it's omenous!

Stranger things have happened my friend - history is full of monuments built on foundations that appeared to initially be as solid as quicksand - why I might pop by here in twenty years time and ask for the wonderful waiter who served me all those years ago only to be told that you now have your own little bistro on Rue de la something or other!

Well I wont deny that similar such thoughts have occurred to me - in fact it even crossed my mind that a much more efficient way to run a restaurant would be to have but a single solitary option on the menu and to mass produce that dish in a thousand such restaurants throughout an entire country - even an entire continent - think of the pure harmony of efficiency that it would entail.

Well let me give you a parting word of advice - take your time - wait cautiously - keep your own counsel - trust no one - watch every move which everyone else makes - and then pounce - realise your destiny... never be on the wrong side of history.

Decrescendo

Thank you most graciously for the wise counsel - I'll try and heed it - I must go now as the new waiter dœsn't quite know how to use the ice pick.

Decrescendo

CHAPTER 7: THE LISBON VAMPIRE

I am the Lisbon vampire. I live in Lisbon and I am a vampire, hence the Lisbon vampire. *Separating fact from fiction with vampires is a most difficult thing to do and no doubt like me you may be incensed at the growing trivialisation of all things vampiric during this twentieth century - not a trend vampires of yore had to contend with - The idea that anyone would serve up as entertainment , stories in which their fellow humans end up as fodder for blood lusting vampires seems to me to be more than a trifle unseemly and one can only hope that it dœsn't signal a coarsening of public taste as the century progresses. My name is De vil era which is merely a coincidence or if one is inclined to use grandiose terms a piece of synchronicity - I have no connect with Bram Stoker author of the novel Dracula nor have I ever been to Dublin. Stoker's book seems to have tapped deeply into some root within the psyche of the common people. Films and plays continue his theme of castles and cloaks and other misplaced artifacts of Gothic style. As I write the year is 1958 and I was born in 1913. My parents were drowned when the cruise liner LUSITANIA was sunk during WW1. I was sent from my birth place (of which I cannot talk) to Heidelberg in Germany to be raised by a relative. I left Germany in 1936 at the unripe age of twenty two due to the fractured nature of that society - even the splinter groups themselves, splintered. Little did I know the wisdom of such a decision which far wiser counsels than I failed to arrive at. By sheer chance I came* to Portugal -again a coincidence since the Lusitania was so pivotal to my childhood.

I am tall and strong and unusually healthy but there my affinity with the count from the Carpathians ceases.

I am not eternal - I never will be. There is no connection between organic and eternal. No vampire is eternal. Perhaps time, carefully used, is the nearest thing to eternity and as a Greek philosopher once almost pointed out, we could in theory keep on subdividing a single second endlessly and whether or not this would stretch to eternity it would surely give us much value for that most priceless of concepts, time. We cannot be sure if eternity as we perceive it truly does exist much less if the arrow of time is in fact an arrow. The clock appears to mark accurately the thing which we call time but perhaps it simply marks the illusion of the passage of time. Wherever you find yourself you say I am here but there is of course no place called here. So with time we are tempted to see it as a progression - a thing heading in one direction only and are confronted by the idea of it being both exhaustible and yet finite.

Our problem with time is it's relentless ticking - it never sleeps but we alas must. It begins with a gentle ticking and eventually graduates to a deafening boom, boom, boom... alternatively it begins with a crashing boom, boom, boom and recedes into a gentle, whispering tick, tick, tock, until finally there is no one left to hear its sound. It then reverts back to its conceptual aura and beats in non beats for all eternity - that of course, assuming that eternity itself exists is an entity. Yet if eternity exists it must then be finite thus we are left with yet another paradox and paradox is the only concept that time seems to bequeath us.

Decrescendo

*I too have not mastered time. To do so one would have
to turn it off much like the throwing a switch. Suspend it.
Freeze it. Strangle it. But as it may not exist in terms which
we comprehend this is fraught with profound difficulty to say
the least. On the mundane life planks on which we monoto-
nously tread, our problem with time is much more basic but
yet again ridden with conundrum. It is this... whether we use
time wisely or whether we waste each moment in sheer frivolity... IT STILL APPEARS TO GO. We cannot store it. Repair
it. Nurture it. Grow it. Slow it.*

*Time is beyond the hand of man and even the hand of the
master watchmaker. This is an irreversible absolute. There
the discussion ends. So, I have not struck any fatal blows
in the unsinkable battle with time. I am not eternal. I have
learned to manage the use of time far better than most which
sometimes leads to the illusion of existing forever yet it is but
an illusion. Once I spent an entire day and night looking at
the Atlantic sea. Wave after wave. Wave after wave. Wave
after wave. Each one the same but different. Convincing
myself that each wave had a birth an action and a crescendo
before its demise. Each wave made but of water - water that's
been present since the world began. Waves that must have
contained connection with Cæsar and with Moses. Immersed
in this communion with the sea, I became full of its presence,
dizzy with its bent, overwhelmed with its twist. And in my
way became as near to water as flesh and blood had ever
done. I never once thought of the Lusitania sinking to the
bottom of the cold, dark ocean. The apathy of the water to
my presence told me it would not shed tears for my loss and I
understood why water would not cry.*

Decrescendo

*I do not drink water. I do not eat flesh. I do not indulge
in banquets. I drink blood and I drink red wine and one day
each week I eat dry bread which fills me with nausea. Like
most human beings I am a raft of contradictions but unlike
others I seldom attempt to conceal them nor do I attempt to
justify them, I even acknowledge them whenever I can.*

*I sense your revulsion at my confession. This I understand.
I too, at first was repulsed and sought reasons to cease living
with myself. But the desire for life is beyond rationale - of
itself it functions.*

*In the end being a man of reason I concocted a loop - I can
call it by no better name -by which I wove a tale of justification and spun it on my loom of logic and although it wasn't
bespoke, it covered the nakedness and vulnerability. I needed
one human corpse per month in order to satisfy my blood lust.
That's twelve a year and since I've begun this odyssey seven
years ago, you have some idea of the huge toll of bodies that
were once human. I don't enjoy the act of the kill, in it I
find no sport. To make some attempt to minimise the damage
which I do, I go to great lengths to select my victims -for that
is what they are. I rule out anyone under forty two years -
this may seem an arbitrary figure and in a sense everything is
arbitrary - I digress - anyway my thinking, such as it is, reasons that at forty, one has had a real taste of existence and is
not quite being plucked in the first bud of youth... so I allow
one more year to pass some kind of symbolic threshold.*

*But after forty one - all are fair game. Forty two up are
still often in prime condition and I don't have too much difficulty repressing whatever small desire I have for younger
blood. I spend two weeks out of each four selecting appropri-*

ate cargo - I prefer this word as it accords a semblance of respect to the human body by way of value and yet is devoid of the hypocrisy of piety. Well I remember my first victim, a journalist - a man full of opinions - wrote a small piece - not quite a diatribe - but nonetheless scathing of some facet or other about Portuguese society - a would be rebel - reformer - seeking change - but vampires don't need change - we seek continuity - status quo - modernity with its incessant evolution is not to our taste - and inevitably we are social conservatives... why would we not be ?... tradition has aided us well and in many ways the entire human race would do well to remember that tradition has served them reasonably well too and it's also worth bearing in mind that each and every system is hugely imperfect - one of the things that helps 'progressives' in their battle to change society is that the real benefits of traditions can seldom be measured by charts and statistics and indices... tradition enriches people in slightly vague almost abstract ways that cannot easily be measured - how dœs one accurately gauge a sense of 'wellbeing' - it's simply a thing that people become aware of mostly when it is absent - unfortunately we are also entering the age of a rights based society - what right should anyone have after all other than the right to exist? So many people whose sole purpose simply seems to be to poke their noses into the business of others - by what right dœs any man or woman have the entitlement to say 'I know what's best for you'... I can already see you pointing to certain contradictions in my orthodoxies... your point is duly noted... I admit that the conservative philosophy has certain paradoxes which can on occasion lead us to take strange bedfellows - I appear to support strong, overpowering government and yet seek less government intervention - well let me try and explain (rather than excuse) the apparent contradictions... conservatives believe that the happiness of the individual is better determined by each and every man, and to a degree, woman, rather than by some intellectual sitting round a table who supposedly has our welfare at heart and whilst I don't deny that many progressives are genuinely motivated their penchant for near total idiocy is so immense that I rarely trust their pontificating on any subjects outside of jazz music and abstract art - we conservatives who inadvertently supported that man from Linz before the war have little problem in admitting that we were indeed wrong and our trust was sorely misplaced and most of the remaining diehards who defended him through the 1940's finally admitted that his escapade was wrong, evil and a very bad thing BUT this very day as I write in June 1959, so many European thinkers and intellectuals still directly offer support of some kind - moral or verbal to those despots in Moscow... how sad is that... what are they waiting for? how many more countries must they annex? how many more gulags must they furnish with human cargo for them to admit that the EXPERIMENT failed and that less rather than more government hands on is a far better thing? That little speech may seem just a bit off kilter with my choosing the state of Portugal to settle in, but please let me explain - there is a subtle yet profound difference between a fascist dictator and a paternalistic autocrat - who amongst us dœsn't secretly seek a wise, kindly, benevolent father figure? Is that not one of the foundations of all images of a personal God? I need not remind you that this past two decades have been turbulent times and if a strong arm

*on the tiller was necessary then it was a strong arm which
saved us from every kind of tyranny be it political or economic
and anyway politics is always a compromise of siding with
he who is likely to do the least damage... so as you see I am
not suggesting the 'benevolent' dictator is the ideal... perhaps
this country should seriously consider restoring the monarchy... perhaps Portugal could again be the centre of the known
universe if she dusted off the cobwebs at Mafra - I can see it
now... after the usual ballyhoo by the liberals and progressives (mind you one way to get them on board for a restora-
tion would be to start up a petition to give equality to such a
threatened minority as a king in exile... surely they couldn't
resist that one? after all, it fits perfectly into their belief that
the vast majority should always make the seismic shift to
accommodate the small minority) the king or queen could be
enthroned... the glamour... the glitter... the awe... majesty and
decadence in an irresistible mix - think of the certainties it
would bestow upon each man and woman - no more petty
politicians pretending to empathise with your every whim
and sneeze - no petty condescension from your idiot neighbour
who earns a few more escudos than you or happens to drive
an eight year old car whilst you drive a nine year old one
and imagine too all those noveau-riche with their airs and
graces suddenly reduced to social nothingness by the trail of a
royal garment - as I may not have already mentioned, I once
worked for a spell in advertising and the habit dies hard so
my prepaid apologies in advance for inflicting this particular
one on you... 'Let's swap our airs and graces for HEIRS and
graces'... now where was I ? politics inevitably cause much
digression... Oh yes... time... and as I've already shown as time*

Decrescendo

is beyond measure, whether one exists for *x* time or twice *x*
time is but a statistical irrelevance. Mind you if victim number one's blood was anything to go by... he had a good heart.
Number two I also remember well - a woman. Yet another
bloody reformer. Talking about the rights of women not being
vindicated - I remember the word well VINDICATED - such
a big word for such a little woman as she scarcely weighed
fifty kilos - that was a lean month indeed.

All of the others loosely met this criteria. People unhappy
with their lot - bleeding hearts that I decided to let bleed for
me. I must mention number fifty - not merely because of its
numeric milestone but also because he had this quaint notion
of encouraging women to bear less babies - to take control of
their fertility was how he put it - having less, he said would
allow better nurturing and also give the mother some other
role beyond childbearing - I need hardly tell you this was in
no way beneficial to the vampiric cause - I mean it's hard
enough spiriting away a few drops of blood from a populous
society, the last thing we need is less souls.

And so on and so on... that is how each one went. Thought
and selection. Proof of the wisdom of my methods were borne
out by the lack of furor at any of these disappearances - what
loss one parvenu more or less. As I write I'm selecting my
next victim - who on paper at least, seems tailor made. She
works in the field of healthcare and is vocal on the need to
monitor the welfare of institutions for the criminally insane
- revealing no doubt her own insanity - as if people didn't
have enough on their plate without worrying about all those
crazies. Wants some of them to be released back into society
- calls it reintegration - and although this too is a big word,

Decrescendo

I must concede her entitlement to so use it as she is a tall and most voluptuous lady - a veritable feast. A point could be made however that the extra blood supply created by their presence on the streets would be welcomed by the average vampire but I hold no brief with this opinion as I feel nausea at even the thought of sipping on blood which has spent years devouring all those toxic drugs they fill those crazies with. Without too much of a reach one can easily opine that my dining off her will benefit all mankind. Why anyone seeks to alter things is a mystery to me. The devil you know is what I always say. Since change is always ongoing and inevitable - why seek to hurry it?

Perhaps I hear you say that by attempting to channel and influence it we can try and influence it for the better - to that I simply reply - who amongst us is wise enough to say 'I know what's best'.

CHAPTER 8: CAUSE AND NO EFFECT

R ita a.k.a. forty two was a spectral figure around the house and for the first time in her young life Kate knew that she had met someone whom she didn't understand at all - someone with whom she was unable to find any remote point of connectivity - any hint of sameness.

Even when present it was still as if she wasn't quite there. Her brother spoke disparagingly of her as he did of most people but even her mother seemed to show an odd detachment towards her as well. Rita's 'problem' went undetected, unnoticed, beyond discussion and unresolved - many of life's conflicts remain unresolved because of the diverse, complex nature of conflict itself but Rita's 'problem' was as universal as it was tragic - her problem was entirely not of her making, in fact quite the opposite and even sadder was the fact that it was one of those difficulties that possibly could have been fixed or at least significantly alleviated. There is no lyricism in the following tale because life's empty corridors don't quite lend themselves to pœtry and on their shabby walls hang drab paintings where the only shadings are confusion. And like so many tragic tales, we've all heard them so many times before that we become immunized - forgetting one of life's single most important lessons which is that each living entity has their own tale to tell and in turn is always entitled to tell it. The art of telling has so many different tones, infinite nuances and subjective interpretations that only those possessed of a beautiful ear can truly listen.

Her parent's were each ensconced in their own worlds and didn't notice the initial change in her personality simply because they had never really been close enough to her in the first place to notice its shift or tremble. Collectively we call it 'depression', an umbrella term that saves us from having to dig deeper, prevents us from having to enter the place where the weeds grow and the lilies are extinct. How to even begin to comprehend that one man or one woman's blue sky appears as a dark grey, wet heavy blanket to another observer. How do we begin to acknowledge that for some the blackbird's song is oddly out of tune. An abstract problem that endlessly manifests itself in practical ways - the conversion of the metaphysical to the physical - no permission sought or needed. My legs, though young and strong, feel heavy, heavy with all the iron ever ored since the world began. I too see the precious baby smile its sacred smile yet it dœsn't fill me with hope much less send my dragons running. For me, hope is a flightless bird. I try. God knows that I try. With each and every waking breath, but no new posture, no different approach, no shift in how I see life's facets, make it sparkle diamond-like. On good days I envy all those who treasure the tender flapping of the butterfly's wings and on bad days I would gladly swop places with a chrysalis. For me there is no turn in the road - the road refuses to rise with me - it continues as a vast, immeasurable expanse of stretch that possesses not even a single curve. Curiously too and adding to such a problem is that within our culture, to be a healer in the profession that claims to assist with the healing of this illness, one need not even possession a single cell of compassion, wisdom or empathy for any who may suffer - one person's hell may lead to a heavenly life style of another - no vocation necessary - just a desire to amass gold and no need to even wash your hands after each transaction. The old maid/housekeeper thought many of her day to day responses were odd but a combination of subservience to her social superiors and the fear and terror of speaking words that those better educated than herself always prevented her from verbalising it - the list of both profound and inconsequential problems associated with depression is endless but most of all the sense of being utterly abnormal and alone always leads back to a signpost marked as inevitable - during these times, colour only appears on the black and white spectrum, a little girl who probably had been an odd, aloof child to begin with became an even odder, much more aloof, young woman.

She led a kind of virtual life - observed everything but rarely commented upon anything.

And though she did at times participate with other children, family and schooling, she did so in a measured, calculating, half-hearted way.

The word ghost, despite it's overuse and its necessary vagueness still best describes how she perceived the world when she looked out and it also best describes the way the world saw her on the odd occasions that it bothered to look in.

The illness itself, who isn't worthy of any real analyses unless we seek to admit that there is not, never was

Decrescendo

and never will be any NORMAL - there is of course the inevitable why her and not him but WHY, understandably asks further whys and, as we begin to subdivide and qualify each one under an incessant stream of microscopes, it inevitably encourages us to mitigate the devastation of the 'victim' - the word victim is so often used with such banality - we hear people talk about A VICTIM OF THEFT, for example - but how many of these victims themselves would steal a thing given the opportunity.

How many 'victims' of a domestically violent spouse would have fought with us to the death for their 'right' to marry that same spouse and would have walked on the old hot coals to prove to us that all our assumptions of what that same spouse was really like, were simply insane prejudices.

Collectively we often debate things not because debate is per se a good thing but because we have become entrenched in the fallacy of every tale having two sides -whatever happened to 'sometimes there's no why but simply an it is' perhaps we also need a debate on whether or not gravity really exists...

My name is professor Tom Smith and I'm here to put forward the facts to prove that gravitation as a provable force dœs in fact exist.

Well Mr. professor, with your fancy title and swanky name, I'm not daring to suggest that it COULDN'T actually exist but more to ask if it might not - I like to keep an open mind on things.

Decrescendo

Well I can clearly and simply show every single time
- without exception - that objects with mass do attract
one another and the most obvious example of this is how
all around us we see gravity give weight to any object of
mass and will cause them to fall to the ground if dropped.

With all due respect to you sir, and you and your fancy
theories, but surely in day to day life the real reason that
things fall when dropped is due to our immense care-
lessness - is it not a fact that if we as a species were far
more adept in our embrace of everyday objects, very few
if any would fall to the ground and so this dubious claim
you make for gravity would have far less validity as there
would be almost no examples.

As a scientist I find your logic preposterous.

You do? ... well that's interesting... history repeating
itself.

I beg your pardon?

I say it's interesting that you find my response preposterous solely because I disagree with you and it's somewhat ironic as it reminds me of how similar my predica-
ment is to Galileo's and your position is to the pope's.

I cannot believe what I am hearing - this is outrageous.

No sir, that's exactly my point, nor could the pope, your

attitude mirrors his exactly when Galileo had the temerity to question his scientific 'facts'.

You are completely twisting the situation - if anything you have reversed the entire scenario.

Well, well, well... I have reversed the entire scenario... let me see... just for a moment... you be Galileo then and I'll be the pope for you see I am so honest and sincere and open that I don't need the security of blindly defending some position.

This is conversation is utterly devoid of any common sense.

Just indulge me a few moments if you will - I take it that your SCIENTIFIC mind is at least open enough for that?

Very well - it's against my better judgment - but go ahead.

Well mister Galileo... I'd like to ask you a few questions about gravity... can you conclusively show me how a gravitation pull works in day to day life?

Yes, it's quite simple really, as Newton shows...

Mr.Galileo... please... I hate to interrupt you so abrupt-ly... but who on earth is this Newton? I sincerely hope that you're not attempting to use the theories of a man who is as yet unborn as you speak, for that would be dishonest, disingenuous and downright illogical and as your beliefs are based solely on empirical proofs I cannot possibly allow the ideas of someone as yet unborn - bad enough to contend with reality without introducing the spectre of theories that as we speak are not even at the conceptual stage.

I am afraid that I can no longer continue with this farce - you are attempting to ridicule scientific truths that all scientists completely concur with - namely the force of gravitational pull.

Well then it's just as well that we do discontinue this debate especially as I see you advancing your ARGU-MENTUM AD NUMERUM strategy and its absurd premise that simply because everyone believes something that it couldn't be incorrect... I'm afraid my mind is too open and rational and inquisitive ever to be a scientist.

So many explanations on so many issues far too simplistic and much too linear for some. Not nearly as complex as we somehow imagine it should be. We are a species of problem solvers, which is perhaps necessary as we also have an immense capacity to both destroy and destruct. Science usually works and when it dœsn't it tends to self correct - it has no mason like guild of shadowy figures intent on protecting inaccurate, non empiric values. Quasi science on the other hand is its polar opposite and its damage is beyond measure for it takes zero responsibility for its idiocy, foolish theories, random guesswork and saddest of all, despite all evidence to the contrary, demands respect and to be treated as if carved in stone.

Thank you for coming along.

Thank you for seeing me doctor.

I'm not a doctor.

Oh - there must be some mistake - the prison warden said that you were a psychiatrist?

His mistake - I'm not - I'm a nothing - just an ordinary person - think of me as the man in the street.

But I can't talk to the man in the street - as a convicted serial killer, I'm aware that he couldn't possibly begin to comprehend the underlying, profound psychological complexities governing my sociopathic behaviour.

I see what you're getting at - he would erroneously think that you cut up the 120lb body of the girl simply because you desired to?

Yes - that's it.

He would attempt to attribute such abstractions as evil as your motive?

Precisely.

May even be foolish enough to believe that you could have desisted from your actions if in fact you had wished to?

I couldn't have put it better myself.

Whereas a psychiatrist would be non judgmental - might understand that you were overtaken by an over-powering impulse that was much too strong to resist?

That's it in a nutshell.

And he wouldn't dare use derogatory or judgmental language?

Definitely not.

Like refer to you as a pervert or a maniac or a weirdo or a nutcase or as an evil sick, twisted bastard - a worth-less waste of space?

Never - such men and women are trained to probe the dark side of the human psyche - to understand that the human psyche is deep and complex and multi layered. They understand the vague mechanisms that make people like me do what we do - they interpret the evidence in an almost exculpatory way - subscribing actions to a com-bination of many overlapping, complicated permutations which overwhelm the perpetrator and indirectly make him too a victim.

I see your perspective and duly note it but I thought just for a laugh and completely off the record and as I'm not a doctor of the mind which guarantees that no-one on earth would listen to let alone give any remote credence to my ignorant opinion, that maybe we two could chew the fat.

I'm not so sure...

Perhaps I could appeal to your ego and your desire to be flattered and respected?

Go on then - give it a shot...

You do understand that anything which I may utter is solely to assuage your ego and temperament and the like?

Unless of course you fall under my charm and become a believer.

Okay... we have a deal.

Let me begin by using a little perspective and may I do so by suggesting to you that your demeanour very much reminds me of another serial killer.

Pray tell who?

Decrescendo

The master of them all.

Surely you could only be talking about one man?

Indeed... for there could be no other.

My respect for you and your insight is already starting
to grow - so few people today are willing to acknowledge
the master as the master - twentieth century life is still
fixated by his deeds yet only insofar as his identity still
intrigues them - he has them hooked still by his enigmatic
persona.

And this saddens you somewhat?

Yes - incredibly so - it would be like people reading
Shakespeare solely because they thought that he might
not be from Stratford.

I see - you feel then that the other aspects of the man
are more praiseworthy?

Yes - just as with Shakespeare - the bard's name alone
makes him worthy of some adulation.

I see exactly what you mean - you're in effect saying
that if Shakespeare had a name like say BOB JONES, that
he would be far less interesting and that we would be less
likely to appreciate his immense literary brilliance.

Decrescendo

Exactly - exactly - you've hit the nail on the head - who wants to read a passionate love sonnet by some bloke called BOB?!

I can see that you're a connoisseur of all peripheral things in relation to your chosen passions.

Why, thank you.

So for you the wizard of Whitechapel is not merely some slayer of bodies, nor some hapless urchin hacking off organs?

No, not at all.

For an æsthete like yourself it's the style of the man that inspires awe?

Well obviously the hacking of the bodies is important too - but the other stylistic considerations are vital also in order to gain my veneration.

His choice of location?

Absolutely.

An area which teemed with the seedy underbelly of all human life?

Yes.

Decrescendo

The twisted majesty which he brought to this glorious decadence - the pœtry of the silhouette?

Continue please.

The black hat, the silk black cape, the soft kid leather gloves, the crisply laundered white shirt with its spotless starched collar, the cane carved from finest oak with its tip of Birmingham hallmarked silver, the hand-made patent leather shœs beating out a death knell with each step on the wet cobbles, and the all black hansom cab with the immaculately groomed stallion of fiery temperament for which to make his clean getaway?

Yes, yes, yes a thousand times yes. Although you may be a tad inaccurate re the rain.

The shrill whistles of a hapless, badly organized force of Peelers heard through the thick London fog, the other worldly atmosphere exposed by the struggling gaslight and the screams of the startled wretches as they come upon the master's craftsmanship.

Again yes and yes.

You're a very sick man if I may say so.

No, not at all, feel free to, in fact it's the general consensus amongst the common man like yourself - not withstanding your ability to present so wonderful a Victorian ambience as accurately as any thrupenny novel.

I see that we're getting a trifle touchy.

It's nothing in particular against the man in the street but you must understand that only a highly trained, even a specially trained mind can begin to comprehend the demons that rage within a man like me or even the master - these intricate things dancing within different levels of both our conscious and our subconscious mind are well beyond the grasp of the normal man or woman - we are haunted by the atomic intensity of our unstoppable drive.

Unstoppable?

Yes - totally - it's like a force ten storms ravaging, rampaging dynamo from nature herself - an organic typhoon of mayhem and brutality for which we are the mere conduits.

An irresistible force?

That's it - as I've already ventured, simply unstoppable.

So what would happen to this unstoppable force if someone took a serial killer and put them on a desert island that was unpopulated?

Your lack of sincerity shows in such a disingenuous

question - even allowing for your non - specialised knowl-edge - you both offend and disappoint me - this is why I always insist on speaking to a psychiatrist, for they would never play such games.

Perhaps I should apologise for the crudity of my ap-proach.

Perhaps you should sir - on an uninhabited island I'm hardly likely to kill anyone... now am I? ... your argument is therefore ridiculous.

So, all that would stop you killing on the uninhabited island would be lack of inhabitants?

Give that man a dog biscuit - YES ! - even a master craftsman like he from Whitechapel couldn't give vent to an uncontrollable urge on a deserted Island - case closed.

One last thing, if I may... what would happen if I put you on a remote island - populated with a thousand women...

Why I'd slay many of them of course.

Let me finish my half asked question - each of the thou-sand women were taller, much stronger and much smarter than you and each had a machine gun as well?

Hmmm... that's a bit of a poser - I'll grant you that but

believe me when I tell you that I'd find a sly way to ensnare one or two.

And if all one thousand swore to look out for and help
and protect each other and further added that if and
when they caught anyone who touched a hair on the head
of any that he'd feel their wrath?

I told you that this force is unstoppable - I'd still go for
it - a lifetime in a warm cell with decent meals and the
odd radio show or book, the ability to correspond with
the outside world - free healthcare - no bills to pay - I
might even take the opportunity to read 'An appreciation
of the career of the great Pinochet' by Professor Thatcher,
which I've always wanted to do... that would hardly deter
me... now would it?

You know how on occasions women can also become
tribal - this is one of those times - there'd be no prison if
they caught you, simply a tribal justice - they'd beat you
for hours with sticks and stones - then let a rat gnaw your
testicles for a bit - then beat you some more - then you'd
be thrown back into your four foot by four foot cell with
no bed nor blankets nor lighting and given one solitary
bowl of soup each day and obviously you'd be castrated
with a rusty knife and the process would be repeated each
and every day until you died.

If it was really exactly as you say, then I must confess
that common sense strongly suggests that I would almost

certainly limit my needs to fantasy and not think of seriously attempting to realise them into reality and besides I abhor any kind of soup.

I don't believe you.

I'm actually being honest - the survival instinct is a strong one too - this you cannot deny.

Stronger than the unstoppable one?

Yes indeed - have you ever heard of a fellow serial killer who sought out only heavyweight boxers to kill and maim?

Can't say that I have... no.

Think about it - so many of my fellow serial killers and not a single one obsessed or insane enough to go after them?

I see your point.

Our unstoppable urge is by necessity tailored to those whom we consider weaker than us or those whom we see as vulnerable.

I hadn't realised that the unstoppable urge was so organised and arranged - I had believed it to be much more chaotic and random and almost pre-ordained?

Decrescendo

Of course not - nothing can really override the survival instinct unless of course you're daring to accuse us of a thing like altruism?

No - I wouldn't dare malign your belief system with such foul allegations.

Thank you for the respectful tone even if I cœrced it from you.

You are right that this is a job way beyond my training - my limited way of thinking - my man in the street mentality is clearly at a disadvantage trying to fully comprehend such complex people as serial killers.

I'm delighted to note your change of attitude - that is in itself a form of homage from your starting position.

You're most welcome - and to think people often describe your caste as manipulative - so in summation may I describe your essence this way... you have an unstoppable urge that is qualified only by an organic instinct for survival and fear of your crimes being replicated on your own being.

Excellent - I couldn't have phrased it any better myself.

So Rita evoked no sympathy, no concern, no anything - marked down as just one more peculiar person in what we all agree upon is a strange world - another social misfit - unable to 'keep' a man - living only for her career - unable to smell the roses - her pain and her degradation would always remain locked away in some compartment or other somewhere, some place that nobody ever sought access to because it appeared that this was just her - some odd facet of who and what she was. As a teenager her mother did take her to some type of counselor - for some apparently unrelated matter and because the woman was kind and soft, Rita found herself opening up these gaping sores but all the woman had to offer was softness and emotional caresses and this was not what she needed or wanted - she wanted to arouse some empathy, some response, she wanted to be told that life often is full of dark terrible nights, ones on which the stars abandon us but that it also has balmy summer evenings when just the sheer act of breathing can fill us with a sense of wellbeing, that we can only describe as wondrous - the counselor herself lacked a sense of wonder and thought of life as a fairly rational paradigm and had never one time in her own life thought deeply about the absurd abstraction that life actually is. Not one time had the counsellor thought about such an obvious thing as how conflicted we all are by the paradox of being some kind of cognitive or spiritual entity trapped inside of an atrophying cluster of billions of cells. Tales unlikely to be true - she did discuss it with fellow analysts but to a man they concurred that it was sure to be the girl's imagination if not some type of repressed desire or urge - and that it was not uncommon for girls - especially such physically plain ones to seek

attention with invented fables of their narcissistic suffer-
ings. Much easier to always give children what we want
to give them - things which assuage our own inner beliefs
- things which make us feel okay rather than attempt to
give the child things that he or she may need.

Giving children what they need, can come into conflict
with our sleeping dogs. To give anyone what they may
need to prosper we have to go to the trouble of connecting with all the disparate facets of their personality and
being - not an easy thing to do -and then we have to
throw away those preconceptions which turned out to
be wrong and override what we had once believed - red
roses in the bedside vase may sound beautiful but they
only emit beauty if the recipient likes red roses in a vase
for if they do not then even weeds might be better.

CHAPTER 9: FASHION.

Elizabeth was old and Kate realised just how beautiful an old lady could be. Beautiful and old. Old and beautiful, meant to be in conflict - opposites. Kate had searched for a word to describe her face but only the word perfect fitted it - there was a thing about it that made it seem so right. The inner and the outer calm blending in a harmonic. Old-worn, weary, weaseled, wasted - but not this time. Kate wished she could paint or sculpt or do one of those things that lent a hint of posterity to an image.

I am old inside and I am old outside but despite the burden of chronology I have retained. Nature, germ, thief, begone. Mirror, reflector of unwanted truth, break into pieces of many. Fresh skin blooming to wither. Last year's model. I have spent thousands of days fighting this unwinnable fight. This battle against nothing and everything. Each step taken. Each one a candidate to be the last. No next breath guaranteed. Randomness. Randomness of all things living. Living of all things - random.

Old - survivor - fingers up to death - death wish absent - fester, decay but still part of a scheme we call living. Old, crumbling facade, decay of majesty's grandeur - crescendo waiting - but each wave must run its course - each stone intent on its own entitlement to roll to the bottom of its particular hill.

Kate felt something strange and wonderful in her presence. Seed of Cromwell filled with humanity. She thought of all those myriad ways in which we inevitably attempt to judge human worth - from the absurdity of beauty to the inanity of intelligence.

All those overlapping, grey, uncertain, barely formed, contradictory, vacillating, feeble ways in which we try to assess our fellow beings. People all of us. Basically simple, millions in common but all a tiny bit different yet bound up in the complex business called life. Still there was a thing that she felt defined people from other people. Wary of words she was reluctant to name it. It named itself inside her head. A thing of kind. A thing that spoke. A thing that was. It was neither quite physical nor meta-physical. What it was?

It was a suggestion - a gist of a thing which hinted that... I am here... I've seen it all... I know things but I also don't know things.

If you were dying on a lonely road in a lonely forest, I probably could not save you (remember, I gave up medi-cine) but I'd acknowledge that you had existed - I would not thieve your pockets - if somewhere in our empire there was some general or other who commanded me to shoot you by firing squad - I'd refuse and risk court martial. If we only glanced at each other from opposite sides of a railway platform in some remote place in some indeterminable time in history, our eyes would meet and in that brief, nothing moment, we'd acknowledge some slight sliver of some shared commonality thing which we are proud to call humanity.

Elizabeth still dressed beautifully each day and this too won Kate's admiration - eighty years and three hundred and sixty five days in each year - that's twenty nine thousand and two hundred and probably twenty more for leap years - all those bodies to be washed - all those dresses to wear - so many limbs to cover - small limbs - growing limbs - happy limbs - blissful limbs - rejected limbs - tired limbs. So many colours. So many fabrics. Folding and unfolding. Creasing and uncreasing. Silk as soft as the skin it draped. Rough wools. Well washed cottons. Hip hugging allure. Garments to taunt. Garments to tease. Clothes practical and restrictive as German bombs rained down, blitzkrieging mannequins and bodies alike and after this all still the colours want to match her mood, still the shapes want to fit that old body. She is old but she's not waiting to die. One thing all the living share is that they've never died before - not one of them. Never.

We all must die.

So it seems.

You're not so sure?

I didn't say that.

No, but you don't sound absolute.

It's outside my domain.

Perhaps, but have you ever known anyone to reverse the trend?

Decrescendo

Can't say I have.

There you go again.

Pardon?

That less than total thing you're going on with.

Dœs it disturb you?

I find it a little disingenuous - that's all.

As I've already said - it's well outside of my domain.

So you think that some people don't die?

That wasn't what I said.

Not word for word, no, but that was the implication.

I apologise for my uncertainty... it's just that...

Yes?

Well, it's just that when we consider that I've never died before - so even if I was shot a dozen times and lay oozing blood, I'd still think, maybe I'm not dying and as long as I was able to think that much it would affirm that in fact I was still alive.

Decrescendo

Okay, I get it - point taken but my comment was slightly different - I was stating that it's the one guaranteed common factor which all living organisms share.

Yes, I suppose that you're right there.

There you go again.

A thousand apologies but it's just that I don't understand death enough to comment so explicitly or forensically upon it.

Okay, okay, okay... let me simplify it for you - if someone threw you into a canyon, a deep canyon, down two thousand feet and you lay at the bottom for six whole months, without any food, you'd be dead right?

Yes, I suppose that I would be.

Let me get this straight - a tiny piece of you still feels that you still might be alive - after the canyon fall and the starvation?

Look, I'll be honest with you, I've had this kind of blind optimism since my childhood.

Blind, deaf and dumb by all accounts.

No need to be too personal.

Decrescendo

But your evasion is so, so frustrating.

I'll try to do better... two thousand foot drop and no food for six months - is that correct?

Yes.

And no water?

Correct - no water.

That's it - no other caveats?

No other caveats.

You're absolutely sure? You won't add any on?

I promise.

Okay.. .well... hmmm... first off I have to acknowledge the colossal, overwhelming, immense probability that I would indeed be dead... 99.999999%... or something like that... BUT... and remember no caveats...

No caveats.

Suppose then that on the morning that you pushed me over the canyon's edge, my body was about 50 kilos overweight.

Decrescendo

We're using metric now?

Sometimes it's handier. So if I was 50 kilos overweight and for breakfast that morning I ate ten eggs, twenty sausages, five large steaks and three cans of beans and ten pieces of thick brown bread.

I can see why you're so overweight.

And let's say I also drank ten litres of orange juice that was laced with super vitamins. My huge bulk would to some degree mitigate my fall - would it not?

Possibly - to a tiny degree.

And if my head didn't hit the ground I might still be conscious when I hit the bottom, at least theoretically - couldn't I be?

Remote as the chances would be... I give you that one... theoretically... yes.

Okay - so far so good - now next let us say that I landed in a patch that protected me from direct sunlight.

Go on...

Well, I could live on my body fat for quite a time and could do without liquids for a few days at least - then if it started to rain I might just be able to turn my head to

catch enough drops to stay alive and if there happened
to be some kind of edible shrub thing that had some
kind of non toxic berries and if I was barely able to move
my hand to snatch five or six every few days - who can
say for absolute certain that I couldn't survive the entire
ordeal.

Incredible... you really believe that insane upbeat explanation which you've just spouted out?

It's not about belief or disbelief.

I should have added that there would be a maniac with
a chainsaw down at the bottom who loved sawing up
people.

Yes, you could have but I'd simply have said that maybe
he'd trip and bang his head on a rock as he was about to
carve me up.

Hmmm.

So, at eighty Elizabeth had had that twilight period
where probability starts to overtake possibility. It was
possible that she could live for maybe another six or
seven years but it was more probable that she would not.
The classic hourglass - eternal symbol of time for all it's
æsthetic beauty never manages to even momentarily defy
gravity. The sands of time do their work as assiduously
and as accurately as any precision built Swiss timepiece.

Decrescendo

They start running in their metronomic way long before the umbilical cord sees the light of day - perhaps from the moment of our conception and the only guarantee which they give is none.

They do not pledge the biblical three score and ten - they do not pledge half of it nor do they pledge a fraction - no matter how small - in short they do not pledge even our next breath.

Each April 24th, Elizabeth held a big party to acknowledge the passing of another year. A celebration. A house and garden party. A champagne and eats party. A musical party. A people party. The older you become, by necessity, the younger the guests at one's party became. What once had been modern culture eventually became ancient. Outdated. Post dated. Dated. Dusty. Half-forgotten. Then forgotten. Almost.

Things multiply. Never decrease. More. More. More. Never less. More stuff. More mistakes. Growing. Adding on. Extra. Surplus. Taller. Wider. Denser. Unfolding. The unfolding itself unfolding. Something out of nothing. No diminution. No abatement. From the ashes a flotilla of phœnixes. On each feather a million atoms and in each atom a million possibilities.

How high can you count?

I once counted up to three thousand and two hundred and forty two - I could possibly have gone higher but the realisation dawned on me that no matter how high would not be high enough. Infinity plus one only seems a really high number until it's surpassed by infinity plus two.

Decrescendo

Mind you infinity to the power of infinity sounds pretty high though there's probably some trick whereby they cancel each other out so that you're not really left with that much at all. New, newer, newest. Fashion - easy to attain - impossible to retain.

I know this really cool, hip, modern dance - it's called the Charleston. It's way out there. Edgy. New. Unwrapped. Pristine. If there's no band around you can play the music on a state of the art gramophone. The records are span new - barely a scratch. What would granny say?

Flappers. Some of those girls who dance it just won't stay home. No sense of timelessness. Don't realise that the jazz age will itself age but the noble art of scrubbing floors for men to walk upon will always be with us. Scrubbing will never go out of fashion. Scrubbing dœsn't slavishly follow a trend - it plays by it's own rules. Dishwashing and baby hugging don't need a P.R. man to promote them but if they did he'd have the best damn product ever made. They'd self promote themselves.

A dimly lit cavern type cellar with those poorly paid jazz men playing their hearts out for peanuts, provocative blue curls of once grey smoke and songs with triple entendres and the odd pop of champagne corks can't compete with an aluminium bucket, new mop and a large fragrant bar of scrubbing soap. True liberation often comes concealed. Masked. Incognito. A wolf in wolves clothing - scratch beneath the surface - those trumpet solos don't really deliver on their promise of escape - their hint that somehow the ennui of routine could some in way be overridden by a vague, abstract, undefined leap of something

or other - somehow - the complex notation itself a slave
to order. They make it look easy but they've practised
day and night for a lifetime to play those notes that ooze
casualness. Nothing on this earth symbolises freedom as
much as spontaneity does. What could be more spontaneous than scrubbing a floor?

Spontaneity demands us to be in the now and floor
scrubbing is of the moment. It has no prelude. No
scheme. No agenda. No ulterior motive. Its very charm
is its simplicity - its lack of artifice. I dare you to suggest
that it's not creative in its own way.

I could stretch the point and compare it to the Sistine
- but I won't. Suffice to say that from the nothingness of
dirt, it produces order, improves the quality of all who
have left the domain of the swamp. And who are you to
say that the doer doesn't glow in its aftermath with a sense
of deep pride and fulfillment. Who made you the arbiter
of what's creative and what's not?

Is there some criteria carved in stone. I must have
missed that one. And if there was you'd be the first to
allude ever so slyly that the man who wielded the chisel
and hammer to carve it was only a labouring person and
not themselves an artist.

Oh yes I forgot... if you personally availed of their
services - say like to have some stonework done in your
garden - you'd say that they were an ARTISAN. Maybe
you're right, maybe he couldn't carve a DAVID but even
if ten thousand artisans carved ten thousand DAVIDS,
you'd be the first to say that they were mass produced and
therefore not worthy of eulogy.

Decrescendo

In your defence you might say that if there were a billion ceilings like the Sistine, we'd never appreciate their beauty but I'd only say that if every floor wasn't well scrubbed, we'd never really be able to truly appreciate a spotlessly clean floor.

And if you saw a floor in a gallery of modern art - who'd know for sure whether it was an exhibit?

Not I - Would you?

Surely the floor in the Sistine not to mention the Louvre is in itself a work of art.

And perhaps the original intention was to highlight the beauty of the floor and as it's difficult to literally 'elevate a floor', what better way to do so than to place a picture of God opposite it.

Meanwhile back at some gallery or other of modern art we see a carefully cordoned off section of floor space. Inside it there is a woman of about thirty three, upon her knees scrubbing. The woman has a not uninteresting profile and is wearing blue and white a la Madonna - whether this is coincidental we cannot say. She is toiling ever so slightly. Bucket of water beside her and a small hard scrubbing brush in hand. Yet the woman seems in control of the situation. On top of it. Almost at one with the task.

Now here's the rub. We are not sure as we go by if she's a lowly paid charwoman or if she's an exhibit. She may be the mother of six and the wife of some unemployed poet or she may be a reasonably affluent arts graduate whose conceptual pieces sell quite well for brass in the market place. We cannot ponder there for a long time to find out as that would be cheating. So we are forced to rapidly analyse the apparent facts in an attempt to find out exactly which she may be... a bona fide exhibit or simply a bona fide cleaning woman exhibiting her prowess with the scrubbing brush. Evidence for her being a genuine exhibit is as follows; her countenance looks a little too trouble free for this to be her vocation and one dœsn't really get a sense of those six noisy brats awaiting her return - mind you they could be well behaved, polite children - the very mundane nature of such an exhibit would be bound to be interpreted as a profound insight into the microcosm that is everyday life - the average conceptual artist can obviously easily plagiarise and copy Michelangelo to perfection but of course wouldn't trouble his or herself to so do and would instead prefer to create new authentic original masterpieces like this one - and last but obviously not least... there's bound to be at least one lunatic who'd offer to buy it for a million or two... far less trouble than taking the money from the bank in unmarked bills of small denominations and burning it - money well burnt and money well spent almost sounds the same anyway.

Evidence for her being a lowly paid worker whose boss insensitively arranged for her to work on the floors whilst her social betters walk off their Sunday lunch in an aura of culture is as follows; she genuinely seems useful with that brush in her hand it dœsn't seem to be a stranger to her - she dœs appear to give off an air of reality... mind you some of those arts graduates have also majored in drama and I'm told that they often chose the method school... so one can never quite tell... there is the merest hint of something noble in her brow and physical labour

often seems to tap into this aspect of the human psyche...
at least according to the good book and a lazy patronis-
ing rich bastard whom I once spoke to - also she seems a
little more troubled the longer I watch her - then again it
wouldn't take too much imagination to envisage her reclin-
ing upon the deck of some yacht in the Mediterranean
- all in all the evidence is quite finely balanced and one
cannot definitively come down on one side or the other.
Solomon had it easy by comparison. Perhaps we'll just
move on to the next room where we're guaranteed it's an
absolutely authentic exhibit... it's a picture of a giraffe taking the pepsi challenge... now that just smacks of reality...

Joanna is now a successful artist.
'Joanna, may I ask you how you first realised that you
wanted to be an artist?'

'Of course Roberto... I first was bitten by the bug, as it
were, on a trip to Florence, as a teenager. So for the next
number of years I devoured all that I could on the subject... all the usual stuff... Medieval, Renaissance, Baroque,
Romanticism, Realism,
Impressionism, Cubism and so on and so on... and
then it occurred to me, in a flash of inspiration - in fact I
shouldn't really take the credit as it was really my muse
who suggested it.'

'Remarkable stuff indeed, so you were inclined to add
your own humble contribution to the magnificent canon
of work already in existence?'

Decrescendo

'Yes, I suppose so, or at the risk of sounding ever so slightly conceited, I realised that art as it existed was somehow empty, some unidentifiable thing was missing from its core.'

'An absent soul perhaps?'

'Yes, that's it exactly.'

'Well, good for you for after all, every creative individual person is fully entitled to add their two cents worth to what already exists.'

'Well Roberto, that wasn't quite it... rather I decided to turn art as we know it upside down... totally transform it... reinvent it... reinterpret it.'

'Ah yes, I'm beginning to understand now... you sought to fill the holes that the great past masters couldn't plug?'

'Not so much the gaps that they couldn't fill but more those gaps that they didn't even realise actually existed.'

'Truly astonishing... I'm blown away... in total awe.'

'Thank you - so I rented a country house in a remote place, one without running water as I didn't wish to be decadent like a Picasso or a Carravagio - I communed with the stars and all that type of stuff.'

'Astounding... unwashed yet awash with awareness?'

'Exactly... and then it came to me...'

'In a meteoric flash, no doubt?'

'Actually no, not at all, more a whimper than a bang (I'd been reading Eliot) but I was aware that this humble admission only made my moment all the more incredible.'

'Joanna, you amaze me and yet I remain ignorant as to this wonderful creation... please go on... I am on the edge of my seat... I feel honoured yet unworthy to hear at first hand the eureka moment that revolutionised all Western art...'

'Fruit'

'I beg your pardon?'

'Fruit'

'Hmmm... Ah, I see, fruit but if I may ever so tamely imply... hadn't this perhaps been covered before?'

'I'm not talking about Chardin's inanimate cherries or Kalf's mouldy peaches nor even Cezanne's over-ripe harvest... I mean actually drawing the fruits in words...
A P P L E - O R A N G E. And so on.'

'Oh, I see.'

'At once I was transforming and subverting the whole genre.'

'Oh, I see.'

'When I painted the word P L U M, by definition it was a perfect plum, no need for the folly of attempting to catch its texture or form or any of those outdated larks - no, here I was painting a plum in perfect aural tones.'

'Oh, I see.'

'Singlehandedly I was becoming the very first practitioner of art to have the sensitivity to cater for the blind... just think of it... a hapless sightless person could now visit a gallery with a friend who on passing my work could be told...' this is a plum.'

'Oh, I see.'

'Naturally I followed it up with Peaches and grapes and so on - and being true to my art refrained from doing banana as I felt it was to close to the bone...'

'What can I say... your conceptual depth truly leaves me speechless.'

'You are most kind sir.'

CHAPTER 10: SUPERSTITION

Birthday time arrives each year and it needs no invitation it's meant perhaps to mark your own little sense of uniqueness - why unique is so revered, it's hard to say - what's not unique... name just one thing... those thousand shiny new cars straight off the assembly line... each one identical... same colour... same model, yet if you had a powerful enough microscope (and big enough) to put each one under it in turn, the tiny, remote differences would slowly begin to appear. At least a birthday proves you did exist and more importantly still continue to exist.

With each passing year there were less and less friends of her own generation to invite. Each year from January to December was like an elaborate obstacle course to complete and each year one or two more succumbed to its hazards. In the earlier part of her innings there had been two world wars and a flu epidemic to navigate and now only the lucky ones remained. Even in a good life, all that one could look forward to was old age and all its attending failures. Leaving aside the obvious physical ones - too many to number - there was the isolation of being last one standing and the well meaning but absurd way in which all and sundry congratulated you for reaching each milestone and whatever stage you arrived at, you had never been there before and you wanted to scream this is not my place - I don't belong here - this isn't familiar

to me - I will rage but you must listen - I'm one of the
lucky ones - living and dying - two sides of the same coin
we've been told - all those neat pœtic metaphors re birth
and death and growth and decay and about a cycle being
completed... who writes this stuff.

Having said all that, she wasn't totally averse to playing
the role of grande dame - there were frivolous perks and
frivolity is to be welcomed at any age or stage. The list
was finished and most of the guests were friends of her
son or the odd friend of her daughter. There were four
or five of the forty or so who were friends of hers. There
are four easily identified types of friend... friends whom
we tolerate... friends who tolerate us... friends whom we
love... and friends who love us - and yes, like so many
things in life they overlap. Kate helped her with some of
the arrangements. A band would be playing and caterers
would bring and serve food. The African woman would
of course have to ready the place but Elizabeth had also
asked her to stay and change and join in with them - naturally Adolph disapproved of this decision but Elizabeth
was firm and he let it go with the thought that the woman
would probably have the decency to decline if only to
save herself from the discomfort of mixing with her social
superiors. Forty two helped too - mainly by keeping out
of the way. Just as well as she was supposed to order flowers but she forgot to and she got all white wine instead of
getting red and white. Maybe it's simply that people are
strange Kate thought.

Elizabeth bought Kate a new dress - blue.

On the evening of the party Kate was readying herself

and went in to help Elizabeth. Her dress too was blue - blue silk - how beautiful it was and the delight on the old woman's face.

'Can I look through your wardrobe?'

'Why of course - help yourself.'

Then it happened - she saw it as though it spoke to her - a dress of dark navy taffeta with folds going this way and that.

'It's so beautiful - may I try it on?'

'Yes you may - though I'm surprised that you don't find it too old fashioned.'

'Class always lasts.'

'Yes, it really, really does.'

'I can't believe that such a beautiful dress exists.'

'That was my exact emotion when I saw it all those years ago.'

'Did you wear it often?'

'No, not often, but enough to know that it must have been spun by the fairies.'

Decrescendo

'I can't believe that you too believe in fairies!'

'Why not - I'm an old crazy lady.'

'And I'm a young crazy lady.'

'Yeats has some wonderful pœms about old crazy ladies.'

'Yes, I know my crazy father loves Yeats - used to read him to me almost as lullabies.'

'That's so beautiful.'

'I come from a land of ghosts - you have no idea - even our ghosts themselves have ghosts.'

We have ghosts for every occasion - ghosts that live in wet bogs, ghosts that scale old castle walls, ghosts that comb their long grey hair, ghosts that bathe naked in the moonlit lake - an island of ghosts - haunting us and in turn being haunted by us.

A land of homage to all things ghostly by a ritual known as superstition.

You must not cut that baby's fingernails before it's a year old or else it will grow up to become a thief - in one fell swoop all sociological research is annulled.

The seventh son of a seventh son has the power to cure all illness by the laying of hands - the drawback of procreating a very large family is somewhat compensated by ridiculously low medical bills for all your kith and kin.

Decrescendo

For a person to win at cards, someone simply has to place a crooked pin in the lapel of their coat - unlikely that he'll be welcomed at Monte Carlo though.

It is lucky to cut your hair by the light of a full moon - even werewolves agree on this.

A dead hand is a cure for most diseases - this presents the ultimate catch 22 for the deceased in question as they are left with the paradox that if they had remained alive their own hand (now dead) could have saved them, or something like that.

If you stumble in a graveyard there's really no point returning home as you'll be back shortly anyway... for good.

And these are the tip of the iceberg - there's many more where these came from...

My advice to you is to find as many horseshœs as you possibly can because these undoubtedly have wondrous powers to bestow good fortune - mind you THEY MUST BE FOUND ACCIDENTALLY - which is guaranteed to equalise the chances of the downtrodden masses with all those noblemen and their silken breeches riding to hounds.

Land of horse - each one shod with iron horseshœs - each horseshœ an object of immense luck in the eternal battle to ward off ill luck.

Rain - each drop sacred - if unwanted by the peasants who rarely had umbrellas.

Rain promoting lush green grass to fill the bellies of each horse who in turn fulfills his or her part of the bargain by promising to occasionally kick off a shœ as he corrals around the endless green pastures...

Decrescendo

General Cromwell... that's a fine horse.

Thank you kindly.

Did he arrive from England with you?

No - I acquired him here...

Well - he's a magnificent beast - will you take him back with you when you return home?

See... that's the problem - he seems to like it here.

Must be all that fine grass... perhaps this isle is sceptred too.

That's exactly it - seems to find it sweet.

So this really is a problem then?

It keeps me awake nights - I'm at my wits end about it.

It dœsn't sound like an insurmountable problem?

Well as you know I'm a devout believer in God and he's one of God's dear creatures, it would be most remiss of me not to take his particular needs into account.

God's?

Decrescendo

No - the horse - CUCHULAINN

That's a lovely and fitting name for a horse.

Do you really like it?

Absolutely - why do you ask?

Well at first I wasn't too sure - you see he was already named when I acquired him and I was about to rename him ROGER but somehow the name Cuchulainn seemed to fit him.

No worry - from here on in all Irish horses will be called names like Roger and George and Charlie.

That's just it - I have some uneasy feeling about converting them here to the tongue of Shakespeare.

You've lost me sir.

This time last year I too would have thought that Roger was an exemplary name for a horse.

Or George?

Yes - of course.

So?

Decrescendo

These people are obviously savages and heathens and all that - no debate there... BUT... one morning in the month of May I awoke early - just before sunrise - God's earth was serene in all its glory - some thirty miles or so outside of Dublin - the mist was rising from the land - the waft of lavender and a host of other perfumes from nature assailed me - I was dumbfounded to be even a tiny speck of this majesty - this awe - this miracle of an omnipotent creator - I stared aimlessly for some time, drunk on the intoxication of it all and was then awoken from my reverie by the thundering hooves of my Cuchulainn as he stretched his legs in an imperious gallop and in that moment when all four of his hooves left the earth mid gallop, it dawned on me how perfectly his name described some essence in him - I didn't know how or what - but this thing touched me more deeply than I can possibly describe to you.

This perfect beast at one with this perfect soil - nature as our lord intended it - this was all that there could ever be - and somehow the very beast's name was an integral part of this celestial equation - and in the moment my head returned to an incident some weeks earlier at some siege or other - a man lay dying - nothing I hadn't seen many times before - some time later he appeared to lie still - the stillness that shows eternity is beckoning but at that moment a young woman ran over to him and wept over him and the dead man as it were found a drop of breath from some remote recess and uttered the word 'macushla'... nothing more - but something told me I had to find out the meaning of the word macushla - I had no idea of its origin - it could have meant help or pain or water or any other mundane, commonplace word except that I knew for sure that it couldn't just be that simple - that it had to mean more.

Much later on I saw a young woman and bade her to tell me what she knew of the word macushla.

'Sir', she said, and not with that usual peasant sarcasm 'it's Gælic and it suggests an endearment, literally... my darling... my pulse.'

I thanked her and after she'd left I sat by a tree - dazed - blood of my blood - a thing beyond love - I was overcome - tears raced down my face - I was awash with confusion.

I - a man sent by God to do God's work - a man of certainty - a man without doubt - without reason to doubt was now being assailed by forces which I could not explain - then I regained some footing but not quite as before - I still was shaky - Now I felt empathy with the creator as he cast Adam from Eden - his mixed emotions - he must reject Adam for it was part of a greater scheme but that didn't mean that each nut and each bolt of the apparatus screwed tightly - neatly - I thought of the natives of this Gælic land and the rapture of their alien tongue which we were taking away to replace with the King's English - and you know my opinion of Kings - and I felt as though it was almost a wrong thing - a crime in the eyes of God - a thing beyond the grab of land - for what is land but a place to lay the head that holds the tongue that speaks the language and again at that exact moment I was inconsolable - I was empty.

Decrescendo

And I sought respite in prayer and I prayed to my perfect Lord that these people who were losing their power of speech would in turn be compensated by him and that he might see fit to tailor the new language to fit - to fit beyond anything else in his perfect creation had ever fitted - a seamless transition of word and thought - that they might match or even surpass the wonder of Milton.

CHAPTER 11: FORENSIC

For many years I was in flight from the church in Rome - a real rebel - as anti clerical as any man who ever lived - the arrogance of papal infallibility, I thought... how dare those puppets in black dare to tell me their philosophical beliefs as though carved in stone, irrefutable, beyond question by man made of blood, the breathtaking insolence and for a while I thought of dining exclusively on those of the cloth, then they could take their chances with resurrection and trumpets and ritual......and yet although not an agent for change a piece of me is still always prepared to be open minded - just like I was in Germany in the olden days, what cared I if gipsy and Jew and Marxist were curtailed in movement or restricted in their freedom? Far be it from me to question a democratically elected leader's wishes to restore glory and grandeur to his Reich. Even I had to acknowledge the æsthetic beauty in the Swastika and the leader's passion and charm, his ability to hypnotise induced envy in me, his power of rhetoric, his ability to twist and turn without movement, the skill to be all things to all people all of the time was a marvel to behold - who can argue cogently with a great nation seeking to enhance their living space? Dœs not the Bedouin seek a cottage? And the cottage dweller a house? And the house dweller a mansion? And the lord of the mansion a palace? And the King an empire? His anti modernity beliefs pulled me closer to his bosom - his understanding of modernism as a plague was akin to my own - who really feels that abstract art is fit *to grace the Sistine? Or that the confused chaos of Jazz music can be compared to the wonder that is Wagner? I once foolishly wasted an entire week of my life attempting to read the wreck of a book called FINNEGAN'S WAKE, but alas I was too literate to succeed, so the leader hit the perfect note on so many important issues - issues the common and the educated man alike agreed with him on - there will of course always be dissenters - so I hear you say why did I leave this burgeoning Utopian paradise?*

Like all of flesh and blood - I have my limit - my moral code - my ceiling - my uncrossable line - this far and no further - as a caveat let me state that I merely disliked the Jews the way I disliked the Arabs - the way I dislike the politburo - the way I dislike all who believe that they are chosen above the rest of flesh and blood as special - there is no special, simply less forms of worse - the leader told us how special he was but looking deep into his eye one could discern that he didn't really believe such an absurdity and that it was merely part of his circus performance - apologies for such a lengthy digression - I was about to inform you why I left this paradise... a reliable colleague whom I knew to be trustworthy, beyond reproach, informed me of a government programme that specialised in medical experiments on healthy babies - this was my wall, my ceiling, my point of no return. Theory, belief, delusion, disbelief, disillusion, insanity, dreams, aspirations, all have, to a lesser or greater degree, their inevitable place in a confusion of human angles BUT no system or whim or belief can ever be entitled to interfere in any way whatsoever with those of such extreme youth... babies have no belief, no creed, no colour, no fix, no chaos, no evil, no hypocrisy, no leaning, no politics, no artifice - they alone are unblemished, beyond all and any judgement - without imperfection, without any culpability, the sins of the fathers shall not.

So, I too was living the life of religious anarchist - and I too had a dream - or a delusion - or whatever one may call it - and no, before you ask, God did not speak to me and no ray of light hit me from an obtuse angle - but in my dream I was walking on a road and yes the inevitable fork arrived and I surveyed the entire landscape - I examined it intensely - under all the microscopic powers which I possessed - I saw each and every crack on each and every surface - there was no concealment - and only two roads at the fork - not three - just two - each road lay wide open to my eye and to my senses - on the first road I looked down I could see very, very little, just vague outlines, jumbled confused things, colours, undefined things, they were so far down the road that it was all that I could do to make certain that they were indeed there, that the road was not entirely blank and bare - it wasn't - the semi visible shapes and things were actually there, at least within the limitation of human senses - if the road had been totally desolate I would have surely recognised that fact but it wasn't entirely desolate - the second road at the fork was by contrast full, vivid, sharp, transparent and easily defined - in many ways its clarity was remarkable.

The second road started with a swamp. And from out of this swamp came THINGS, I call them such for no other name is more appropriate - things is what they were - they were semi formed - semi conscious - semi beings - they were foul and they were slimy and if they possessed a few brain cells then that was their limit.

Decrescendo

They were shuffling and falling and crawling and squirm-
ing and bumping in chaos - they were without sense and
devoid of any real purpose but even at that I could tell that
they had an immense will to survive. This fact became even
more apparent as I looked further down that second road, sec-
tion by section, the further my eye went the more the swamp
creatures grew and the more they collided with each other
and I imagined that each gained some strength and purpose
from crawling over their fellow creature - down and down,
still they grew and still they reeked, their hideousness not
diminished by their apparent progress of a type and in an
instant I was aware that if this road had no end the crea-
tures would go on 'developing', at least in a fashion and that
they would slowly, gradually gather a personal power and
an affirmation and of course some ability but that no matter
how far they went down this interminable road the source of
their beginning would always be a swamp. Gold and jewel
and rocket to the stars would not, could not erase this birth
from swamp, their foul origins, their slime ridden past, their
putrid source would always cling to some aspect of their being
- no rose or scent could ever obliterate such a stain - I must
admit however that a part of me was fascinated by them and
in a perverse way almost admired their profound will to pow-
er, their lust to progress and more than once I wondered why
they just didn't return to swamp and lay down within and
die. But I chose the first road - the uncertain road - the vague,
hazy, ambiguous one. The improbable one. The one that may
be smoke and mirrors. The raffle that may have no prize. Yet
I did this in the knowledge that no matter how remote the
chance of those hazy figures materialising into some Eden, I

*would rather its mathematical improbability than the abso-
lute certainty of the swamp - from swamp origins there can
be no Eden, no risk of Nirvana, no return ticket - this was
the choice which I made.*

*So I accepted mother church with its flaws and farce, its
ritualistic order. The possibility, however remote, that a
kernel at its core just might contain a thing beyond measure,
a thing to unwrap all those secret boxes which we've amassed
since life as we know it began. Imagine even the possibility of
life eternal. This was the promised package of mother church.
With the potential of such a wondrous payoff there were
bound to be a few hitches along the way...*

SO I SURMISED THAT GOD COULD POSSIBLY THINK...

*Such a journey would necessarily contain some awkward
curves, rough rapids, pitch black turns, the odd dead end.
Such arrogance of human thought to dare suggest that such
a profound, magical odyssey should be without danger and
uncertainty. What insanity to even expect such a miracle to
be black and white in its design. I set ye but one conundrum.
Faith... Blind faith. Suspend the thing which ye call rationale. Drown your doubt at birth. Do not nurture it, revere it.
Deify me, not your doubt.*

*Yes, I confess, I withheld some pieces of the jigsaw called
life. Of necessity. Think of it as a giant lottery, sweepstake.
A poker game in which I am the sexy dealer. Yes, I could deal
each and every man and woman a royal flush... in hearts...
but what would that tell me of your ability to play the game.*

Decrescendo

*Again of necessity, I deal you deuces and threes, occasionally
the odd ace but only in your willingness to play the low cards
well, attentively, with courage, with grace, with dignity, can
I know anything of your worthiness. There can be no winning without risk. I ask much but I offer more. In your genesis
I give you pain and toil and uncertainty. I bestow you with
gifts both mediocre and beauteous. I pave access to perfection
through the tortuous path of chaos and decay. I inflict burden,
I give sufferance, I give fragmentation, I lay potential pan-
demonium at each step, I send prophets, I send false prophets
and shamans. I bequeath comprehension and cyphers beyond
encryption both at the same time. Think of me as your muse.
I am everything. I was there at the birth of the stars and I
shall still be there as they perform their last cosmic dance in
a synchronised suicide which only I can choreograph. Many
things have some kind of value and just as many things
have some kind of merit. I will not weigh you down with the
weight of detail by listing what they are but one thing I let
you know is that over and above all these things from small
fish to vast stars, but two things should concern you above
all else... Good and Evil... these two entities exist almost
as of themselves and are well beyond my remit... of these
two things I have no control whatsœver as of necessity I did
relinquish it a long time ago as part of my grand creation...
my entire creation would be empty if I still held dominion
over these two things... how I too would have loved to nullify
the sperm and egg that brings the Mengeles alive to breathe
my air and a million other trials that beg me intervene but
each application of my hand in man's affairs would of itself
undo all design and in a sense reduce mankind to the role*

Decrescendo

*of programmed puppet incapable of input in the blueprint
of his own destiny. Easy to ask why a wave of my fingerless
hand refuses to wipe out all your pain and obliterate all your
suffering and the only balm I can offer here is to remind you
that all suffering is finite but all glory is without end. Just
as you are my creation - your creations are your own. I did
not fill Shakespeare's quill with ink nor did I mix Raphæl's
palatte, much like a father dœs not directly create the child
of his child but simply is part of its link. I have no hand in
your good and none in your evil. These come from within
you. They are not inevitable and are always in doubt until
they come to pass. At times circumstance may drastically
limit your options but even then there is always choice - no
matter how profound its limitation. The sole purpose of your
existence is to exercise these choices... everything else is but a
backdrop. Your journey is not simple nor was it ever meant
to be or that would be to set limits and for all the frailty of
flesh and blood and all other fragilities of the human bond -
you are without limit. Access to the furthest reaches of a vast
cosmos are yours. Within the finite nature of your organic
being, there is something of the infinite - a suggestion that
you can one day return to spirit. Even within the limitation
of the human body and mind I have factored in the random
growth of evolution to permit you to evolve into other things.
This metamorphoses can be achieved individually but will
of course flourish far better in collective harmony - a coming
together of all skins, all genders, all ideas. The only barrier
to the stars is the reluctance to choose good over evil. I am at
a loss to describe 'evil' to you. It is not a thing easily quanti-
fied. It is as you might expect, shapeless, multi-dimensional,*

abstract and at the same time obvious, clear and definite.
This is not an attempt to absolve myself from the equation of
responsibility, rather it is an acknowledgement that it would
wither without your nurture.

I will refrain from really giving examples as there are too
many to number and besides in that heart of hearts each
knows its essence and yes it is ALWAYS borne of elevating
one's own needs, desires and whims above the welfare of oth-
ers - everything from healthy individuals insisting on those
less fortunate to scrub their floors to megalomaniacs believing
that they are entitled to abuse any and all living things.

And merely as a postscript of sorts, let me add; you can keep
your big bangs for it implies very little and proves even less - I
was around long before its noise was ever heard - to me its
sound was more akin to a tiny, tiny feather dropping onto a
vast large satin pillow - so you must not stop your quest for
knowledge at the big bang, you must ponder what occurred
before such an event took place and what if there were 'gas-
ses' - what would that prove or disprove - whatever medium
I chose to deliver my blueprint for life is beyond relevance -
what would it matter if I selected blocks or circles or strings
or liquids or gasses or particles so minute that they made each
sub atomic particle seem vaster than mount Everest - why
would size matter - why would matter itself matter?

These things are simply the means and you could do far
worse than to concern yourselves much more with my mo-
tive and remember motive is best analysed beyond the reach
of a telescope's lens - the microscope shall never be built that
can divine motive - as a caveat let me withdraw part of that
last statement, for I too am loathe to use a word like 'never'

Decrescendo

- there is no limit to what you may build or destroy for that matter.

'Elizabeth, I think I like that book about the vampire, I like both his certainty and his confusion, his moral immorality, he seems to be writing just for himself as any great poet should of course do.'

'That must be why you never seem to put it down, tell me more of Yeats.'

'My father the unpublished poet loves Yeats and loves Eliot too - sometimes I think he would have liked them to merge into a single voice, then he would have had his ultimate poet... Eliot Butler or some such silly thing. Do you know of a man called Parnell?'

'Well, my Irish history is a little barren - we tend to minimize and bury our colonial sins as you keep reminding me - but I have heard his name - a nationalist parliamentarian, I think.'

'That's only part of his story and like all great stories it affects us in conflicting ways - it gives to us and it takes away from us.
Yeats in his homage to Parnell endorses the common belief that he was an uncrowned king but in many ways he was crowned - a king needs only subjects to validate his kingship not a crown - by this reckoning Parnell was indeed a king.

Decrescendo

In a different context altogether, Eliot, writes of a broken king - this is what Parnell really was.'

'That's such a sad, poignant image.'

'I think so too - broken by men in black who chose to worship a man from Rome and they have one thing in common with the communists - they'll never say sorry - they'll never show error - to show vulnerability would loosen too many tightly nailed sacred icons. When Yeats calls Parnell a lovely man he hits the spot - for this is what he was - but all of history's villains are of necessity dead and just as corpses cannot wear robes of silk, they cannot wear blame - as a species we sometimes forgive the living too little and forgive the dead too much.

History is such a sad tale and it's a tale entirely man-made by man - spun by man - revised by man.'

Kate tried on the dress and fairytale like it fitted her perfectly.

Gordian knot - tightening - woven by the strands of chance and all the stronger for it.

Cinderella from the streets of Belfast... continuing to tread softly. There are still many thousands of my soldiers on your streets and although they're basically decent lads, their orders may not be so decent. They may not know that a man like Parnell ever existed.

They may not have heard the purity or beauty of Yeat's words nor have the ability of Madame Blavatsky to read minds. They may not know you don't hate them but

simply hate their guns and their masters. They remain...
waiting... for what exactly they are not sure... they may
not know that Godot never arrives. Their guns are heavy.
Heavy guns can only lighten their load by firing off bullets. Their guns are new not the old ones that helped save
the world from the Austrian artist. They're not the same
guns that stormed the beaches at Normandy nor the ones
that jammed in the hot north African sand as Rommel
achieved heroic status for delaying the final score. They
are not the same guns that said we may well fall but fall
we gladly will rather than pretend we eat cheese and wine
and love impressionism - there's no Champs Elysées in
London town but if there was we'd never let you have a
gay jaunt down it in an open top car and we don't have
a Parisian opera house but if we did we wouldn't show
you around it so as you could espouse your knowledge of
its design. This sceptred isle has no phantom in its opera
house. And no phantom line of defence named Marginot
and of course no phantom soldiers.

On your streets our soldiers only fire guns at your terrorists.

And obviously we hate all terrorists - even in the future
it shall never happen that an elected prime minister of
our great land breaks bread with a South American dictator who fitted electric wires to men's testicles and tortured
them till they were reduced to human shells. And if they
then went on to do their best to exculpate him and to do
their best to make his latter life comfortable... wait... we're
straying into the realm of futuristic fantasy... such a thing
could never happen... never... never ever.

Decrescendo

All night long Elizabeth made sure that Kate got introduced to some of the more interesting guests - ones to
whom she just might have something to say. Often Kate
hated her own spontaneity - tried so many times to measure and wait - but it never came- she had no real control
of its trigger - she always seemed to expose some part
of herself - people of course found her incendiary, com-
bative and profoundly judgmental but she explained this
away by believing that all her judgments - no matter how
scathing or subjective or insane - stopped short of what
she described as ultimate judgment - she nor anyone else
was entitled to ultimately judge anyone - anyone - but
as most of life was played out on a minor scale - she felt
it okay, even necessary to form opinions and even found
consolation in the fact that time and analyses didn't of
themselves guarantee wisdom or knowledge or accuracy.
What was the purpose anyway in showing restraint... the
graveyard's long term tenants floweth over with restraint.

'And you must be Kate? What a lovely smile.'

'Thank you - and you must be Mr. David.'

'So refreshing to see a young lady smile and not taking
life too seriously.'

'You're most gracious.'

Decrescendo

'I'm a historian - a friend of Adolph's.'

'That's so interesting.'

'Would you feel patronised if I commented on just how pretty your dress is?'

'No - not at all - and it is very pretty. Can we talk history now?'

'You're unusually direct - I like that.'

'Thank you - what period of the past do you specialise in?'

'Twentieth century - let's call it past present'

'History is full of grey areas - forgive the cliche.'

'You're so right my dear - but I have made it my life's mission to explore all those grey areas - even if it unsettles the status quo or rattles a few sacred icons'

'That's so brave of you.'

'A historian must also have courage - not fall into the trap of seeing everything the way of the victor.'

'Do you really believe that the victors do write history?'

Decrescendo

'Can it ever be any other way?'

'You have a point.'

'History is full of nuances - that disturbs people - but when it's presented as black and white - however inaccurate that may be, it reassures them, affirms their world view, when we start to forensically examine things, we discover uncomfortable truths which deeply disturb and unsettle us - we prefer to bury certain things.'

'You're so right sir, we must never slaughter sacred cows for they serve the purpose of fear's banquet.'

'The historian's job is not to apportion blame rather it's often his job to show that there's usually blame on all sides.'

'I think that's mostly right. Sometimes in my land we insist on interpreting history in a narrow subjective way... I know it's one of my many faults... you're such a brave soul to take this approach.'

'In history all swords have been dipped in blood - it's usually just a question of degree.'

'I think I'd make a terrible historian as I almost always take sides.'

'That's understandable - one of the many problems with

taking sides is that how do we decide which side to take?'

'I am very simplistic in that way - I simply choose whomever I feel to be the least evil.'

'That's very good! I'm amazed that you're so interested in how the dust of history settles.'

'Yes but you're only surprised cos I'm a girl.'

'No, not at all, mainly because you're so young.'

'Mozart would have surprised people much more if he had of been a girl - we don't expect girls to be touched by genius.'

'Ha ha... is the lady informing me that she's a little genius?'

'No I'm not a genius.'

'Well that's a relief - we're both mortal!'

'No one is a genius - the very concept of it is flawed.'

'Well, perhaps it's extremely rare but it obviously does exist... just think of...'

'No names please - I'm sure that all the people who spring to mind are incredibly talented - I do believe that some people have moment's of ingenuity - touched by genius if you like but not that they themselves are geniuses.'

'Let's not use semantics young lady.'

'I have the inherited genes of a pœt - this gives me the right to be semantic - if I can't on occasion be semantic, who can?'

'Anyway it's been so lovely chatting to you and when my book comes out I'll send you a copy.'

'That's very decent of you - what's the title?

'JUDAISM AND ITS CONTRIBUTION TO WW2'

'All the subtlety of a panzer.'

'Young lady you continue to amaze me.'

'Which aspects of the war dœs it focus most on?'

'Using much research, profound analysis and a totally unbiased approach I've discovered that the holocaust never really happened or should I more accurately say that the magnitude and scale of it has been completely misrepresented by almost all other historians.'

'So you're a holocaust denier?'

Decrescendo

'No - I'm a HOLOCAUST MISINFORMATION DE-NIER... it's the job of the historian to deny all historical inaccuracies.'

'So I was misinformed?'

'You and every one else who simply swallowed the allied version of events.'

'This is so shocking and repugnant to hear.'

'Yes it was to me too - when I was a student in London, I too was spoon fed the standard line and believed it - it's not easy to go against such a well worn grain.'

'So it didn't really happen?'

'Sure there were atrocities committed - by both sides - but the idea of vast numbers of people being systematically euthanised is a fairy tale and at odds with the evidence once we examine it minutely and with total impartiality.'

'This has me so terribly stunned - I'd always believed what I'd read as being reasonably accurate and thought all the stuff that my dad told me was true.'

'It's not your poor father's fault - he was no doubt well meaning - it's not his fault that lies and exaggeration have replaced fact - many people share the blame.'

'Has everything which I've read on the subject been totally wrong then?'

'Well obviously not everything - I'm not some Walter Mitty type character who's attempting to suggest that Germany in the late 1930's was always welcoming the Jews with open arms - that would be ludicrous.'

'I suppose that stuff like the Nuremberg laws must be lies too.'

'Not exactly... I mean the democratically elected government of Germany may have decided to impose certain slight restrictions on certain sub cultures in an effort to redress inequitable social imbalances.'

'So those laws really were enacted?'

'Yes.'

'What created the huge social imbalance?'

'Certain sub groups had come to monopolise certain critical financial areas and other important areas within the society.'

'How did this come to pass? They must have greatly outnumbered the REAL Germans then?'

'No not exactly.'

'So how could say ten percent of the population come to amass so much - it was ten percent wasn't it?'

'Well not quite.'

'How much then - just a mere five percent?'

'Maybe one percent.'

'Or even less???'

'Maybe, but it's not solely about numbers it's more about power in key areas.'

'So they must have been a sub group that controlled all the universities?'

'Not exactly.'

'The judiciary then - that must be it?'

'Not quite.'

'The church?'

'That wasn't really it either.'

'Well then they must have come from some native soil

rich in gold and diamonds and pearls - pockets stuffed deep with stolen treasure?'

'I'm not so sure of that one either.'

'Oil - that's got to be it?'

'No.'

'Well, then it must be a group who had it so easy throughout their history that they amassed much goodwill and trust to always be in a position to pull all the levers of each society that they inhabited?'

'No, not exactly that either.'

'So how did they ever monopolise the German state to such a degree as you assert that they did?'

'By much cunning and guile - that's how.'

'They must have been smarter than the ol' Krauts then?'

'Are you crazy girl... Hegel, Wagner, Mozart, Gœthe, Kant - surely even you've heard of some of these illustrious names? How could a nation with such talent be beneath any race?'

'You forgot Wittgenstein.'

Decrescendo

'A minor thinker by all accounts.'

'Still, I'm reliably told that he was a decent enough carpenter - made his own furniture.'

'The real genius from Linz was Herr Hitler - not that I condone everything that he did.'

'I'm so relieved - not that you don't condone him more, pleased too that you're not on first name terms with him.'

'One shouldn't speak ill of the dead.'

'Have they extended the slander laws?'

'Can we please be serious again for a few moments?'

'My apologies for the poor attempt at sarcasm and levity - perhaps they were a parasitic people - gave nothing to any other tribe - made no contribution to culture or science or erudition?'

'Yes - that's it - they only took and took and took and engendered resentment amongst the rest.'

'Those dirty tookers... They gave nothing to religion then?'

'Well... perhaps some trifle.'

Decrescendo

'They gave nothing to the sciences - I'm especially thinking of chemistry and physics?'

'Well perhaps a scintilla but what's a few test tubes here or there'.

'They gave nothing to the arts then - I'm especially thinking of literature?'

'A few simple folk tales, no doubt.'

'Art?'

'Not my field.'

'Music?'

'Don't talk to me of music - after Wagner, there is no music - sublime beyond words.'

'I can only apologise Mr.David - he was indeed one of nature's true gentlemen -an uncanonised saint - the original biophile - a man for all seasons - his deep, in-grained love of humanity rings from each and every note - his boundless compassion for all living things leaves me breathless - and that allied with his profound sense of humility puts him right up there with Jesus.'

'Young lady I don't value your sarcasm nor your gross ignorance and besides one must always separate art form the artist's personal life.'

'Of course we must - in fact I often think it's a disgrace that the Fuhrer's art is so undervalued simply because of other aspects of his life.'

'You must be genetically programmed for sarcasm - the point is that this parasitic sub group were hated and Herr Hitler simply responded accordingly.'

'The only other conclusion I can come to is that they must have had a history of waging war - killing tribes - I mean, they must have annihilated peoples like say the Persians did?'

'No.'

'Or the Romans?'

'No.'

'Or the Turks?'

'No.'

'Or the Mongols?'

'No.'

'Well then their only crime must be an unwillingness to

assimilate on terms laid down by others - but that should always be an option and never seen as a crime - by the way, did they assimilate more than say the Arabs?'

'I'm not a statistician.'

'The Orientals?'

'I refer you to my previous answer.'

'The defence rests then - and we hope that you still consider her dress pretty.'

'Whether all or any of your clever, selective words and immature, superficial semantic games are true or false dœsn't really alter my main contention one tiny iota - there never was any mass extermination of any race of people and equally as important there never was any attempt to so do - this is irrefutable to any non-partisan.'

'If this had been a debate Mr. David - a mindless exercise in puerile point scoring - which of us would be ahead?'

'To be brutally honest... I suppose that in such narrow, shallow terms you might possibly be.'

'Thank you - however as I feel no need to vanquish - I'll be generous - I'll concede a DRAW if you answer one simple question.'

'Just one simple question?'

'Just one - and take as long as you need.'

'Fire away.'

'Why... would the state we call Nazi Germany, NOT have exterminated the Jewish race - give me one single reason? Mr. Dav...
....
....
.........................Time up.'

CHAPTER 12: VIEW FROM A GLASS SLIPPER

It wasn't quite Oscar's night in Hollywood but for Kate it may as well have been. The affluence wasn't staggering and the opulence wasn't overwhelming and ostentation wasn't all around but one of the many peculiar things about money and luxury is how relative such terms really are. This is such an obvious point that we may be tempted to refrain from saying it too loudly but that would be a mistake. This wasn't a bash thrown by a Rockefeller or a Sheikh or a medieval King but to Kate it could almost have been.

The social ladder has many rungs and each rung is by definition equidistant from the next and in this complex hierarchy that we have either invented or accidentally ended up with, these tiny spatial separations of the rungs are difficult to bridge.

It is most likely that such separations are actually both deliberate and inevitable. Whatever position/opinion which we may take on the issue we will find a wealth of 'evidence' to back up our beliefs. Jesus it was who once said that the poor will always be with us and no doubt this is equally true of the rich. The question must be asked... who doesn't want to be rich?

Except for a small number of people who include lunatic, idealists, those who've achieved some alleged higher consciousness and perhaps some selfless altruistic souls, the answer must be... Everybody!!!!!

Decrescendo

People, conscious of the hint of selfishness and greed
this can imply may cloak this most human of all desires
with all kinds of caveats...

It's not that I'd like to be rich really... it's just that one
could do so much good with it, help friends, family, etc...
And that priceless gem, 'It's not the money itself I'd
like... more the peace of mind it brings' or even 'It would
just be interesting to see what the money was like... that's
all' and not forgetting 'I wouldn't like it... I'm happy as I
am'.

Well, I mean you could always take the billion dollars
- a billion escudos wouldn't be quite as impressive - and
burn it at the bottom of the garden of your mansion if
you didn't really want it - you'd have to take it there first
in order to get the chance to turn it to ashes - still, you'd
have a posse of servants to help you bring it from the
huge reinforced safe in the east wing of the house into
a large dug pit somewhere on the vast estate - I'm not
sure how faithful the faithful old retainers would be in
the performance of this duty as it would by definition be
their last paid task. There would also be the inevitable
risk too of some of those apparently faithful old retainers
being light of finger and swift of thumb and pocketing a
few wads of the soon to be incinerated cash - who'd blame
them, and although you probably aren't the petty, niggling
type and wouldn't normally quibble over a buck or two,
in this particular instance you couldn't afford to be laissez
faire - doing such a symbolically profound thing as the

torching of a billion dollars, quid - I suppose a billion lira is out as it's fractionally less than it sounds and possibly would only pay for the champagne to toast the bonfire with - but anyway, its impending immolation on the altar of... not sure what we can call it... nothing quite fits... but I see that cash and ash are quite close to each other, that has to be synchronicity... so anyway you'd have to plan this destruction of the lucre in military detail.

Again not that I'm suggesting you're such a mean oul bastard that you'd mind them taking a crumpled twenty dollar bill or even a crisp hundred dollar bill but get this... the logistics of the actual burning would be far more complicated than you can possibly imagine. Even if we stretch a point and allow that the bills are in large denominations and that the safe in your mansion was a large walk-in type, it would still take a fair amount of muscle to transfer it from that particular room to the dug hole way down the estate - far to much work for you and old Babbington to do alone - his bones aren't what they used to be - how many years of faithful, faultless butler-ing service has he given to you and your family, anyway it would take a few sturdy lads and lasses to carry down those boxes and a fair number of trips and regardless of their individual honesty surely one or two would be tempted to grab a bill or two - who'd blame them. They wouldn't see it as thieving especially if they'd thumbed through that old copy of Das Kapital you'd read for a laugh during your college days and simply never bothered to throw out from your library and so wouldn't have any qualms about lightening the load and by the way I am still not entirely convinced that dear old frail Babbington isn't gifted with sleight of hand - I once thought I saw him reading Robert Houdin's autobiography and perhaps there's more to the average butler than meets the eye - I mean they all can't possibly get inner fulfillment from waiting hand and foot on other's even if they are one's social betters... up and down those long winding staircases all day long -

Lady Camilla would like you to fetch her mail Babbington and please be prompt about it as she's in a hurry... meeting minty for lunch at the Ritz......your mail lady Camilla...

O Babbington be a dear and open them for me... I'm ever so tired after all that dancing and being jolly at The Savoy last night - I was just remarking to Lucy Hazlett Smythe the other day how demanding social life is for people of our generation compared to mater and pater's... Babbington, can you please warm young master Henry's slippers and bring them up to him and please take him a hot mug of drinking chocolate as well, he's in the observatory.

Thank you Babbington old chap, those slippers sure are toasty and the choc is scrummy.

Has the young master discovered intelligent life forms on distant planets so far?

No Babbs but I know that I will - even microscopic life would do - imagine it!

Decrescendo

O indeed young sir it would be most riveting... all those hyper intelligent specks of dust.

Indeed Babbington indeed... why, we'd have to treat them like royalty!

Indeed we would sir, nothing but the best, we could install them in some palace or other.

Babbington, I'm not joking... their discovery would be unparalleled... wondrous.

Indeed it would sir, indeed it would young master, pardon my ignorant levity... perhaps we could keep them in sterile beakers which cook could wash and I could fetch and carry.

Yes... of course but you'd have to be extra careful when carrying them.

O indeed sir... I'd treat them like one of your father's rare cognacs.

And there'd be lots of esteemed scientists visiting here to analyse them.

They'd need a lot of sandwiches and tea then?

Yes, they would and perhaps a few plates of crumpets.

Decrescendo

There'd be a continuous flow of extra visitors then?

I'm afraid so old chap.

So this would be Babbington's bind. A lifetime spent to the loyal, dedicated service of others and now coming to the realisation that even the discovery of magic and extra terrestrial life wouldn't lessen his load...

The philosophers stone - alchemist's base metal to gold - the fountain of youth - none of these shattering magical events will remotely alter his lifestyle or his role. The die is cast, unbreakable, permanent, irreversible. His head would be bound to race... who invented the idea of a butler? Someone who liked penguins perhaps?

Someone who thought that whodunnits should always have an obvious suspect?'

Someone too lazy to pour their own port.

Perhaps the original 'user' was a wonderfully decent, kind man or woman who actually had philanthropic intentions.

I live here in this big old mansion. I am fit and well and strong and like going down to the cellar for my own port. I can use a corkscrew quite adeptly and have no problem fixing my own cocoa at night BUT I'd like someone to chat and converse with... mmm... someone versed in the ways of my nobility yet not of themselves noble as that would be too similar... one perhaps of humble origin and no formal education yet with quick clever wits and adaptable - they must be observant but not judgmental and only speak when spoken to - not that I wish to silence them but as I already have many peers I sometimes need an unequal... someone far removed from my social strata... I will not abuse him... will respect his status and in fact accord dignity to it and will on occasion heed his words if they are dipped in wisdom... I will call him by his family name not from any form of condescension but simply as a sign of his professionalism... unfortunately I can only control my own behaviour and attitude... I cannot control that of others... if they need to highlight the social gap between themselves and my butler by demanding that he be prompter it's outside of my control.

Like all social experiments with good intentions it takes very little movement for the original idea to be distorted and corrupted.

So this gave us Babbington who at age seventy had to concur word for word with snotty nosed thirteen year old master Henry and his monologues re distant galaxies.

With all respect to Babbington's previously impeccable record of scrupulous honesty, I'm afraid I have to put him in the frame as the most likely suspect to pocket a considerable chunk of that billion which you're about to torch to prove you're a bit of an æsthete at heart and Babbington who hasn't had your upbringing and education - you can go back to your profession of classical music or aristocratic origins or being an industrialist or whatever content in the knowledge that you had sufficiently mastered the purpose of human existence enough not to need the stain of silver whilst poor old Babbington who hasn't yet acquired so high a chakra as you must scrimp and scrimmage to cope well with his impending, arthritic laden retirement - keep your eye on his soon to be bulging pockets, that's my advice to you...

The partygœrs had a lifestyle that was well removed from Kate's personal experience - each of the wines on the table she knew cost nearly as much as her mother earned for a week of scrubbing floors and she had no way of knowing that at other parties in other places people would be drinking wine that cost as much per bottle as her mother earned scrubbing floors for a month. There was no obvious answer to this apparent dilemma - if almost everyone (who answered honestly) desired to be rich instead of poor - people's only quibble with all social injustice was that they were on the wrong point on its pyramid.

Even the poor weren't against poverty per se, they were simply against themselves and their kith and kin being poor.

If capitalism 'succeeded' like it had since the beginning of the industrial revolution and each passing generation in western society became more prosperous than the previous one then inevitably at some stage in the future - however distant - everyone would (allegedly) be rich or something similar. If nobody in that society needed to scrub the floors then the only way to have them scrubbed would be to bring in others from an economically inferior

society to fill the gap AND if further on all societies had
the chance to develop similarly then they too at some
stage would run out of people willing to service the menial needs and whims of others

...Aha... I see what you're getting at the old 'robots will
do it for me scenario' - well let me tell you, that just won't
wash and before you yell technophobe or technoramus
(one who is ignorant of, rather than fears technology)... let
me explain... and by the way, explanations don't have to
be perfect, they simply have to fill a space waiting on an
explanation and they serve their purpose and of course
some explanations are better than others but any explanation is better than none... the dog ate my homework
teacher, may sound wooden and limp... but the teacher
cannot prove that you don't have a dog and once it's
established that you might have a dog, who's to say that
it's well fed and docile, so if it's both hungry and mad it
might well take a chunk out of some non food item and
as paper comes from trees which are sort of a vegetable
thing, then just maybe the crazy mutt may have snatched
a morsel or two from a book and as canines tend not to
distinguish between the merits of that print of Macbeth
lying near your school copy, would the teacher risk all his
chips on a spin of the roulette wheel? I think not - mind
you if it happens on consecutive days then you're probably stretching the laws of probability too far especially if
it's the maths teacher as she is liable to be familiar with
probability theory, still one could counter her brilliant
analysis of the unlikelihood of the mad dog mopping up

your homework two or three consecutive days by suggesting that the mongrel may have developed a taste for
copybooks after his first feast and if anything it made the
second helpings even more rather than less likely - your
psychology teacher would be sure to swallow this one
and if they did there'd be no stopping you as by now the
poor beast has become addicted to homework copies
and there's no valid reason why you'd ever be expected
to deliver homework again... so the robot would be metal
and noisy and all those cogs to oil - who'll do that? Also
they'd play chess with you perhaps but how will they make
a cup of coffee? And if they did it'd probably be too weak
and when it comes to the real litmus test - floor scrubbing
- whatever about their intellectual superiority it's very
unlikely that they'd have the requisite flexibility and mo-
bility to do it well... Yes, I'm stalling here... the thing we
call technology can by definition have no limit - no ceiling - bound by no parameters - how could it be any other
way - whenever we develop X, it only takes one budding
Einstein to improve X by one millionth and we now have
a superior X - this process can and will go on as long as
we do and even this slow gradual increase would do and
no doubt there would be the odd quantum leap along
the way too - so in time the robot is guaranteed to easily surpass us in each and every task - only then a matter
of time before they acquire some type of consciousness,
for want of a better word, and with that must come some
type of survival thing or some inkling to place itself at
the head of affairs and put its own needs above we whom
have enslaved it to do our will - it's hard to say how and

when the robolution (revolution of the robots) or robellion (you guessed... rebellion of the robots) will come, but
come it will - don't be lulled into a state of false security
just because they can't yet quite get your latte or cappu-
chino the way you like it... time is on their side and they
have us aiding them in our own ultimate downfall - one
positive outcome of the robellion is that it would at least
unite all humankind on the same side - a brother and sisterhood of harmony - that's not to say that there wouldn't
be a tiny hardcore of sympathisers with the rebel bots...

They deserve their freedom... let's support them...by
what divine right do we dare enslave these advanced,
complex entities?

Perhaps Adam and Eve too were robots as this would
account for one or two tiny unexplained details in genesis... after Cain slew Abel, Eve just simply replaced his
damaged part with some fragment of herself... this is the
real meaning of the term MOTHERBOARD - so with all
these possibilities as to their origins and ethnicity the
robots would have a certain core support within an otherwise united human race - no doubt they'd leave the robellion until we had made them indestructible by bombs
and weapons and if the bots are successful in their efforts
to overthrow us - and why would they not be - they too
will need menial tasks done - the odd oil change and so
on and get this... as they'll be so intellectually advanced
compared to us - a typical run of the mill robot will have
approximately an I.Q at least one hundred times that of
Einstein and one hundred times the physical strength of

Frankenstein - so they aren't likely to discriminate between professors and pot washers when it comes to divvy-
ing up the chores - all those years seeking equality within
the human race and the robots achieve it with one single
stroke of a pen - in a sense that puts the human race to
shame - and though we're tempted to think that in some
dramatic last minute climax as the robellion is about to
win, the human race taking one last throw of the dice
puts Einstein and Frankenstein into a blender machine
thing and invents a new FRANKEINSTEIN... that's frank
and einstein... FRANKEINSTEIN - a creature so full of intellectual attitude and monstrous ability that it wipes out
every machine on the planet... wishful thinking no doubt.

Perhaps our main reason for having others do our
menial tasks has nothing to do with necessity and more
to do with the need to feel superior to someone - anyone
- why would any healthy man or woman ask anyone else
to do their laundry? Why would some sense of shame not
kick in at the very idea of it? It can only be because we
feel above them - nothing else.

An eminent brain surgeon would never ask a fellow
brain surgeon - even a retired one with time on his or her
hands to mop out his bathroom -

Excuse me Professor Von Something or other but I was
just wondering if you're not too busy tomorrow afternoon
whether you'd be so kind as to mop out my bathroom
floor - there's a grand sturdy mop in the press and a
unopened bottle of bleach in the cabinet under the sink -
you may need to dilute it, I'm not too sure as I wouldn't

Decrescendo

be caught dead mopping a floor myself - oh and by the way I just wanted to say that I so much admire that paper which you published some years back on the subject of dealing with arterial sclerosis...

...nor would a concert pianist ever dream of asking J.S. Bach to wash his dishes even if Bach was penniless and needed every cent.

I say Johann old chap but I'm rather busy tonight as I have a prior engagement so I was hoping that if you're not too immersed in putting together another one of those endless toccatas as you sit in the gloomy candle-light, if you'd be so kind as to bring my dustbins down to the city dump - there are only two of them and if you put them on your shoulder, you'll have it done in a jiffy and please try to remember to close the garden gate after you as I seem to remember that you carelessly left it open after you the last time.

So the poor would always be with us... poor Pierre driving a second hand Ferrari... poor Araminta has to make do with a hundred yard yacht... poor scrubbing lady just wants to swap places with the mistress of the house, dœsn't really aspire to end slavery... poor robot, spent his life at our whim and now just seeking the reasonable entitlement of self determination... poor, poor, poor............

Kate thought of the pœt and his unease around both the rich and the poor and although he too was poor, he wasn't really and although he had never sought riches or ambition, she knew that if he could press a button to have a bag of rare diamonds, he'd surely press that button.

Elizabeth glided. Place to place. Person to person. Kiss her. Hug him. Parties brought out some simple, shallow but wonderful thing in any who wanted to enter into their spirit. Forty two laughed and sang - unusually outgoing her mother thought. Of the moment. It's here if you want it. Won't give us world peace but it'll let you dance and defer all those unfixable things you've been meaning to mend. All healing is temporary. Nothing ever even half fills that vacuum which we're born into - that circle can't be squared - all existence a diversion - pœtry, music, icecream, wine, sex, satin, silk, sunshine, snow, Mona Lisa and on and on... all of these things and a thousand other things gave magic to a moment... put balm on the wound but life itself was the untreatable wound... the vacuum and the void were there whether we acknowledged their existence on a minute by minute, day by day or once in a blue moon basis... sense could only be made of things by reduction...

macrocosm to microcosm...
my universe...
my planet...
my continent...
my country...
my city...
my neighbourhood...
my street...
my house...
my room...

Decrescendo

my bed...
my pillow...
my side of the bed.

Kate, I want you to meet Senhor Stephen, a very old friend of mine, he's an astro-physicist, you might like to play with him.

At your service Miss Kate... here to answer all your queries about deep space.

Is it really as big as it seems?

Yes, I suppose that it is... it's not called infinity for nothing.

Can anything really be infinite though?

It appears that way.

Too hard to believe.

You're right... it causes me problems too - we're used to everything else being finite - we're finite, our planet is finite, its resources are finite, everything which we touch we can measure and the idea of an immeasurable thing terrifies us.

My father says that space couldn't really be infinite.

Decrescendo

Is he a physicist?

No, just a crazy pœt.

An unpublished pœt?

Yes... how did you know?

They tend to have the most outlandish theories - in a sense being published calls writers to account - makes them responsible to some degree for their thoughts and theories... but those unpublished pœts tend to rave on.

So you're expecting his theory to be insane?

Cuckoo.

Mad as a hatter?

Madder.

Being a pœt he was well prepared for this eventuality.

I suspected as much.

Says that all things lunar deserve a lunatic response.

Words alone won't mask its craziness.

You have a point there.

Decrescendo

Pœts use pœtic words because their ideas break down under any microscope.

Such as?

Well, here I'm spoilt for choice... Helen's beauty when analysed under a glass that magnifies it a thousandfold reveals pores and spores that would scare not lure - shall I compare thee to a summer's day... a typical summer's day in the sixteenth century would have sped up the rate of all those plagues that were ravaging half the population... pœtry must stay close to the shadows in order to retain its effectiveness.

I didn't realise you wrote pœtry.

Who dœsn't. I once had a cat who attempted to write pœtry.

Did she write well?

Hard to say... seemed full of half scratches... very intro-spective stuff I suppose.

Did you write of stars and dust and primordial soups?

Who better than a Scientist to do so.

Again I can't disagree with you - can you recite me a

Decrescendo

line or two?

The naked star
stripped
of its gasses,
embarrassed with wound,
slinks
stutters
to a halt
that has no end,
save.

Mmmmm... perhaps you could rewrite it.

That was the rewrite.

Perhaps you could tinker and tweak.

It's been tinkered and tweaked.

Perhaps it would grow in translation.

You can't dilute water.

The pœt says that you can in fact dilute water.

How so?

He's a pœt... normally people don't ask him to explain...
so he rarely uses a plan B.

Decrescendo

Apologies... about that space not being infinite theory... if you still have time.

Oh... If I must...

We've come this far.

Well... he maintains that if you go out really, really far enough into space you come across a wall.

A wall?

Yes, a wall.

What type of wall? Can't really believe I'm asking this.

Don't be too hard on yourself... people always ask about his wall theory.

Oh... it's already accepted as a credible working theory then?

Well it is at least amongst the cognoscenti in the drinking clubs in west Belfast.

Go on then...

Just a big huge wall... really huge.

Decrescendo

Yes, it would have to be quite big as space itself is a decent enough size.

As well as being really long, it's also very high.

Yes, it would be... and I suppose very dense too?

You seem well informed already on the theory - are you sure you haven't come across it already?

I don't think so... my textbooks at college weren't nearly so advanced as you suspect... they didn't quite include everything.

Again, no need to apologise, it took the pœt an entire weekend to arrive at his conclusions.

An entire weekend?

Yes, and even then he still needed to tweak it a bit.

And tinker?

Yes, and tinker... hard not to believe that you've encountered this idea before.

Scout's honour.

Yes, the wall is extremely dense... he estimates it could be as dense as that huge big dark lake in Russia is deep.

Decrescendo

I am impressed... that is deep.

Profoundly so.

How high is it again?

Huge.

Just approximately?

Oh, I don't have the exact measurements on me right now but take it from me... it's really, really, really high and then some.

What's on the other side of this wall?

People always ask that.

And what do you tell them?

Nothing.

Too difficult a question?

I mean there's nothing on the other side.

Very interesting.

Yes, I thought you'd like it.

Decrescendo

The only wall ever with nothing on the other side.

Yes indeed, no doubting its uniqueness and it certainly adds to his theory's validity with an astro physicist like yourself admitting as much.

By the way... who exactly built the wall?

Funny you should ask that as it's the one tiny part of his theory that's a fraction incomplete.

Ah well, even the greatest theories are open to some adjustment.

That's pretty magnanimous of you - he'd appreciate that.

Tell him he's welcome.

He says he'll arrive at its architects by the old Holmesian method.

Process of elimination?

Good to see that you're up to speed on England's greatest detective.

England's? I would have said the world's.

Probably, though that bloke from the story about the

purloined letter might give him a run for his money.

No doubt, no doubt.

Using the Holmesian method he's already ruled out...
the Romans - not enough slave labour in space and besides those chariots weren't all that they were cracked up
to be - each one could have only held a few stones.

I suppose they could have made a lot of trips.

Good to see you using your head but I think it's fairly
safe to omit the Romans though especially as there's no
road leading up to the wall.
We can also rule out the Irish, he says as there's no bars
where a decent honest hard grafting Paddy can get a jar
after work to slake his thirst.
The Portuguese as there's no sign of deep waters in
space to permit them to sail, ditto the Spanish - also the
French can be safely ruled out of calculations as they'd
never create anything that the rest of the world couldn't
come and stare at admiringly.

We're starting to run out of nations - what about the
Russians?

I'm glad you asked that... they had of course to be
on any shortlist... sputnik... the bloke in star trek called
chekov... one hand not knowing what the other one's doing... each gulag built further from civilization than the

previous one and also a country built on slave labour... yeah it's easy enough to put Russia in the frame...

And they've enough romance in their pœtry to conceive of such a thing.

You're right there senhor Steve... never a truer word spoken... and those old troikas were certainly built to last... but I forgot to tell you that the theory was constructed after he watched a murder mystery so the whole thing was of course modeled on a WHODUNNIT so on that basis alone Russia seems too much like the butler... they look too good... so with that as our guideline we must alas rule them out.

I see... the Chinese?

I can see where you're going... and that whole Zen thing would explain it all... but I can't honestly see them building two huge walls, can you?

No... Genghis Khan?

No... space may have seemed a trifle claustrophobic to him.

I have a strange feeling that we'll shortly be arriving at 'it built itself territory'...

It seems that you haven't wasted that analytical mind of

yours... the gentleman wins a teddy bear.

So... the wall effectively built itself... that's the sum total of the theory?

Yes... it did... but that's the beauty of it... its very simplicity.

Who'd have thought... it built itself...

Indeed... the wonder of evolution and all its attending magic.

Has he published his findings in any scientific journal yet?

No - he wasn't chasing the glory - I think that he feels it was enough to solve the riddle of space.

Yes, it's definitely out there, I'll grant him that.

Yeah who'd have thought it that a man who's afraid to even fly on a plane would figure out such a complex mystery.

So the wall just built itself then?

Yes - so it seems I mean, there are one or two tiny loose ends and the odd technical aspect to work out but basically as I said... it just built itself.

Decrescendo

Probably all those absurdly small particles of cosmic dust floating about for æons and æons and then forming accidentally into small masses which over time formed a type of astral boulder and so on.

There you're starting to get the hang of it now - I did say that the theory simplified a lot of complex and astral and molecular stuff... didn't I?

So you did... so you did.

See it as a thing to liberate you from the tyranny of living an existence that demands empirical proofs ad nauseam - with its eternal catch 22 - the more you prove the more you have to prove - this simplistic linear version of events is chain free and in the long run much more likely to do your head and your heart more good - I mean, what if space were infinite - what would that in fact mean? Where would the profit be? How would that satisfy any remote part of you? Or as is much more likely... the proof of its infiniteness would and could only ever be based on a pre set of clearly defined assumptions which you were already working off - a chain of many links stretching from Aristotle... What if even a single link that you had thought of as absolute, forged in certainty ultimately proved to be false... paper... illusion... human error... what then? Your 'defense' would be from Nuremberg... you were acting in good faith... just obeying orders... not your fault that some fifteenth century physicist spilled his tankard

Decrescendo

of ale on the parchment on which he had done his tally of irrefutable proofs and accidentally smudged an x or a y - how were you to know that he had a clumsy left hand - not your fault that one tiny brick in the wall was a fabrication - an untruth - an empty cavity - how were you to know that? Not your fault too that Albert got a nice handy job in the patent office leaving him with too much time on his hands that he'd nothing better to do than ponder time itself - imagine if he'd instead taken employment in a factory that made cuckoo clocks. If that had of been the case I've absolutely no doubt that special relativity would probably have been closer to cuckoo clock time than space time and have you ever seen one of those cuckoos returning to the clock? Talk about the speed of light... why, they positively fly, zoom and so on - really, really fast they certainly are. I'm not so sure that Albert wouldn't have been more than a little entranced by their antics and would probably have spent his entire life working out the complexities of their mating habits and the idea of wooden birds 'mating' would have just been abstract enough to hold his attention and his wondering mind from wandering. While we're at it... that was a real piece of Teutonic genius to disbar the one man on earth who could have helped them build an atomic bomb or even if he'd never split the atom he'd at the very least have livened up the Fuhrer's nauseatingly dull monotones each night at table talk -

So Albert, my adjutant tells me that your surname is Einsten... well that's a fine German name... I wonder if you're any relation to Baron Von Frank Enstein?

No Herr Hitler, I can't say that I am.

Well... not to worry... he was a particularly fine German - in fact he single handedly transformed medicine - turned the impossible into the possible.

Ah yes I do seem to remember something about him - created a perfect specimen of German manhood if memory serves me correctly... tall and strong and gallant and noble and sensitive and...

Yes, that was him my dear Albert and his creation also had the most adorable long blonde curls and of course a fine straight nose.

Whatever happened to him? I imagine some crazy, jealous Zionist assassinated him or something?

Yes - that was probably it - some sick, twisted, worthless Jew probably swopped his perfect Aryan brain for an idiot Jew brain.

Mind you Herr Hitler it's hard to believe an incompetent Jew would have the know-how to perform the necessary surgery to switch the brain in the first place.

Yes, yes, of course you're right my dearest Albert and by the way you may call me Shickelgruber - indeed how could a member of a race that has given so little to science possibly have the werewithal to accomplish such a thing...what was I thinking of?

Much more likely Herr Shickelgrubber that the Baron's creation eloped with the wife of one of those romantic English pœts like Byron or Keats or the other fellow whose name I can't recall.

I think you've hit the nail on the head - I can just see him with her now on some deserted island as they raise a brood of beautiful little blonde haired children. I can so easily visualise them all in their little pairs of lederhosen which she lovingly and painstakingly stitched by candlelight as he hummed her one of Wagner's arias.

You paint such a believable picture mein Shickelgrubber of how perfect the nuclear family can be not that I can claim to be an expert on nuclear things by any means.

What did you say that you do then?

I make cuckoo clocks.

Do you indeed - how very interesting and you won't be surprised to hear that I have some interesting theories on that very subject.

Why my dear shicky your breadth of interest never ceases to amaze me - no wonder your public so adore you.

Thank you but as I was saying... I have a theory that the cuckoo and time and the atom are all linked...

Do you mind if I write this down?

Of course not - and feel free to use it - I see myself solely as a conduit for genius as I'm a very modest man myself anyway as I was saying... on a cuckoo clock and here I'm not talking about the one's cheaply made for penny pinching Jews to buy... I mean the precision built ones made by perfect craftsmanship... well as you probably know the bird retreats ever so swiftly after it has cuckooed...

So I've heard somewhere before...

Well all you would need to do would be to speed it up a little further...

Perhaps say by another 300,000 kilometres per second?

Possibly - the petty details are of no real concern to a mere conduit like myself - then after speeding it up a little, throw in a few bits and pieces the odd wire and a bolt or two here and there, perhaps a few cogs and rubber bands too and I'd be amazed if it couldn't be turned into a time machine...

Decrescendo

Or perhaps even an atomic bomb?

Perhaps, but as I may have already said I'm a very modest man and using the cuckoo clock to master father time would be enough for me... I'll leave the splitting of atoms to the fantasists...

I understand... if you had a time machine you could go back to THAT day...

Yes, I know what you mean... I haven't forgotten. I can still see them now... the entire board telling me that my artwork was inadequate for a place in their university.

I can only empathise; the same type of men told me once that I wasn't qualified to teach children.

Did they indeed - mind you as it turned out they did Germany a profound favour as I'd never have become a soldier if they'd have given me a place in art school.

Destiny is a funny thing my dear Shickelgruber and I'll bet none of that class went on to hang in the Louvre whereas you now basically own the place.

Mmmm... I hadn't quite thought of it that way and I'll bet you that the teacher who took your place never went on to dismantle that old cuckoo clock of Isaac Newton's and then to reassemble it again...

Decrescendo

By the way Shickelgrubber, what do you think of modern art?

I'm glad you asked me that as my favourite fairy tale is THE EMPEROR'S NEW CLOTHES and this sums up entirely my views on contemporary art appreciation.

I couldn't agree with you more.

You and all your rational certainties gleaned from the head of man - himself the most frail, fragile, uncertain creature to ever draw breath - I can hear you now... we called it infinity because we had no other word... how were we to know that romantic pœts would run with it and that it would be so distorted beyond our original meaning... we simply meant a thing too big to measure... too vast to comprehend... how could anyone ever have thought we meant a thing that had no end... that would be absurd... if it had no end it could have no beginning and if it had no beginning, how do we know it was born and if we don't know of its birth how can we prove that it exists?

I don't even believe in science - after all what is science but a temporary stopgap to fill the vacuum of our profound ignorance - what scientific truth isn't open to being replaced by better knowledge... why did you all take us so seriously?

Everything which we told you was predicated on what was told previously to us and so on.

When I told you that the earth was flat I acted in good

Decrescendo

faith and you didn't complain - did you want me personally to sail single handedly across the globe and measure
it with a giant ball of string to prove the point? When I
told you how far the stars were apart from each other...
surely you didn't expect me to personally measure the
distance with a stick and tape? You didn't complain when
there was gain and prosper to be had from my scientific
truths... when I told you how electricity behaved and how
to be its master or how sound could travel or how to save
your dying lover by operating on their body sick and
now in my moment of lapse... you pounce on me ? How
could I have known that somewhere in the remotest spot
in darkest space in the deep bowels of a vast cosmos that
there would be of all things... a wall... brick by brick...
stone by stone... the debris of an infinity that promised
to be so much but ultimately never was... this far and no
farther.

CHAPTER 13: THE AFFLUENCE OF THOUGHT

I have just returned from the game and if I tell you most forcefully how seething with rage I am, you will still have no real idea of the depth of my anger.

Naturally enough my club of choice is the mighty Benfica - for after all I am not totally crazy.

So with the score at 0-0 and with but just two minutes left to play, we were rewarded a rather dubious penalty but let's not dwell on the merit of that decision - the point is that our penalty taker strode up to the ball with such an air of nonchalance, I suspected the worst, it was almost as if he was strolling in the park with his great grandmother on her walking stick - so he strikes the ball with all the power of a butterfly and the fool naturally enough misses it - our opponents break quickly and in turn score a goal - this is not the first time this season that this incompetent has behaved as if he was simply playing a game - football is not a game - it's more a statement by civilized people that war can be contained within a very finite arena and this civility is taken to an almost Utopian level by the ensuing lack of casualties - some fools see it as tribal savagery or primal chaos but you may take it from me that it is exactly the opposite - it is the ultimate in physical decorum - it makes no demand on the supporter other that he should always support the club through good and bad - he need not offer any other single attribute and for the player himself all he must do is always attempt to play to his maximum ability - he is never expected

*to do things with the ball for which he is not gifted enough
to do - it bears no comparison with all those other sports in
which one is allowed to use one's hands - what a joke - why
would anyone be impressed by the ability to do a half clever
thing with a ball using the human hand when we consider
the profound adeptness and near miraculous ability of the
hand to do many other staggeringly complex and beautiful
things?*

*If there were no Sistine chapel or no skilled surgery or no
David, etc, etc, THEN perhaps maybe I could be somewhat
impressed by a man throwing a ball into a basket or to hit it
a distance with a piece of stick - but otherwise...*

*These football players come from the rank of the common
man as do surely ninety percent of the supporters and it dœs
grieve me a little at the paucity of their remuneration - in
some instances it is roughly about the same as a tradesman
and when we consider their artistry and their ability to en-
thrall a crowd of many thousands it really dœsn't seem fair at
all - it is indeed a form of exploitation and although I never
thought that I'd hear myself say it, I actually think that a
Marxian approach to the situation could solve their dilemma.
If only they were paid for the fruits of their labour... could
somehow take control of what they produce and exploit that
rather than the other way round but alas this shall never
happen as such a concept is beyond them... simple boys playing a sport for the love of it, for the sheer joy and exuberance
of showing their God given talent - in fact I have little doubt
that each and every one of them would do it for absolutely
no monetary reward whatsœver - what boy wouldn't turn
up once a week at the stadium of his favourite team to kick*

a ball around for ninety minutes? The privilege of treading the hallowed turf, of wearing the sacred garment that is the team strip is of itself a thing to savour beyond all else - what would he do in lieu of this anyway?... wait on tables... paint a bathroom wall... drive a bus... sweep the streets?

It has just occurred to me that the aforementioned striker may qualify as my next cargo - I must give it some serious thought - it would serve a dual purpose of satisfying my blood lust and more importantly force the club to seek out a (hopefully better) replacement.

But you have no idea how difficult it is to actually score a goal!

It seems quite simple to me - it's not rocket science.

Rocket science is easy by comparison.

Yes, of course it is.

You may mock but I assure you it is a most complex thing.

Perhaps I have misjudged its complexity - my mistake was to think that it was simply a matter of whacking a spherical piece of air filled leather into the back of the clearly defined net.

If it's really so easy may I ask you how many goals Einstein has scored? or Newton? or Michelangelo?

Decrescendo

I see your point - I hadn't thought of it in such terms before.

Why do you think that some people actually choose to study rocket science?

I had thought it was because they were interested in all things Cosmic but of course I am open to persuasion on that point.

We football players also have to take the Cosmos into account.

Please pardon my profound ignorance, I hadn't quite realised.

The concepts which we use may be instinctive rather than intellectual but they are none the less complex for that - imagine a player stepping up to take a penalty kick - as he walks towards the inert object that we call the ball, he faces an infinite cosmos and yet he must place the ball within the tiniest confine of what we call the goalpost - this narrow, finite, limited almost claustrophobic space is the only part of the vast cosmos where it is acceptable for him to put the ball - this micro speck - this infinitesimal dot - any other part of the entire heavens and he is a total and utter failure.

Hmmm... I hadn't exactly perceived it in such terms but sure enough as you say it, it does of course make perfect sense - so all those young boys who dream of being the first kosmonaut or astronaut into space are in fact choosing the easy option rather than facing the near impossible challenge of playing as a centre forward for the mighty Benfica...

A harsh conclusion but alas so very true.

Who's that new striker that's just come on the pitch for Benfica?

He's some Russian named Gagarin.

Hope that he has enough skill to play for us - I think that it's a bit of a gamble signing him - he's an unknown - a nobody.

They say he's a bit of a wizard - very good in the air.

I hope he's a brave player.

He's supposed to be absolutely fearless.

I wonder if he's easily brought to ground by a strong defender?

Someone said he can almost defy gravity.

Hope so as the player who's marking him tonight likes to bring fancy new signings down to earth quickly.

All we need to be champions is a striker who can put the ball in the back of the net and if he can do it for us then the

Decrescendo

sky's the limit this season.

All night I have observed my sister, a woman of forty two, and noticed her strange behaviour. As a trained experienced, fully fledged psycho therapist I am well placed to comment upon the actions of all living things - both the conscious and the unconscious behaviour and as a man I am also well placed to comment on the behaviour of women. And before you dare suggest that it would be fairer or more objective to allow a female therapist comment in lieu of myself let me tell you something about feminine psycho therapists... there are none.

Of course they may be female in biological construction but their inclinations have been well suppressed. They work in a paternalistic field and accept all the patriarchal aspects of psychiatry - how can they not - we had designed the jigsaw before they had arrived and they jumped aboard the good ship. In many ways they have benefitted our profession. They show the zeal of the convert. I hear you say... what woman would let a Freud define their innermost needs? Well, you'd be very surprised.

Perhaps it's their delight at storming our male bastion that blinds them to its raison d'etre... and of course our focus will no doubt change somewhat as time gœs by... we've built up a nice little earner based on half-truths, incompetence and general fraudulence so we've no real objection to ditching certain wayward phony theories as they become unsustainable and untenable.

Money is our true God and before you begin to wonder

if we've coined a term for those addicted to exploiting other human beings for profit... no, we haven't as that would hardly be in our self interest... now would it?

And remember unlike some professions... we are apolitical... we have no objection to working within a democracy nor do we object to helping dictators of every hue devise the best most efficient methods to break down the people whom they wish to break down with torture, humiliation, etc... why would we?

Tyrants especially like the way we don't acknowledge such banalities as good and evil - Perhaps even Hitler wasn't evil... he just had some stuff which he hadn't 'worked out'... perhaps he was infected with a disease from a Jewish hooker... that would account for everything - the chairman isn't evil... he just has a tendency to want the spotlight... do things his way... mustn't have gotten enough attention as a child. Our own, modest, humble, altruistic, ingenius leader here in Portugal... Salazar is a fine example of how well a dictator can work... he personifies how benevolent a dictator can really be... he built his concentration camps far, far away so as not to have an eyesore in the land he truly loved, refused to acknowledge our city slums in case it insinuated he felt better than the slum dwellers and censored all our reading material in case the doom mongers printed things that upset the delicate psyche of our fragile people.

So listen to me when I talk about my sister... and I will put this in slightly non-technical terms... she's fucking crazy.

Decrescendo

Sigmund darling are you ready yet - our cab is waiting?

Joost one moment my liebling.

What's keeping you siggy?

I'm trimming my beard dearest.

I don't understand why you don't just shave it off?

Are you mad? Shave it off !!!

Well, I was only...

That's a good one... shave it off... I'd have to give up psychoanalysis then.

Oh... I'm sorry... I didn't realise just how important it was.

Important? Important? It's absolutely essential - who'd listen to such outrageous ideas as mine from a clean-shaven man - I ask you?

Well - if you put it that way.

Yes I do put it that way - a beard is vital in my profession - it's as essential as a crucifix is to a priest - obviously spectacles and a waistcoat and a pocket watch are necessary too but they're not indispensable.

Who are these people whom we're having dinner with again?

Important people from the film industry - naturally they're interested in my ideas and theories on the nature of good and evil.

But Siggy darling you don't believe in good and evil.

That's the beauty of it - they make fantasy films.

Please say we don't have to play the role game again in bed tonight...

I told you a thousand times that role play is healthy.

But it dœsn't sound normal.

How many times have I told you that there's no NOR-MAL.

Well, couldn't we play a different role play game then?

There'd be little point as being a female you wouldn't get pleasure from a different game either.

I suppose you're right but...

Decrescendo

No buts - I'll be sweet, cute, pretty little Siggy aged four and you be momma - sweet scented, soft but firm momma.

O.....kay.

I assure you based on all my clinical expertise that it's a particularly ordinary, common thing for a man to desire - would you rather I played the goat fantasy then?

No.

Good - let's not discuss it again.

But sometimes I get these deep urges from some distant place in my body.

Liebling, how often have I proven to you that you have no desires - well?

But Siggy darling, it's just that... I saw a man the other day and for a split second I thought that maybe he and I...

I've never heard such nonsense - absolute utter rubbish.

But he was so young and strong and detached.

My sweetness... it's so obviously a case of transference.

I don't quite understand.

Decrescendo

Look... let me see... how old was the young man - what height - what colour - what individual traits did he possess?

Let me think... mmm... about twenty seven... six feet tall... blue eyes... and a strong inquisitive visage.

Hmmm...tut, tut, tut...hmm...aha....mmm....tut...hmmm.

I love the creative way that your analytical mind works.

Hmmm...tut, mmm,...hmmm....aha - I've got it - it was so patently obvious that it took me a few moments to quite get it.

My husband... the greatest ever therapist... greatest ever clinician.

Please - refrain from the praise - you know my opinion of the ego - well as I was about to say - the young man whom you imagine that you had these feelings for...

But Siggy I had those feeling - warm ones - very warm ones.

Anyway my dear - the young man is merely a representation of your brother Hector and in his absence you've simply transferred the affection onto this anonymous young man.

Decrescendo

But I never had warm feelings for Hector.

Perhaps not but I can assure you that it's still a case of transference onto a very similar young man.

But I haven't seen Hector since before I met you all those years ago.

Still...

And Hector was only five feet tall and had brown eyes and a nasty disposition.

Well perhaps it was one of your cousins who was the object of it.

Darling I don't have any male cousins.

Then it was probably an uncle.

But...

Don't tell me... no uncle? Well, then perhaps it was a son of a female cousin?

All my cousins are childless.

Ah yes it should have struck me before... a next door neighbour when you were growing up - yes that's it - fits like a glove.

Decrescendo

Well if you say so - my next door neighbour was indeed a man and a really nice one at that.

My diagnostic powers are impeccable, razor like as near to infallible as one could reasonably hope for.

I remember Mr.Otto so well.

See... I told you... you were probably in love with him as in your mind he idealized everything that a man should be.

I remember his one hundredth birthday so well - we gave a party for him as it was also my seventh birthday.

One hundred!

Yes Siggy dear - he actually lived to be one hundred and six.

Well the age is not so important anyway it's more the strength and masculinity he represented - a proud man of action and so on.

He was a dressmaker.

Yes but as a child you would have seen a dress as a symbol of power - your mother who would have controlled the house and the servants would have worn one and in this old neighbour you would have been aware that he went even a step further by actually being the one who clothed the powerful mother figure.

I suppose maybe - it just seems a little bit shaky.

Hmmm... let me see... did the young man you saw look like he may have had a grandfather?

Well... possibly.

Aha... I knew it - I knew it - my clinical instincts are seldom wrong. You simply transferred the feelings onto the grandson of the old man.

The one that he never had?

Exactly! That's the beauty of it - the very fact that he never had a grandson in the first place made it totally safe for you to complete your deluded transference cycle thing.

Elizabeth and Kate too noticed forty two's odd beahviour. Odd little nothing things like walking around with a glass of wine in each hand - saying to Elizabeth things like, 'I know you... don't I?' - putting napkins into her pocket. Nothing things. Yet sometimes it is these nothing things which reveal everything. People rarely behave out of character - this is a truism which has much merit.

Decrescendo

A different woman could have done big things like strip naked and dance on the table and it would have revealed nothing odd because it would be part of their normal behaviour and not in the least noteworthy of being classified as strange.

Elizabeth thought too of other little unusual aspects of her daughter's life in recent weeks - again, things so insignificant that they went unremarked by all and unnoticed by most. Twice she had locked herself out of the house within a one week period and Elizabeth couldn't recall her daughter doing this even once in the previous twenty five years. On one occasion just an hour after she'd eaten Sunday lunch she started to prepare food again and when questioned as to why, she swore blind that she hadn't eaten and when Kate and Elizabeth both agreed that she had, she simply shrugged and said that it was her business if she was hungry again. Perhaps it was all those invisible stresses of twentieth century life that everyone talks about all the time.

Life was fast and probably would only get faster. No one single thing or idea had made it so. A culmination of many processes converging with all the nuance of a runaway train throttling downhill. Each born into a world that moved faster than the one who bore her had been born into. No one to really blame. A thing bigger than all. Magic seeds. Beanstalk. Killing giants.

Slow just a derivative term. A minus. Obsolete. Obsession with speed. Rate. Velocity. Acceleration. Quicker=better.

Decrescendo

Lets go back to single lane motorways. Lets go back to
cobbled streets. Use cars that only travel at forty miles
per hour. Use hansom cabs. Use ponies. Use single engine planes. Use gliders. Use balloons. Use steam engines.
Computers are the source of the problem. Spaceships are
the source of the problem. Blame rock n' roll. Blame the
moving pictures. Blame abstract art. Blame the impres-
sionists. Blame Darwin. Blame the industrial revolution.
Blame the enlightenment. Blame the renaissance. Blame
the printing press. Blame the magna carta. Blame the
crossbow. Blame the bow and arrow. Blame the Romans.
Blame the Greeks. Blame the iron age. Blame the one
who discovered fire - must have been a repressed arsonist.
Blame the hunters who for reasons unknown moved into
agriculture... what about all those crazy alchemists?... Men
and the odd woman too of much learning living out their
days in some old dark cave. Cold and dreary. Damp. Penniless. Forsaken by their fellow man but bent on proving
in their own inarticulate way that some quantum leap was
possible. Too ignorant to know what a Newton or a Bell
or an Einstein or a Edison might ever do but somehow in
some vague abstract way sensing that magic was feasible
- something out of nothing - unable to hear the bloke in
the next cave shout but eerily thinking that maybe, just
maybe it might be possible to talk to a bloke half way
round the world.

So, you're an alchemist then?

Yes I am.

Decrescendo

And what exactly is it that you do then?

I change base metal into gold.

Well that's certainly clever.

Thank you.

Is it difficult then?

Pardon?

Is it difficult to change the metal into gold?

Let us say it's a trifle time consuming.

Oh... I hadn't realised... I'd imagined it was fairly straight forward for a person of your learning... may I ask if you read Latin?

Yes, I do.

Greek?

Yes.

Mathematics?

Yes.

Philosophy?

Yes.

So it shouldn't be too hard then?

Well as I may have mentioned it is a little time demanding.

May I ask exactly how long it's taken you so far?

Forty years.

That's quite a long time.

Yes.

Still... it was worth it all... gold is of such immense value
and now that you've cracked the secret there'll be no
stopping you - by the way how many tonnes of the stuff
have you so far?

No tonnes.

Still... even a few stone weight of pure gold ought to
bring in a decent few bob.

No stones weight.

Decrescendo

Mind you gold is so rare and precious that those few pounds of it you've made are still of huge value.

No pounds weight.

All those years for just a few ounces?

No ounces.

Dust?

No dust.

Mmmmmmmmmmmm... I see... simply hovering on the threshold of greatness.

That's it... each time I go over my recipe I find something missing. A different thing each time. Always a thing bereft.

Perhaps you're simply crazy.

Some say so.

Perhaps you're simply delusional. Too many nights burning endless candles in the unending dark. There is no magic. No quantum leaps.

Forget Zeno. There are no short cuts. Toil and sweat, that's our lot. No magic carpets to fly to distant lands only boats built by bloodied gnarled knuckles and reluc-

tant timber. Only a fur skin keeps out the winter's gnawing bite. No way to trap sunlight - only a candle illumi-
nates the blanket darkness. The moon cannot ever be
reached by foot of man and the stars but serve as beautiful, useless metaphors.

The hand once severed cannot be reattached and blood
spilt can never be restored - these are self evident truths.

Go home to your family - if they still remember you - il-
lusions are but well carved mill stones. There is no shame
in base metal remaining as but base metal.

I thank you for your critique... and yes base metal is
blameless... in its way it is as worthy as gold... indeed I
have in my way wasted my entire life and as must has
been said before, our problem with time is that whether
used wisely or in errant fashion as I seem to have done...
it still gœs... we cannot pause it... the hourglass has a will
of its own and only flows in one direction.

It's true that I could have translated texts of ancient
Greece and the wise words of Æschylus and Sophocles
or written learned treatises on the irrigation of land and
analysed sacred texts for hidden meaning but somehow
these things, noble of themselves, were not my calling
- how many early mornings I awoke cold, frozen to the
bone with a growling belly and hands cramped by repetition, barely able to stand and swearing on holy books
that that was that. Walking in the fresh bracing air as I
vowed to turn my hand to tasks anew... yet somehow the
images carved into my brain would not begone... The
mighty oak but from acorn... the butterfly from a larva...

Decrescendo

the harsh winter snow turning to the glory of spring... the
clumsy inept baby to athletic brave warrior or graceful
majestic dancer... something miraculous from nothing...
always but always these images drove me on... braver
and braver or if you wish foolisher and foolisher... keeping deep inside my real thoughts... why not travel to the
moon... after all it is but another place... why not talk
to one in distant lands... sound travels... and if we could
master fire, who knows if it could rival daylight... and yes
if the birds can fly... why not we... wingspan can be explained... that magic is magic there is no doubt... but who
can say we do not have magic within us... there is much
still to be explained, of this I am certain.

So I shall go back to the dark... seeking illumination...
of what exactly I am not sure... and if I do indeed manage to turn base metal to gold, the magic will have only
begun for gold will simply be a better kind of base metal
to begin my task all over again with... next stop never.

Decrescendo

CHAPTER 14: DOTS AND CIRCLES

Today I visited my publisher - such a difficult man - he dœsn't seem to understand my dilemma.

In previous discussions that we had he seemed to think it an excellent idea that a practising psychiatrist like myself should in fact write a book - thus I began my memoirs a.k.a. THE LISBON VAMPIRE - but he was under the impression that my book would deal with my work as a therapist but this was not my intention at all - our conversation went something like this.

I thought that as you had been a therapist for many years after your brief stint in advertising and that you would use a lot of that subject matter in your work.

That is not my wish.

But surely it is your profession which defines you?

No.

There's a significant market for such opinions.

Be that as it may - it's not what I desire to write about - I am writing about much more real things - truth and beauty and so on.

Decrescendo

But you must have had some interesting patients - that one of whom you told me before for example.

The woman who's husband was cheating on her?

Yes, that's the one - please tell it again.

Well it was a very beautiful thirty five year old woman who'd been married for ten years and found out that her husband was seeing a vivacious eighteen year old girl - the woman was quite upset - the husband seemed a decent up-standing chap so I recommended that she forgive him - let it go - move on - just forget it.

Then what happened?

They appeared to put it behind them for a few months but then she told me that the husband was cheating on her with the sister of the eighteen year old... a stunning nineteen year old - naturally I encouraged her to forgive and forget - to put it behind her - for after all we are all imperfect - with great effort and much reluctance the lady forgave and achieved a level of intimacy with her husband once again.

And?

She returned just a few short weeks later in tears - this time he was now having an affair with the luscious thirty seven year old mother of the afore mentioned sisters - after a number of sessions and much careful and sensitive persuasion

Decrescendo

I managed to readjust her perspective and so she agreed to give her floundering marriage one last try.

What a story - a real credit to your immense skills if I may say so.

Yes you may but the story doesn't end there - some short time later the patient returned this time more dazed than sad or hysterical - her unfaithful spouse had been at it again - this time it appears that he had successfully targeted the fourth and surely final female member of that same family... the mother's mother - a particularly well preserved fifty three year old woman - an amazingly elegant, charming creature - perhaps there's something to be said for early motherhood - anyway the husband was besotted by her - her blood relation's views are not on the record.

Don't tell me that you simply told her to forget it, move on and try again?

Do you think that I'm a complete idiot? Of course not - I knew that only a Herculean effort by me could avert disaster and that anything less would terminate the marriage not to mention undo my previous good work - so after much painstaking effort and intense research, I arrived at a possible solution to the incredible fragile and delicate situation - so I gave it a try:

Doctor before you waste your breath and tell me to move on and try again... don't bother... I'm all out of forgiveness.

Decrescendo

(I knew that I had to soften her up, that I couldn't pitch my idea straight away).

Well let me begin by extending my profoundest empathy to you on this perilous and immensely difficult situation in which you find yourself through no direct fault of your own.

Thank you doctor - you are most understanding and sympathetic.

No thanks is necessary, it is the job of the trained therapist to be a font of compassion, wisdom and understanding - each and every therapist would bring the same in depth concern and knowledge to your situation.
I have given your situation much thought, much rumination, much analysis - I have read copious amounts of a range of diverse psychoanalytic literature on the subject in hand and I have naturally enough drawn the only possible conclusion that is accurate and proper.
You mentioned to me in one particular session that we had about how your husband was an orphan.

No - I couldn't have as his parents are both still alive.

Well then you definitely must have conveyed such a thought to me by some means... possibly suggesting that your husband felt orphaned in some symbolic way?

I don't remember ever hinting at such a thing... but I sup-

pose that it's possible.

Of course it is and it's entirely understandable for you to suppress the thought - indeed it is - most natural.

So what my profound, extensive research arrived at after hours spent with voluminous, heavy books that were full of dust, is as follows; Somehow your husband has carried around with him a lifelong sense of abandonment - of being emotionally orphaned - whether or not his feelings were justified is of no real concern but the point is that within his own emotional compass he believed it to be so.

Here we have a grown man with a splendid wife and a child who has a successful career yet inside this gnawing, incessant belief that he somehow dœsn't belong within his spousal family - a part of him wants family more than ever yet another part of his divided self feels unworthy of it - so the divided self seeks to rebuild another family - an artificial one yet one of which he shall be worthy of.

He subconsciously searches for an amoral family which in a sense is a mirror opposite of the idyllic family which you present to him - his subconscious feels that by accepting this new family and then ultimately rejecting it he will then be worthy of you - so he picks the perfect amoral family of the sisters and their mother and their grandmother and instinctively knows that by each one's lecherous, bed-hopping behaviour they are an artificial family unit so he dismisses each one in turn and by doing so feels one step closer each time to being worthy of you his real family.

Doctor, it all makes such sense now... truly you are a ge-

nius... I could have thought about all that stuff in my head for a million years and never arrived at such a solution.

What a story - we must publish it - absolutely brilliant.

Alas I am bound by ethical codes not to reveal such scandalous stories.

Such a pity doctor - remarkable story to end that way.

Actually I'm not so sure that it did - because even though I never saw the patient again someone told me that they happened to see her husband in a restaurant with a sophisticated, garrulous lady of some seventy odd years and for a moment it passed my mind that the family he'd been 'seeing' had in fact a great grandmother of some eighty years... C'est la vie.

Adolphus I'm so sorry to call like this - I hope I'm not disturbing you.

It's quite all right - we're just having a little bash for my dear mother's eightieth birthday - is there a problem at the clinic?

No - everything's fine at the clinic - it's something else entirely. As you know my cousin João has excellent contacts in the regime and he just rang to tell me that there's some rumblings going on.

Decrescendo

Rumblings?? What are you on about man?

Something about a group officers attempting to over-throw the regime - he wasn't sure exactly but he said that something significant was definitely going on.

My dear Roberto you are such an alarmist - relax - sit down and have a glass of port.

Why thank you - I will - calm my nerves down - it all seemed so frightening.

Obviously there's some little matter up but that's about the gist of it - probably some Bolshevik or other has per-petrated the ranks of the army - bound to happen even in the most disciplined of forces.

Do you really think that's all it could be?

Of course - absolutely - our officers are men of the highest integrity - carved from the very rock of patriotism - they will always put nation above any petty grievances which they may have.

It's just that my cousin is quite a calm, collected charac-ter and is the quintessential civil servant and not given to fits of fancy.

Well as I've already said there probably was some trifling disagreement or other in the ranks - possibly a dispute over the state of the cooking in the officer's mess or even about some promotion or other but these little aggravations go on all the time.

Yes - perhaps you are right - we are blessed with a particularly loyal bunch of military men - always interested in the collective good of their fellow Portuguese.

Indeed, and I'll wager that the so-called uprising has been dealt with by now - I can just imagine how forcefully our fine generals will quash even the slightest dissent in the ranks.
All those junior officers will quake if our Generals just so much as wag their little fingers.

You must be right of course - nobody dares to stand against a general - unless the problem is with the generals themselves?

The glass of port must have gone to your head Roberto - why on earth would any general ever dream of overthrowing a stable, competent, efficient, much admired and respected governing class?

I suppose if you put it like that...

There's simply no other way to put it - who ever heard of the military overthrowing an unelected government in a Latin country? If anything we tend to do it the other way round.

Decrescendo

Thank you for your words - I feel most reassured now.

You are most welcome - revolution is the last thing that the country needs right now - if such a thing ever came to pass it would be an unmitigated disaster - revolutions are invariably bloody, chaotic, barbaric - vehicles for mayhem and anarchy - often they simply replace an apparent despot with an even worse tyrant - why just look at history - we are a proud but melancholic people - much of our greatness lies in a distant past - it's not a living thing simply a shadow long since gone to rest - we had the world in our hands and then...

We let it slip Adolphus... didn't we?

We did - but it could never have been any other way - our position at the top of the pyramid was artificial - it had no real root - just a couple of generations of inspired individuals who rode a flight of fancy into the storm and found the wind at their sails which enabled them to momentarily become masters of the universe but despite this it is not within our nature to be conquerors - we are a nation of reflective souls - contemplative - we are that bit more comfortable in the internal world which in a sense makes our seafaring exploits even more remarkable - you could think of us as somewhat reluctant empire builders - perhaps it was more destitution rather than destiny which made us set of for distant shores.

Decrescendo

Revolutions take blood and bullets in a vast amalgamation - sacrifice for the good of others and personal lust for power vie equally for the prize - and whœver lands the crown finds that it never quite fits the way they had thought it might as they laid their blueprint in the smoky backroom or the Turkish coffee shop - the Russian revolution may have been right and proper in a moral sense - it brought an end to the tyranny and apathy of Czardom but only a fool would say it was an improvement - admittedly it was under siege from the very first - and for the wrong reasons - but it then went on to totally prove its detractors correct - small men with even smaller outlooks went on to suffocate an entire people - demagoguery and paranoia are the only currencies to flourish in the Soviet union - ironically its belief that the individual is far less important than society has to destroy it in the end, for what value is there in being human if it is not the apogee of virtue - what kind of parent would tell the child that the notion of family was more important than them and that although they were the soul of the family they were at the same time less important than it - this contradiction is apparent in every aspect of such a society - having said all that it is doubtful if many of these maniacs really believe their own words - far more likely that they simply use it as a means of self aggrandizement - under a Soviet style system there can be no place for a thinker like Marx who challenged conventional orthodoxy - his only reward would have been his very own gulag.

Decrescendo

Comrade Karl, I am sorry to inform you that the Polit-buro has decided to declare you an enemy of the people and so I must ask you to accompany me on a long, ardu-ous, dangerous journey of thousands of miles to spend the rest of your days in the wasteland that is Siberia.

Me? Me? Surely there is some mistake?

I'm afraid not comrade Marx - in fact, the committee has shown you great leniency by allowing you to reside in a remote part of our great Socialist republic.

But without me and my work they'd be nothing - where would they be without all my clauses and sub clauses?

I personally am not unsympathetic to your plight you understand - but in building a socialist paradise there has to be some hard decisions taken.

But I thought we all were in agreement that it was capi-talism that was the enemy?

We are, but your analysis of the capitalist society for all its brilliance was limited and error ridden.

I don't understand.

That's exactly my point - the capitalist system is seri-ously flawed, unjust and unfair but for all that it allows, even encourages, the individual to challenge the beliefs of

that same society - it discourages socialism not because
of ideology but because it believes that it dœsn't work
- dœsn't do what it says it will - that the theory breaks
down during application.

It feels that people and by definition society is too complex, too multi faceted for such a rigid blueprint to ever
work.

But my clauses... my sub clauses.

That's all very well and good but for a system to work
successfully it must have no opposition - it must have free
reign - a monopoly.

But I understand systems - I can make such a system
work for the greater good.

You still don't get it - you are a product of the capitalist
system - you value individual input - new ideas - individual brilliance - flexible approaches - why I'll bet you
could continue to evolve your political beliefs - hone them
- pare them - reinvent them - renew them - even change
them... in fact you're probably not even a Marxist.

But Jesus wasn't a Christian - I can change, a work in
progress - I haven't even started to develop some of my
ideas - socialism would only be the start.

See - that's just it - communism dœsn't want new ideas
- social evolution, adaptability - a wooden horse is easier

to tame than a wild mustang - who did you think would buy your product - Men like Jesus? Or women like Joan of Arc?

Your manifesto was tailored to perfection for men like comrade Stalin - it's almost as if you personally measured his inside leg.

You misconstrue my entire life's work - people are beautiful - the be all and end all - nothing is more sacred than the newborn baby - I love humanity - my entire dream was to remove the shackles - to ennoble the common man.

Then you should have been a musician or a poet or even a philosopher.

I am a philosopher! I realize that man can never fulfill his potential so long as his belly is empty and another controls his working hour.

Do you think that the Pharaohs didn't realise that too? Did you think that they imagined that the slave enjoyed the lash of the whip and unending hours digging dirt in that hot sun? Did you imagine that the Romans thought for one moment that the Christians enjoyed being eaten by hungry lions? Or that the Kings of Europe believed their peasant subjects were happy to be beheaded for hunting deer to feed their starving bellies?

You taught history nothing new - nothing that it didn't know since before the birth of time.

Decrescendo

The flaw is embedded deep within the human heart - in the recesses of its darkest side.

Man has always known injustice was wrong, that tyranny wasn't a beautiful thing.

Before you we had Shakespeare and he showed us every imaginable facet of the blackness of the human soul and the frailty of its ego - all you inadvertently did was unleash a mechanism whereby all the uncle Jœs could incorporate all their wildest dreams for human domination in a single document - in effect all you did was to enable all those despots who can use your fine words as a decoy to subjugate till their little hearts and little minds content... it seems that you understood everything except human nature.

I reject all this - all of it.

Well, that will only make you an enemy of the state - for in practice that's how communism works - and by the way, if you require a slightly bigger wooden shack you'll have to cross the warden's palm with silver - for that's also the way communism works too.

So, all in all my dear Roberto you may take it from me that there will be no revolution in Portugal for the foreseeable future - our people are a broadly contented lot - I'm not suggesting that everything is perfect but they have their football, fado and their Fatima - and whilst Marx's opinion on Fado or football are unknown, I have no doubt that he and I would concur entirely on our views of religion, not that I object to the masses being hooked on opium.

Perhaps there could be a gentle revolution?

Are you mad altogether?

But...

A gentle revolution??? We are a nation of warriors - proud to the last - our history shows that we fear no-one - even the idea of going fecklessly into brave new frontiers - uncharted lands where no European had dare set foot and we did it all on the back of a thing called courage - not because of size or overbearing strength or vast wealth - we fear nothing.

Adolphus... if I may...

What is it... go on... have your say... I'll suffer it.

You are right about the fearless thing but if I may add a thing or two... we are unafraid of the unknown but some-times I think, especially in my work as a therapist, that for all our bravado in facing invisible giants, we are actu-ally more afraid of the known.

The known?

Decrescendo

Yes... I think that we Portuguese are less afraid of the unknown - which is the opposite of how it should be and how it is for most other peoples - we are more fearful of the known, the obvious, the tangible - many of my patients are afraid to talk - to talk to those whom they love - to those whom they should be close to - so many spouses tell me how they never communicate all kinds of solvable problems to their mates - husbands and wives living together separately, afraid to talk over deep emotional feelings, never discussing elephants in the room or even the bedroom - parents and children discussing every issue on earth except the ones that may show how they feel or how things the other dœs may affect them - to me this is why we are so courageous at facing the unknown - it's because we have a profound fear at facing the known - look how we build bridges half way across the world and people still live in shacks in our great cities here in Portugal.

Enough - my dear Roberto, remind me as your much senior colleague to have your prescription refilled for you - such unadulterated bunkum - baseless – rubbish - almost treasonable.

You say you want a revolution... I seek to upturn your entire society... you may call me a member of the intelligentsia... I do not seek piecemeal change... not for me the idea of fixing and mending broken things for I am not an artisan... I need complete and total revision of all things... there can be no half measures... that was Mussolini's big failure as a schoolteacher too, he bribed the little children with candy in order to get them to behave... his biggest mistake in my opinion... I reject all of the status quo... I wish to throw away the baby with the bath water because the baby has been too long in that filthy water and has become contaminated... it reeks of all the things which I despise... besides there is no shortage of babies... I do not believe in renovation... only total destruction of the existing temples to rebuild anew... bottom to top... my idealism is the cure to heal all your germs and the existing society is the disease...

The tyrant you know may be better than... all actions potentially have unforeseen consequences... why take the risk... why gamble with the lives of others - things may be bad now but remember that they could always be worse, much worse.

Revolutionary... who or what is it? What is he or what is she?

What is to revolt? How many revolutions offer anything other than to replace one ISM with another ISM - why must you always seek an ISM to solve all your problems?

The entire planet seems to be simply full of ISMS - ideas with at best a scrap of merit that some joker or clown is hell bent on blowing up into a fully fledged belief system to deal with all problems - one size fits all - why would a single system fit every contingency - capitalism, theism, Marxism, hippyism, psychism, monetarism, Buddhism, vegetarianism, nationalism, racism, narcissism, whiskyism, radicalism, absolutism, constructivism, conservatism, determinism, existentialism, Gnosticism, hedonism, materialism, objectivism, pantheism, optimism, pessimism - have we left any out ?

Yes... most of them... the list is endless and growing... a single fix... a grand unifying theory - a cure for all ills - a system to liberate human beings from being non systemic - somewhere right at this moment in time some idiot, well meaning or otherwise is racking his or her brains to invent a new system (presumably this means that they reject all other systems as inherently flawed) and no matter what the system is some other idiot will attempt to show you its failings by... yes, you've guessed it... another system.

Having said all that... I do have just a slight, sneaking regard for SCEPTICISM.

Imagine a revolution.... where but a handful of bullets are fired... so few that they can be counted on the fingers of a single tiny child.

Imagine a revolution... where the revolutionaries fired so few bullets... that they could be counted on the fingers of a man without arms.

Imagine a revolution where the soldiers really put flowers down the barrels of their guns? the genus of flower would be irrelevant but I hear there's a particularly large crop of carnations this year - just imagine...

A revolution
spun out
like a fragile
silken thread
each second of its life
so close to snap.

Decrescendo

The revolution's heart
is full to brim
of pumping blood
contained for now
but spill and gush
hover, haunt
and hang
waiting a sign
or a symbol
that cordite in the air
is the breath to take.

Revolution happens
only happens
when the puppets
disenchant themselves
from the strings
of the puppeteer

The centre can and did hold, mere anarchy avoided.

Decrescendo

CHAPTER 15: FAIRY TALES AND MONSTERS

Babysitting - Kate for Jose's parents - she liked it - the responsibility - the sliver of independence - the silver of independence - the child himself.

Nighttime - a time of its own - absence of light and more - its own peculiar aura - as different from daytime as two things could be but to define why, impossible.

Nighttime a time for adventure... high heels and romantic moonlight... champagne glasses... handsome strangers and mysterious women... the promise of promise - the shadow of intrigue and the intrigue of shadow.

Nighttime a time for consolidation... locked doors and warmth... comfort... safety... sanctuary... calmness... serenity... peace... sleeping flowers and motionless bodies.

Bedtime stories of impossible tales - beanstalks and beasts and reckless princes and unloved princesses. No wrong way to tell a fairy tale - the story tells itself - unlike ghost stories where the haunting is within the teller - fairy tales happen to somebody, somewhere and maybe, just maybe, can happen to you - each tale a moral fable and open to all interpretation and any slant.

Cinderella dearest sister you know how much I love you and that there's nothing in the world that I wouldn't do for you.

Shut up bitch!

Decrescendo

Please sweet sister don't be so harsh on me.

Your ugliness revolts me to the pit of my stomach!

But...

Ugly!

But...

Ugly!

Please...

Ugly, ugly, ugly.

Your sister and I only wish to help you - we're so concerned about you, that's all.

I DON'T listen to ugly bitches and their opinions - how many times must I tell you that?

We'd love to see you be a little bit motivated, go to college, train for a career, take an interest in your appearance by wearing some of the pretty dresses that we've bought you anything at all darling once it breaks your habit of drifting aimlessly...

I do exactly as I like and the day I take advice from two

fat hideous wretches like you two will be the day I jump under a stagecoach!

But we swore to dear papa to look out for each other - it was his dying wish.

God, I used to wrap the old man round my finger... those were the days.

So is this how you repay his concern by wasting your days sitting around unwashed lying by the ashes?

Just you wait - I'll end up with a thousand times more than you two ugly old bitches - I won't end a barren spinster who spends her day bringing soup and bread around to the doors of the poor and crippled - what a pathetic thing to bother with.

Please...

I think I'll get me a hot young prince like the one who's throwing a ball on Saturday night - he looks cute and somewhat naïve and I've heard he's a sucker for pretty blondes like myself.

What a terribly calculating thing to suggest and besides they say he's a born romantic so, though you're pretty sister, you haven't the most tender of souls.

Tender my ass - I'll lay a snare - romantics are the easi-

est to ensnare as they're entirely predictable - looking
for a thing that dœsn't exist - so if I don't dupe him, he'll
dupe himself with some other... hmmmm... hmmmm...
Bessie, be a sweet servant girl and bring me those elegant
golden slippers, I have an idea.

Jose lying in soft warm bed - pyjamas - snug - Kate
weaving tales and the little boy being entranced and terri-
fied by turns.

Kate... where do the monsters go at night?

They go to a great big cave... huge and deep and very
dark.

So, they can't get me then?

No - of course not - every monster in the whole world
gœs into this big, big, big cave each and every single
night.

But they might sneak out and get me...

Aha - y'see that's the best part of the whole thing -
when they go in they must stay in until daylight cos the
guardian of the cave won't let them leave until the sun
rises all the way.

Is the guardian like God?

Decrescendo

Like God?... I suppose he might be... possibly... perhaps... maybe.

Are the baby monsters afraid of the dark or afraid of the big monsters?

Even monsters have it hard - embryonic monster deep in its mother's womb - may be a monster but it's my baby - baby monster nursed lovingly - more baby than monster - big monster as role model - do as we do - follow the path of monsterdom - the only true path.

Belong with us - you can never be like them - we don't fit their æsthetic - wrong shape, size, colour, species - named at birth - you are a monster - not for you, monster is as monster dœs, for you there is only monster and all its attending glories...

Monster hierarchy - as in all social groupings - baby scaring monster the lowest rung on the ladder - lowest of the low - the granny mugger of the monster world.

Monster reduced to caricature by modernity - days long gone, we roamed when and where we wished - all feared us - Kings and tramps and churchmen in their purple silk robes - all nations, all cultures... those were the days... we conquered all before us... the very mention of our name was more than enough to unsettle tribe of mankind - the hint of our presence was sufficient to shatter nerves and send Shakesperian monarchs into madness's descent - that was then and this is now - now relegated to the shadows and beyond - we struggle for bare survival - our identity lost - our sense of purpose fragmented past the point of no return - our great past now condemned to fable and the imagination of small children who by their innocence and lack of guile invite us somewhere near their space.

We note your ongoing response to our existence but what is your solution?

Who is the arbiter on the right to exist?

What do you suggest we do?

For each mother monster to drown her baby at birth?

I see that you stop short of this advice - you refrain at following the logical conclusion to your intolerance - your courage deserts you - content you remain to vilify all things monster.

Perhaps you believe that we should use science to alter our construct? Shed our birth skin for one with your stamp of approval - in short, be like you.

Courage would tell you that there is no other answer to this problem that plagues some black recess within what you are and what you deem yourselves to be.

Evolution, whether dubious gift from wayward Gods or random occurrence from infinity's spark, deals out its own brand of chaotic justice.

Single cell amœba looked down on by some bi cellular dot who in turn induces feelings of rank superiority from the tiny grub worm - so to all three, common marsh toad must appear as majesty or beyond.

Thanks a million Kate - sorry I was so late - how was

Decrescendo

he - good - he is a little darling.

I told him that his papa would go up to see him when he arrived home.

Oh... he won't be home tonight... we're separating... there's no more us... I can tell no-one except you as I don't know you well and this makes it possible.

Jose's mother Alice paused - momentary confusion - temporarily caught unaware even though no-one had sprung a trap. ...

Alone. You are alone. His footsteps will be heard no more by your ears - they will still make sound but only for the ears of another.

Bottled up things - hermetically sealed vault - contained things within other knotted.

Secrets... but to what purpose... who amongst ye is fit to judge... you there with the impeccable veneer and untroubled surface... how well you hide your own underbelly... so well do you conceal it that it empowers you to point, sneer and comment.

Who does what to who, why, where, when... what's it to ya?

Alice stood in the center of the room, alone. Vulnerable. Exposed. Layers of social circumstance and conformity woven over many years, paper sword.

All those snotty nosed 'friends' whatever would they say? Whatever would they think?

Decrescendo

Their beak like noses would pitch that bit higher and mightier than usual?

They would offer the 'consolation' of 'I told you so'.

From beneath the intact canopy of their own hollow relationships, from the vacuous chambers of their empty existences, they would be there for her - like a friendly storm in a hurricane - a dirge at a requiem - a black hat in the dark.

Schadenfreude... did ever a word so accurately distill a thing within.

Would be Juliet, your balcony too lies in ruin and rubble.

You laid your wares out and though he took them home for an extended trial he did not buy - he did not seal the deal with the stamp of eternity. Seller beware. You were possessed of many charms but the only one that really counts is the one we name eternity.

He came to the well and he drank long and deep but somehow the thirst was not assuaged.

All your magic bag of tricks couldn't contain. Coloured hoops and black silk garters.

Each night you looked at the stars and felt worthy to share the same setting.

In a world of emptiness and an overflow of nothing - you had something - a thing that made it all worthwhile - a single tiny spot, place, thing - an accidental collision of heart and soul.

Now you cannot say that word - the one we all overuse,

misuse, abuse.

The word that makes us float but is of itself too heavy to weigh - this word has ripped more hearts asunder than we can count.

This thing unquantifiable and beyond any real analyses - its joy beyond all and any and its loss a thing beyond a thousand deaths - we use cliché to explain it because we dare not use the language of logic - under rational thought its disintegration is guaranteed so instead we use the imagery of pœtry - good pœtry, bad pœtry, any pœtry.

She cried tears - warm empty tears - useless tears. She felt hollow within because she was hollow. Raw.

The recentness and the newness and the suddenness of it destroyed her - the chairs in the room looked the same as before but how could they be - nothing could ever be the same again - of this she had no doubt.

The thought went through her head that if she had been hit by a train earlier that morning and now lay in intensive care in a coma with her very existence hanging by the most fragile thread imaginable... she would still have him at this moment - he would still belong to her - Oh for a runaway express.

Doctor... how is my wife?

Well I'm sorry to say that she is unconscious and has multiple fractures and may not walk again and she may also have a brain clot and has punctured both lungs and the coma may be long lasting.

Decrescendo

But she is still alive? She is still breathing then?

Yes.

Oh thank God for that much at least, as long as there's a breath in her body I can carry on living.

There's Alice's husband again, poor man - that's every single evening for the past three years - how does he manage to carry on?

I think he just adores her essence - her presence - her very being - organic and inorganic.

Last week I noticed that tall, leggy, attractive temporary night nurse trying to flirt with him but, poor girl, he didn't even notice that she existed because he was so absorbed holding his wife's inanimate wax like hand.

Poor woman, imagine being hit by an express train - could anything more tragic happen to a woman in love.

At her bedside he hangs.
Broken... distraught... inconsolable... but within that grief, a piece of him has calm, peace, joy - joy at knowing this half woman who lies deep in her coma. The oneness of their combined presence. To hold her non throbbing hand for a few moments, better than being stranded with a troupe of dancers from Les Folies Bergère, on a desert island.

Decrescendo

Again only cliché and repetition can even begin to convey how her love makes him.

It was love at first sight - I caught her eye and just knew - two huge metal cogs clicking into perfect calibration - at last he understood Tennyson and Keats and Byron and Yeats.

Existence had no other purpose other than to love and in return be loved - there was no second most important thing.

She was a Goddess - words were inadequate to express the depth of his feelings - pœtry fell apart and reassembled itself when he thought of her.

She makes the void a little less void.

She makes the futility less futile.

She makes me, me.

Lying inanimate, ghostly, vague, apathetic, suspended - hooked up to her life support and still the only woman on the planet to hold his heart - he remembered the day he had given it to her......................take it....it's yours....and yours alone....handle it with all the care that you possess..... mark it fragile... very fragile..... you are its guardian... you above all others.... entrusted to my distilled essence... all that I am and all that could ever wish to be is some small attachment to you.

After you there can be no such thing as love - you are its origin - I am honoured to be within your orbit.

Kate stood and Alice stood - the comfortless giver and the uncomforted - she is passionate but she is young - she cannot know my pain - I am tumbling down and my fall has no limit - no end. You do not know what it is like to build your entire existence around a single individual and to use them as the cornerstone of your life - be all and end all.

I live on a planet of billions of men but I cannot see them - each one invisible - I only have eyes for him. You cannot know my pain - no one can, except perhaps those who've been here and even then I'm not so sure as I honestly feel my pain is more unique than theirs, my suffering much more profound...

It fell - it fell like a hammer blow - swift, clean lethal... or should that be a cleaver - either way it was cold, clinical, brutal, and final. It came from nowhere and from everywhere both at the same time. From the moment his lips started moving I sensed something was up - not a small thing - not a crashed fender or a lost cuff link - not a flat tyre nor a broken china teapot.

His lips moved and I saw them talk to me as if I wasn't me - solid, logical, business like - in control of all the words - afterwards the first thing which occurred to me was that it should have been harder for him to get the words out - they should have spluttered rather than flowed.

The land of I love you but.

With you
and you alone
I want to sail

to the land of I love you
but
I am unworthy
of the vessel.
My world
consists of
but one space
the land of I love you
but
my compass wavers.
I shall crown you
queen,
queen of
the land of I love you
but
the queen is dead,
bring in the pretender...

As soon as the sentence was passed, I knew that there could be no reprieve and no appeal.

There was a bluntness, a crudeness in their mouthing which the civility of the language could not mask - this was it - you are alone - take back your soul - soul for sale - one careful owner. No reasonable offer refused...

If only she'd discoursed with Newton or Einstein or any mathematician at all...

Okay young lady... I see that you're twenty years old and you've met this boy with whom you now claim to

be madly in love with. You describe him as your SOUL-
MATE... the only soul on the entire planet who can throw
some imaginary switch within your being... am I correct
so far?

Yes - everything is as you've outlined it.

Fine, fine... now if I may attempt to put it into some
kind of logical, coherent perspective and here I will
attempt to use rough, easily understood numbers and
definitions... is that okay by you? At no stage will we seek
to subvert, diminish or undermine your feelings, beliefs
or your right to claim this cosmic oneness which you've
suggested exists except if the empirical evidence points
that way - in short we will gather the data and see what it
suggests on the balance of probability - okay?

Yes, that's okay although it dœs seem a little dispassionate a little too mechanical.

Love is beyond the measure of science and remote from
the lure of calculation, it is a thing without boundary,
tangible only to those who ride its wave. It has no tem-
plate and has no domain. It is of necessity unbridled and
untamed, it is the mustang that cannot be corralled. No
thing in all existence is more personal nor more subjective.
But that's the beauty of science - it's not a little bit dispassionate, it's entirely dispassionate and it's not a little
bit mechanical, it's entirely mechanical - think of it as a
Bhuddist like equation - I take it that you have a basic

grasp of probability then?

I suppose so.

Imagine if I told you that there was to be a chess match between two players - X and Y, and then asked you the likelihood of the chances of each player winning the match - in percentage terms - what would you say?

Well as there are only two outcomes - if we exclude the possibility of a tie - then I'd say 50/50.

You'd say that each has a 50 percent chance of emerging victorious?

More or less... yes.

Very good answer - very good indeed - two competitors, one prize... sounds rational enough.

Thank you...

Except that if it then transpired that the two combatants were Joe Bloggs against Bobby Fisher - you're 50/50 analysis goes out the window - think of it more likely to be 99.99999999999999% to 0.000000000000001%.

Oh!

Please forgive my manners for that little party trick - I

had wanted to demonstrate it merely to showcase my own cleverness - but to get back on track with our demonstration and agree that with two possibilities there's a 50/50 chance either way - and even using this very crude, basic device, let's continue.

If there are approximately say one billion men on the planet whom are eligible to win your heart - and this is a conservative number, for convenience sake - and there is in fact a unique, cosmic mate that destiny has in store for you... what do you think the chances are of you finding this mate?

One in 1,000,000,000?

Your numeracy does you credit - you are completely correct - 1 in 1,000,000,000... think of it as walking down to the shop to buy a lottery ticket and on your way there you find a thousand dollar bill - you then buy your lottery ticket and then take a totally different route home and on your way there you find a diamond encrusted ring - you arrive home and switch on your T.V. to hear your numbers called out as the sole winning numbers... this is roughly the probability of you finding that cosmic soulmate - assuming that he exists in the first place - as you may have gathered, I tend not to read too many love poems. But I am also a human being and so have some concept of what love really might be. It is a balm, a cream, a cool bandage or even a glue, yes a glue. One to stick back together all those tiny broken pieces which we've amassed since that umbilical cord was first cut. It's a blind throw of multi faceted dice, ones that have so many dimensions attached we cannot even begin to add them up. It's the hands with boxing gloves on as they vainly attempt to un-tie a myriad of tightly bound knots - each knot overlap-ping and labyrinthine beyond description and of course, each knot a scar which we've picked up somewhere along the way. This and only this is what romantic love's only purpose and usefulness may be to our species.

Kate listened in that way we do - no right thing to say - refraining from saying some stupid, insensitive thing in itself a success. She had seen the couple together a num-ber of times and although they seemed content enough they didn't strike her young mind as especially passionate or connected - what does anyone know.

Her only framework of reference outside the fiction of books and drama was her own father and mother - they were close - they were passionate - they were playful - they argued and they sulked and they occasionally raised their voices but they had this thing for each other which she could only describe as awe - a thing which could not easily be supplanted - one day he wrote a poem on some global atrocity and the next day he wrote one about the shape of her lips - sometimes she caught her mother looking across at him and the look suggested... he's the guardian of my heart and it will always be this way - or so it all appeared.

Age old conflict between appearance and reality - out-side of two plus two is four, very few things were verifiable - abstract things too impossible to measure - too vaporous to explain - the ingredients too subjective to list - too many variants - too much fluidity - flux and more flux.

Love itself could be an aberration - a beautiful hazy cloud - one minute you see it next minute you don't - the eye of the beholder territory...

My man is a work of art - more priceless than Michelangelo's David - more valuable, more beautiful.

Here's the difference... I've seen your man... if they put him on a plinth at the Ufitzi - nobody's jaw would drop - other women wouldn't wish to run their hands dreamlike over him - and if he came up for auction at Sothebys there wouldn't be a bidding war... trust me.

I talked to your man once and his passion wasn't so obvious in fact I'm not even sure that he has a warmer heart than David either...

My woman is the most perfect picture - by comparison Mona Lisa is a train wreck.

I must agree with you that the lady with the smile is a trifle overrated in terms of otherness but to me your woman would inspire about as much romantic poetry as bucket of wet coal on an unlit fire.

... however we must concede that amour is mysterious

Decrescendo

and subjective and in a sense anything is possible...

The coal bucket stands alone but proud
and to me each piece signifies solidity
power, beauty and a rough, wayward grace.
Its solitary way of being
infuses my senses to overload.
In its blackness, I see only light
and in its limitations
I see only possibility,
Bucket of wet coal
you and you alone
are my one, my all.

Decrescendo

Decrescendo

CHAPTER 16: GREASEPAINT

As a therapist, I Dr.Adolphus, single-handedly created a system whereby ALL couples could live their entire lives together in perfect unison. My system guarantees total harmony and complete balance. I can understand your scepticism at such apparently outrageous claims. Inevitably you must think that there has got to be a catch, a trap, a sham... you think it must equate to building on quicksand and I understand such obvious, legitimate concerns. But again let me reassure you that this rainbow delivers its crock of gold.

No sleight of hand, no smoke and mirrors, no false bottom in the cabinet - this rabbit really comes out of the hat... anytime... anywhere.

Imagine a planet where all man/woman relationships were without all those endless list of petty, pointless grievances and squabbles. Neither one seeking to undermine, to humiliate, to punish, to overwhelm, to possess, to limit, to dominate, to hurt, to exploit, to abuse or to conquer.

Without backtracking or reneging let me insert one or two tiny caveats - again no traps will be sprung by me but as it is a system there must of necessity be some procedure to its operation. Forgive my defensiveness for the world is full of cynics.

The caveats, such as they exist, are rudimentary and easily understood - and as I say, their application is essential in much the same way as it would be necessary for such a marvelous invention as a motor car to need petrol and for the engine to require switching on.

For my system to run and work it is vital for both partners to agree to the following:

1. Both participants must be totally willing to conform to all and every aspect of the procedure.

2. It must be tried and tested over a period of weeks rather than days.

3. It must be remembered that all partial inequalities and injustices within the system will work themselves out to the total satisfaction of both parties provided each adheres exactly to the guidelines.

On the night before the system is agreed to come into play, a coin must be tossed to decide which of the two will start in the passive role and which will start in the active role - I personally suggest that the coin should be tossed on a 'best of five' basis.

He/she who 'wins' the toss gets to select whether they wish to opt for passive or active role on the following day (day one).

Let us assume that she wins the toss and chooses to pick the active role for day one - this means that she has to spend say an hour of the evening prior to write her script for the next day. And so to the all important script - the script can be flexible with regards to quantity, timing, emphasis, theme, scheme, etc... but of paramount importance is that each participant MUST adhere slavishly to the tone, sentiment, essence, mood, and above all else the direction which the author takes - in effect he must follow the words as accurately as possible that she has written for him. The following night the roles will be reversed and so on each alternate night.

Already you can see the real beauty of my system - in how each author will be mindful that the player whose script they now write, will themselves be in the same position very soon.

Those tempted to force their partner to mouth humiliating language will be mindful of the next day's payback - those who wish to cœrce their partner into any act with which they are not comfortable must suffer the consequences - this of course is not simply a system to deal with the darker side of human relationships it is equally well designed for encouraging and stimulating all those positive aspects of the man/woman orbit - a sensitive, caring, attentive, complimentary script is likely to be met by a mutual reward... Here comes my first couple now... Let us follow my impending triumph...

Day one of the experiment in which Marguerite has written all of the responses which her partner (Terence) MUST make - he is given no room whatsœver to deviate from the script and any time he appears to do so, she is entitled to sternly rebuke him and to insist he recant and continue.

Marguerite's responses to him are only loosely scripted - more as a guideline and as the active participant today, she is free to ad lib, change, etc... at will or whim.

M: Hi sweetie, good to see you and how was your day

today?

T: Lovely to see you too my princess - my day as always was bereft of your divine presence.

M: Shall I cook up a nice cosy meal for two or do you want us to eat out?

T: Let's eat out honey - I so want to try that new French bistro.

M: Oh... that's a pity cos I spent ages sourcing ingredients for a new recipe that I so wished to try out for you... but it's okay, it dœsn't matter... maybe another time.

T: Great - I don't want to be late there as Greta said it's the best French cuisine that she's ever tasted.

M: Greta? Oh... I see...

T: Jesus honey... why the face every time that I mention her name... she means nothing to me... just because we were once married... that's all in the distant past now.

M: Sorry for any insecurity but it's just that you still seem to care about her opinions... that's all.

T: If by that you mean do I still respect her then the answer is yes, after all we were married for seven years and had a child together.

M: I am being a silly - ignore my foolish, obsessive behaviour... I really am sorry for over reacting.

T: It's understandable for after all she is a remarkably successful woman.

M: You still seem to admire her so much.

T: I'm just trying to be honest and accord her the respect which she deserves - we had seven good years and now it's well over.

M: I'm so glad that you love me a million times more

than you ever loved her.

T: Yeah.

M: You seem unsure?

T: It's just that I don't like the idea of measuring people as though they were objects.

M: But at least I'm a far better lover... more sensual... sexier... much more fascinating.

T: You're not just the best lover that I've ever had - you're the best lover ANYONE ever had...

M: She probably bored you to death in bed... I can just imagine her there with her awkward body and total lack of imagination.

T: Honey, can we please not go there?

M: Why - are you afraid to admit it?

T: People are simply different - no better or worse - just different.

M: If I didn't know better, I'd think that you still have a crush on her but you'd have to be mad to prefer her over me.

T: You're my only desire now darling.

M: Now??? Now??? Why on earth did you say, Now!!!

T: You're being petty and ridiculous - I adore you - you're everything that I ever dreamed of in a woman - I couldn't draw breath without you.

M: I'm so sorry for my stupid insecurities - I feel so ashamed - can you ever forgive me?

T: Come over here - For you anything - You are my reason to be - you're pœtry as yet unwritten - I'm the unworthy one - to be in your space is to be past the point of happiness.

M: I'm so glad that I still excite you a little.

T: A little? Are you joking? You excite me beyond my wildest fantasy - I get dizzy sometimes at even the thought of your fingers running a casual touch over my body.

M: Stop... you're embarrassing me... you don't have to flatter me.

T: Whatever else I'm guilty of, it's not flattery - if anything I've understated the effect which you have on me - I really am the luckiest man in the world - can we go upstairs now?

M : Yes my love...

They go upstairs.

ANALYSES: Well as you can clearly see day one has been as expected a spectacular success.

Think of my system as a start-up business - quite simply the more effort one invests in it, then the more one is rewarded.

As you also saw, Marguerite was willing to own up to some of her insecurity and as you also saw by the respectful, strong language that Terence used in his reply, which after all was scripted by Marguerite, that she wanted him to be both respectful for the mother of his child and unwilling to be browbeaten by Marguerite's own petty behavior - each of them will have derived much wisdom from the episode - learning toleration and also that a little uncertainty is permitted even a healthy thing provided the situation is dealt with maturely.

Decrescendo

Day two, as scripted by Terence:

T: Hi!... how's my girl?

M: Fine.

T: What's wrong?

M: Nothing.

T: Are you sure that you're okay?

M: I said that I'm fine.

T: You seem upset?

M: I read it.

T: Read It?

M: Yes - I read it.

T: I don't get you?

M: You don't know what I'm on about?

T: Haven't a clue - not an inkling.

M: I read that notebook diary thing that you're always scribbling in.

T: I can explain - really I can.

M: It dœsn't matter - go to her if you want to.

T: You've got it all wrong - totally.

M: Look, I can't talk about this right now - I'm too upset.

T: It's nothing at all - it's just some loose ideas I have for my latest theatre piece - that's all.

M: I wish that I could believe that but it's too real - it can't be fiction.

T: You crazy little beautiful confused woman - It's you and you alone that I adore - I've never so much as thought of another woman since I first laid eyes on you.

Decrescendo

M: May I read from it?

T: I'd prefer if you didn't but if you must go right ahead - be my guest.

M: 'I lie awake here as she sleeps deeply and I painfully realise that I'm all alone - she fills me with warmth and a profound tenderness but even as these emotions go through my head, from out of nowhere the thoughts of HER flood my desire - my wild, untamed other creature whom I let slip through my fingers - her being haunts me in ways that are beyond the scope of mere pœtry - her perfect shape, her heavenly restlessness, her almost mystical sexual presence which still after all this time fills the fountain of my pleasure to overflow and makes the communion of pleasure impossible within the arms of any other - Oh to wash her excess over my senses for even one more time - even the image dœs things to me I had not thought possible - nerves which I had thought dead were but dormant and ghosts whom I had imagined buried, rise again to walk the spaces I had perceived as filled by this other comfortable existence - I have been the prince of fools and must now pay the ultimate price - perhaps, one day, our ghosts shall together conspire in that breathlessness which we once shared - to my dying moment - this shall be my heart's lonesome burden'.

T: As I've already said - just a rambling synopsis for an over the top piece of romantic mush which I thought would make a good popular play - you know how women love that stuff.

M: Please be honest with me - that's all I ask.

T: Look deep into my eyes - do you really think that I

could ever say such things about another woman?

M: No... of course not... I don't know what came over me... I can only beg your forgiveness.

T: It's easy to forgive a princess - or should I say MY QUEEN.

M: I'm so lucky to know a man such as you - can we go upstairs now?

They go upstairs.

ANALYSIS: Remarkable stuff - truly remarkable - beyond even my expectations and as you can see the couple are dealing with important, substantive issues, they're not merely going through the motions like couples do in normal discourse - they're delving deep into the obvious insecurity which Marguerite seems to possess (and in my prior therapy this also was the root of their difficulties and he denied that he was in any way the cause and as the unfolding 'drama clearly showed she had simply misinterpreted one of his notebooks in which he had written some completely invented scenario)... there's really little need for me to monitor tomorrow's drama but just to show you how ingenious my system actually is, I shall roughly describe to you what in all probability will unfold and we will in fact take in the ensuing action. The 'bogeyman', in the relationship - the insecure woman's paranoid meandering has now been outed and 'embraced' by both participants and from here on in the relationship should freewheel - in fairness to her - she has immense regret for her behaviour and has shown both remorse and the desire to practically apply herself to compensating her beloved for her erroneous behaviour by acknowledging her weaknesses and has used her obvious idolatry of him as a further means of atonement.

Day three - Marguerite's script:

M: How's my honey bunny?

T: All the better for seeing you my dear!

M: What are you up to?

T: Just have to ring Greta over a problem Alison's having in class.

M: Go right ahead darling.

T: (picks up phone and dials) .... Greta... Terence here... about Alison... please don't talk - let me speak freely for a minute...........................Greta, I still love you, I think of you constantly... I was crazy to ever lose you... you're still everything to me... she means nothing...

M: I can't believe what I'm hearing... oh my God.

T: Greta are you still there? Just give me sixty more seconds... I love you more than ever... please darling I'm begging you to give me one more chance... I'm gonna hang up now and if you're willing to try again - ring me back in exactly five minutes... goodbye.

M: How could you do this to me? I'm numb... numb.

T: I didn't plan it this way... it's just that I repressed so many things.

M: What's next... you tell me that you still care about me... is that it?

T: But I do... it's all so confusing.

Decrescendo

M: Jesus Terence - spare me the guilt - that's all I ask.

T: Forgive me - I'm not worthy of your humanity.

M: God... I'm gonna puke with all this sanctimonious bullshit...

T: You see me as I am - exposed - naked - vulnerable - useless.

M: You took the words right out of my mouth - I'm walking out the door now and I won't return - don't say another word - don't follow me - just be silent for only in silence will you discover what you really are...

(She walks out).

ANALYSIS: I must apologise for although my system WAS indeed perfect, I had not factored the degree to which sly, self serving female cunning could and would come into play - we men foolishly assume that the female of the species will reciprocate our honesty and our openness - still it's of some consolation that the poor suffering spouse won't have to encounter that harridan again.

Further analyses:

On mature reflection I realise that my system is even better than I had at first imagined - I have rid that man of that blight of a woman from the landscape of his life - only a miraculous system like mine could have exposed that worthless witch for what she really is - my system unmasked her almost instantly for the manipulative whore that she is - I have saved him from a lifetime of wretchedness.

Decrescendo

Decrescendo

CHAPTER 17: LIFE - SUCH A SMALL WORD

Ihave examined your daughter Rita thoroughly over a number of weeks and put her through an exhaustive list of tests and analyses - from a neurological point of view I can find no obvious problem. You had said that you were especially worried about her apparent loss of memory but on this score again I can find no real prob-lems - in fact her memory seems to be particularly strong and her power of recall is pretty remarkable for a woman of forty something. She has recounted numerous tales from her childhood and her attention to detail is amaz-ingly accurate - both you and her brother Dr.Adolphus have confirmed many of the stories like the one where she recalled many of the items from the nursery when she was scarcely aged three. She is able to hold an intelligent con-versation on a wide range of subjects - such diverse topics as the Versailles treaty to the plots of many old film noirs and especially on the subject of the Titanic which appears to fascinate her.

Her ability to do mental puzzles and crosswords seems fairly unimpaired - she dœs forget the odd little thing but then again don't we all. I always think myself that if someone can remember the past then there can't be too much of a problem.

'Doctor in some ways you've eased my worries over my daughter but in other ways you've increased them - in a sense if you'd have found something wrong with her, anything, then I'd be relieved as you could then focus on a cure.'

'Elizabeth - I understand completely your situation and being a parent myself can empathise how we worry about our offspring but your daughter is almost certainly suffering from what we call stress or some associated illness - this type of illness is best treated by sympathy and time itself.'

'Doctor let me tell you a story... a few months ago myself and my daughter went to a restaurant for lunch - it was a Lebanese restaurant and we enjoyed a long, relaxed lunch.

One of the items on the menu was a dish called falafel and as I had tried it one time before, I urged Rita to give it a try and after much discussion she agreed to and she absolutely relished it - she even made a running joke over how to pronounce the word falafel.

This lunch was particularly unusual as I went to her workplace to meet her so we could go there together - this was the first time ever that I'd gone to pick her up at her place of work.

She had never tried Lebanese cuisine before in her life and only went at my request.

About a month later a friend called off an evening for a chat and in the ensuing conversation she agreed to lunch the following day with both Rita and I.

As we bandied about various restaurants as possible venues, I suggested the same Lebanese restaurant and it soon became apparent that my daughter had zero recollection of it at all - nothing rang a bell with her - not the ethnicity, not the falafel and not the unprecedented step of I collecting her from her work place - naturally I let the incident pass rather than get into some petty argument as it was clear that she had no idea what I was talking about.

But doctor, let me tell you that the alarm bells were ringing loud and wild in my head - something major must be wrong or so I thought - this just wasn't right - how could she not remember such an obvious thing whilst an old lady like me could remember it in detail.'

'My dear Elizabeth let me put all of this into perspective - your son whom I know quite well and have the height of respect for asked me to look into this little matter as quietly as possible and almost as a favour to him I did - I had no preconceptions and at the time didn't even ask him to provide me with any personal history of the patient until after I'd done certain basic tests - I brought all of my expertise to bear on the subject - your beloved daughter and was more than willing to diagnose as I found her.

I am not of course saying that her memory is perfect or her attitude for that matter and I am now aware of some little problems she has had as regards to her personality and outlook, etc, but I can assure you that my examination was far from cursory - it was long and probing and varied. The results are inconclusive only in the sense that you insist that I may have missed something and whilst I cannot claim to be infallible, I can tell you that there appears to be nothing much amiss with her. The memory is a strange thing and we are learning about it all the time but I honestly feel that you are probably blowing a tiny problem out of all proportion - if she was forgetting big things, important things, if she misplaced a bag with a million pounds or tossing a Rembrandt into the dustbin then of course I too would be very worried but a trivial incident like forgetting a lunch in a restaurant - no matter how excellent the fare - is not a serious enough lapse to over concern us.

I will of course give her something to relax her a little and to help her to unwind and will see her again in six months time and in the meantime try and forget these silly lapses and hopefully the difficulty will remedy itself. There are certain types of disease which affect the mind and the personality but these diseases which we loosely call dementia invariably apply to people far, far older than Rita. So on that score alone we don't have to worry too much as she is still a fairly young woman. Feel free to give me a phone call should anything else crop up.'

'Thank you for your time doctor.'

On the way home Elizabeth tried to heed the doctor's words but found it difficult. They carried no real solace. She knew him to be an accomplished practitioner of medicine and that he knew a thousand times more than she about medical matters but somehow she had a problem accepting his expertise as accurate - the gap between an expert and expertise.

She recalled Mark Twain's definition of an expert...

Decrescendo

someone from out of town... and this only reinforced her
sceptical frame of mind. She was also aware that we put
too large a burden on our experts and none more so
than in the field of medicine - How much did one have to
know in order to become an expert - more than the average man or woman, that's for sure, but beyond that point
who can say. Science itself was simply the best know how
available at that particular time - something to fill the
vacuum of ignorance and no matter how smart it was it
would almost certainly be surpassed by better knowledge
at some future date.

What right had anyone to dare question an expert in
their field of expertise. If we thought that the expert was
wrong but ourselves lacked the expertise to factually
prove it, dœs that make our suspicion irrelevant because
of its unproveability - what was smart and how exactly do
we define intelligence...

I am smarter than you as proven by my I.Q.... it's a full
forty points superior to yours.

I feel so ashamed that you can fit geometric shapes into
a box far quicker than I can.

Yes I can - yes I can.

And you can probably work out the square root of a
banana much quicker too?

I hadn't thought of that one but now that you mention

it...

Aged just three years I could recite the alphabet backwards in Aramaic in less than thirty seconds.

Truly remarkable, mind you I was busy at the time playing with my little red car.

Oh... I had a red car too and the unrealistic combustion engine really bothered me.

I simply went vroom, vroom, vroom with mine.

I also worried that the scale model was inaccurate in many features.

I loved to play football as a child.

Me too although I always wondered why the other seven year olds seemed unwilling to deploy more strategic thinking to their offence and defence formations.

As a child I loved going to the beach - building sandcastles.

I also - although I loathed the misinformation re sandcastles as I was only too aware that sand would make a ludicrous fortification and besides structurally speaking they were doomed.

I loved watching the tide coming in as it ran over my

Decrescendo

little toes.

I too welcomed the incoming tide as invariably it contained a member of the phylum cnidaria and all the different morphologies represented by the many species.

Did I mention how I played with the jellyfish.

I've just been talking about jellyfish.

Oh...

I come from a long line of intellectually gifted people - my father was a ground breaking inventor and my mother was a gifted engineer.

My ancestors broke ground too - digging ditches to help build the railroad but for all that I'm still intrigued by your ancestry.

Oh yes - we were involved with the sciences and technical and artistic spheres for many, many generations.

You probably helped build the hydrogen bomb?

Funny that you should mention that as a cousin of my mother's actually worked on some project or other in Manhattan or Tennessee or somewhere.

How reassuring.

Decrescendo

Yes, that's it - we were always to the forefront.

So your ancestors must have believed that the earth was flat at one stage?

Well, I suppose so - at some stage.

And that some women should be burned as witches?

Well - I think we all thought that.

And that people should be thrown to the lions?

Well actually that made sense because at the time lions in Rome were a bit of a rarity as they disliked breeding in captivity whereas the Christians bred like the proverbial rabbit.

Do you read pœtry?

Well naturally I respect the construction of iambic pentameter and the structured mechanism of the quatrain or sonnet.

Whereas I just like the wash of the words.

The human race fascinates me.

I thought that it would.

Decrescendo

The magic of evolution with all its myriad stages from single cellular life to all those complex creatures.

Yes - it's certainly heart warming to think that we may have come from a swamp.

Now you've really fired me up - the primordial soup, all those array of gases and chemicals buzzing about in total randomness.

Indeed - I'd say it was great fun sailing on the beagle - champagne, girls, music - the celebration of life.

Oh - I see that you're mocking - sarcasm is a sure sign of an intellectual deficit.

Well I am at least forty points inferior to you on the I.Q. scale after all.

Yes, you are - please forgive me - I should not expect so much.

It's not my fault that I live in a society that values such quaint attributes as character and humour and intuition and all those other non intellectual abilities.

You make a very valid point - one can only hope that in a futuristic society that measureable intelligence shall be prized above all else.

Decrescendo

So that my cerebral superiors would be able to make better decisions on my behalf?

Yes - just think about it - every decision only made after the cream of our mental geniuses were consulted - the average man and woman would benefit tremendously.

All those boffins constructing the best solution to every eventuality in life and all for my benefit.

Imagine the joy of it - only those of the greatest I.Q making the important decisions.

God, you make it sound so tempting that I almost wish that I could join in.

I take it that's your wit again.

Apologies - I seem to use it to compensate for my lack of intellect.

That's quite alright - as my intellectual inferior it would be rather remiss of me to expect any better.

Again you humble me sir as you combine graciousness with brains.

Think nothing of it - the entire gamut of my immense intellect is at your disposal - I only wish what's best for you - ultimately I have high hopes for the humble working man and woman.

Sir - you really are too much and besides I've taken up far too much of your valuable time already.

Think nothing of it my good man, for after all, your petty, trivial concerns are important to me as I seek to build a better world - one where the common man and woman will have a vital role to play - in fact my latest fascinating theory just gœs to show how highly I think of the common person - I have calculated that if a large enough quota of common workers were put into a room with a typewriter each and granted that they were given enough time they could eventually type out the complete edition of 'Origin of the species', without a single mistake.

Remarkable... truly remarkable.

Elizabeth's dilemma seemed unfixable to her - where to go after the best knowledge available dœsn't seem to help us. So she wanted to believe the doctor's words very much but they just wouldn't gel with her instinct that something was very wrong - something very sinister. In the background too she had the ever present feeling that she had let her daughter down over a lifetime. This was not just the usual guilt that a parent may feel but more a sense that she hadn't quite known how to be a mother. She wondered if the parent/child relationship was a two way one or if all the onus was on the parent.

What, if anything, should the child contribute? What happens if you somehow loved the child on that maternal/primal level and yet a significant part of you didn't actually like the child's personality - did this by definition make you a bad parent?

Were children beautiful? Were all children beautiful?

Was it easier to like some children over others - was filial love compulsory and if a parent didn't love a child... who exactly would?

She had thought these confused, contradictory, tangled things about her children many times before, especially about her daughter - she remembered very little about being pregnant with Rita - she did remember the year - 1931, but very little else - it was a thing, an inevitable thing and the key to it was to hurry it along with as little fuss and as little mess as possible. It was not a thing to experience, to feel, to interpret. The end product would be celebrated but not the journey along the way to its conclusion. Her long since dead husband whom she still missed so very much was kind and thoughtful to her during her pregnancies and if anything he was more interested in the process, much more than she was - that was easy - and he thought it a wonderful thing to feel her tummy as the baby inside pulsed with life - she did of course remember the pain and the fear - the total uncertainty - the primal nature of it all - and then the relief - immense relief - a thing done - a thing done well - a healthy baby whom you were entitled to name after some maiden aunt or other on your husbands side - task

complete - task just begun - unfinished task - unfinishable
task - work in progress - work in regress.

Some people adore children and some people cannot
stand them... I am neither one, she mused. I like them but
they could never be my raison d'être... my epicentre... my
all.

I am many things and baby can never be all things to
me. Yes, I love him. Yes I love her but I love all my family
because I was taught to love blood. Taught to love but not
how to love and not to know if in fact love can be taught.
Children are nice. Lots of things are nice... music... sea-
side... picnics... animals... pœtry and so on. How can anyone be guaranteed to love someone whom they've never
been properly introduced to and not allowed time for the
love to develop - love this stranger - your baby was born
at thirty seconds before midnight and by the time the
hands chime midnight... you must love it.

There are a variety of ways to demonstrate this love
ranging from a soft, ticklish rub on its little tummy to
running into a blazing house fire to rescue it should the
need arise.

It will have its own little personality which you may
shape and hone anyway at all which pleases you. There
is no belief system so absurd that you are not permitted
teach to it. No matter how insane your own ideas and
creed is, you are perfectly entitled to inflict them on baby.
If it's your own personal belief that God made the world
from rotten tomatœs... well then that's good enough for
baby... or if you feel that the rotten tomatœs made God,
well then that's equally okay and more than good enough

for baby. If you wish to tell baby that different ethnic peoples are like rabid dogs this is of course well within your rights or that the odd slap makes a woman behave better, that's okay too. You may teach it to respect their fellow human and to revere all living things but naturally enough you can indeed teach it to hate and despise anything that moves - if that's how the whim takes you. You can punish it as you see fit - within reason of course - baseball bats are not recommended but a thick leather belt is permissible. There are also a range of psychological humiliations at your disposal too - you can humiliate it whenever and wherever you so choose to.

If it's to your liking, you may crush its self esteem on a minute by minute basis or on a daily basis - call it fool, call it nothing or not call it at all - alternatively you may put it on a pedestal and elevate it beyond the stars - convince it of its angelic prowess.

The point is that literally anything gœs and obviously in this blueprint there are no criteria which you must meet in order to obtain the thing called parenthood - no exams to pass - no bar to jump - no lakes to swim - no knowledge necessary - you may not sexually abuse it but in case you feel this ruling is a little to rigid and impeaching on your rights and entitlements, it should be noted that in the event that you disobey this last dictate, we as a society will avail you of many opportunities to evade punishment - we will ignore the child's claims and protestations for as long as humanly possible and even then we will try our hardest to disbelieve the child and if at all feasible we will label the child itself as the problem and diagnose it as defiant, wild, maladjusted, etc...

So Elizabeth had her babies, two bundles created in a
moment but lasting a lifetime.

Sex.

A moment of pleasure.

I've heard tell it can sometimes last a shade longer
than.

She thought of sex and what it was - it was everything
and nothing both at the same time.

Pleasure and baby - no correlation.

Created by sex and haunted by its shadow for ever
after.

Born of, by and for pleasure.

Hedonistic by-product.

At least I was a wanted baby - my parents had been
trying for ages.

They weren't trying for you - they were simply trying
for A baby - any baby - did you think they'd have returned the baby from down the street if she'd been born
to them - they can't have wanted you specifically as they
didn't know of your existence for the simple fact that you
didn't exist - they're stuck with you and you with them
- no return address - care of God's pocket won't quite
work. It's true that they may have found your tiny, fragile fingers amusing even touching but that's because of
the vulnerability of those same fingers, not because they
were attached to you. They gave you a name - they could
hardly go on referring to you as baby or worse still, as

'it'. The name didn't suit you because it wasn't you - no matter what it was it wasn't you but you must try and grow into it. Anyway, none of this really matters as once the act is done it's done and it can't be undone and don't ever wish that you hadn't been born because that's a really stupid thing to do, for if wishes don't come true then what's the point in wasting your breath and if they do come true then why not use the wish to cure what ails you unless of course it's the very fact that you exist that ails you because there's no cure for that.

I'm you fairy godmother and this is my magic wand.

I can't believe it! Does this stuff really work?

Casting aspersions as to my ability to cast spells isn't really the way to go.

Sorry... I just can't believe my luck.

Didn't you know luck was a lady - lady luck and all that kinda thing.

Well I thought lady luck was like fickle, dark, even a little twisted.

Oh don't mind that... that's just a male thing... always making us out to be irrational, unpredictable and unfair... I mean who else would pick a deadbeat like you and offer to do this magic stuff.

Decrescendo

I'm so excited - I'll have to try and use my three wishes wisely - not waste them.

Come again...

I said I want to use them wisely.

There's no them - there's only it - one wish is all I grant.

There must be some mistake - I thought it was three wishes... in all the fairy tales...

Ah yes the fairy tales - did it ever occur to you that fairies don't write those tales - they're usually written by some bloke with nothing else to do - no proper job - no woman - no life.

I see what you're getting at - wish fulfilment.

Got it in one and besides why give three wishes to one person, much better to give three sad bastards a single wish each.

I can't make my mind up - with three it would have been easy.

God - you men are so predictable - let me guess... a big huge chest of gold and diamonds - a beautiful woman and your football team to never lose a game again.

Decrescendo

You're a mind reader too - but I really am stuck.

Let me help you out... I can provide you with data from the last ten years... 51% of participants went for UNTOLD RICHES... which in some ways is a surprise as I'd have thought that there were far more greedy bastards than that out there - 19% went for ETERNAL LIFE... which again is a lot less than I'd have expected as anyone living for eternity would be pretty likely to amass untold riches - 10% chose TRAVELLING BACK IN TIME... and again I'm surprised at this one being so low as again if you travelled back in time you could pick up a few Van Goghs for a few schikels each and make a packet when you returned - 5% chose to be famous.

Let me guess... again you're surprised at the figure not being far higher as when you're famous you get the bonus of being super rich.

Wrong smart ass - I wasn't going to say any such thing - what if you came back as Jack the Ripper - you'd be famous but you'd hardly be in a position to profit from the best selling autobiography - would you? Four percent picked to change gender and this one always makes me sad when I think of all those others who will never get their wish - 4% also chose to have a perfect body.

Isn't that a little low?

Decrescendo

Not really - it just goes to show that beauty or rather the lack of it has a 'price' - power and money and fame can transcend any physical defects - did you ever hear the words ugly and billionaire in the same sentence?

Can't say I have.

As for the rest there were all the usual standards... world peace... a thing called happiness... a woman who wished for her ex to be turned into a snake, or should I say an impotent snake... an alien who wished to return home and a man who was lost in the Sahara and just wanted a bucket of clean icy water.

Thank you for that rundown fairy godmother but I'm not sure if it made things clearer or not for me to chose - can I just ask you for sure if the wish really, really will come true?

Yes of course it will come true - no backfire, no ricochet, no miskick, in short no trickery, but still you should re-member exactly what a wish really is - a wish is simply the filling of an empty space and empty spaces have a knack of replicating themselves ever so quickly.

Okay... I wish I was Adam.

Adam... the one from Genesis... mate of Eve?

That's him.

Decrescendo

Sure?

Sure as I can be.

Whoooooooooooooooooooooooooooooooooooooooooooooo
ooooooooooooooooooooooooooosh

I'm Adam... I'm Adam... I really am Adam... I can't quite believe it.

Of course you're Adam honey - who did you think you were - you've been dreaming.

You're Eve then?

Silly boy - of course I'm Eve - who did you think I was...

Hmmmmm... any sign of God then?

He was here earlier - I think he said that he had to see a man about a dog.

Ha ha... that's a good one at least she has a sense of humour.

What's the joke Adam - he really had to go and see about a thing which he calls a dog - it seems that men really love them and quickly become good friends with them - I think it was an idea he had to give you a gift.

Decrescendo

Oh... My, you're so exquisitely beautiful.

Beautiful? What's that... I don't get it...?

You - your face - your body - your æsthetic... it looks so perfect.

I still don't get it - what's this beautiful thing?

You're the most beautiful creature that I've ever set eyes upon.

You're really weird today sweetie - unless you're including the serpents and the goats and so on, I'm the only woman that exists, so I'm the only woman whom you've ever set eyes on.

Oh yes - I'd forgotten that but even if there were a million others you'd still be the most beautiful.

How do you know - what if there was one or a hundred more beautiful?

... I'm guessing.

And besides if it just happened that God made a woman in this way which you describe as 'beautiful', why would it be a compliment to tell me so - it wouldn't be anything intrinsic to do with me at all - what's the opposite of this beautiful stuff anyway?

Ugly.

Ugly? What's ugly?

It's the opposite of beauty - the serpent over there is ugly.

He is? I don't get it - why is he ugly and even if he is what does it mean - how does it affect him or any other serpent?

Well he's ugly because he's not beautiful and I suppose it wouldn't affect him too much if he didn't know that he was ugly and it would only affect it if the other serpents thought that he was ugly.

And do they find him ugly?

I don't really know whether they do or not.

So maybe he's not ugly after all?

I suppose not.

Adam, this is so interesting but it's also very confusing - how is this beautiful defined exactly?

Well... it's hard to explain... it's a kind of visual and

Decrescendo

sensual interpretation... causes a type of inner delight.

If you'd never set eyes upon me and were sightless and then met me would you describe me as beautiful?

I'm not sure.

But I'd still look the exact same way.
So then beauty of itself dœsn't really exist - it has to be affirmed by some external source?

Yes - maybe that's it - a man and a woman find each other beautiful - it's natural.

That's very true - but maybe a man could find another man beautiful too - don't you think so?

No - speaking for myself that wouldn't be possible.

I like the shape of you Adam, so I guess I find man beautiful too, see - that's what I mean but I also love my own shape and the curve of my body and its soft unexposed places and have imagined many times if it would be nice to feel those parts in another woman.

God - you're a lesbian!

Lesbian?

Nothing - it's nothing - forget that I said it.

But you told me that I'm this beautiful thing, so why wouldn't another woman find me so as well?

Well perhaps she might but it wouldn't be normal - that's all.

Adam, what's this normal which you speak of? And why is it wrong for me to imagine kissing the tips of a pair of full, heavy, ripe breasts?

Stop asking me all these things - I can't answer everything.

Don't talk so loud Adam - I'm only asking about things which you mention - you used the word 'normal' - so I wish to know exactly what it means.

Normal is like a standard - the way most people behave - the usual way of being.

But as I'm the only woman alive it must follow that whatever feelings I possess as a woman are normal as they're the standard, as they're the sum total of what all the women in existence feel.

Perhaps, maybe, possibly.

You don't seem very sure darling but according to your own definition it must be normal for a woman to want to touch another woman in the same way a man and a woman touch.

I'm not sure - it just dœsn't seem right - it seems undignified, sinful.

You're really gonna be pissed at me now but again I don't understand this sinful thing - what is it to be sinful?

It's to do a thing that we know is not nice - that feels bad - that is against God's law.

But God made me and if I possess those feelings to touch another woman then it follows that he designed me in that way so it couldn't be against God's law - now could it?

Look there are things - lots of things which you don't even begin to remotely understand and they're too complicated for me to explain to you.

But...

Please don't cry Eve - I'm sorry...

But you said that I was beautiful... I heard you say it.

Please stop sobbing - yes you are beautiful but there are still many things which are too complex for me to show you.

Decrescendo

Well what use is beautiful if it dœsn't help me to know
things which I want to know - there must be something
in beautiful that offends you - what is it - tell me and I'll
change it....

No - you're perfect.

Is it my hair - don't you like its dark colour - I can
change it - I can dye it lighter for you.

... I don't mean to upset you - forget everything which
I've said since I woke from my dream.

But I like you calling me beautiful - I just wondered
what it meant and why you never mentioned it at all
before.

Then I'll still call you beautiful and I never mentioned it
before because I'm a fool.

Fool ??? That's a lovely word - you know so much - I
know so little by comparison - all this time I had been
searching for a word to describe man and couldn't find a
suitable one but you've helped me so - man is a fool - it
sounds so good to even say it - come over here my fool so
that I can kiss those lips.

CHAPTER 18: NO STRING ATTACHED

I *have here in my hand a magazine and on the cover is a picture of a woman - the blurb underneath her picture informs us that she is in fact the most desired woman in the world.*

The article inside further regales us with tales of how she is any man's dream date - these magazines are a trifle conservative in their usage of language - so in effect DREAM DATE translates to FUCK MATE - the necessary euphemism doesn't alienate all those respectable readers who spend their entire lives repressing all those primal urges - so those of you who may have sensed me to be ever so slightly misogynistic will be surprised to hear the following critique of my gender -

Why on earth would this technically perfect specimen of womanhood be their dream date as in best fuck mate?

How do we arrive at the deduction that simply because she has excellent bone structure, good legs and wonderful skin that it translates into the conclusion that she would be the best lover - the most engaging - more sensuous - more tender - more imaginative - sweeter - sexier - more lustful - more willing - more giving - more accommodating - more appreciative - more beguiling - more mysterious - more seductive - more enchanting - and I could go on and on. All of this is without even touching on the whole area of personality, charm, soul, depth, humour, and a whole host of attributes that are necessary for the perfect pleasure partner - we are being led to believe that human sexuality is a single dimensional thing -

meat - and not just meat - the idea that regular, æsthetically pleasing meat is of itself all that's required to reach the highest plateau of human sensuality - why would her pretty face make her any more likely to be sexually charged?

At times I can only despair of humanity - sometimes I run out of excuses and explanations - my reservoir of mitigation dries up - no matter how far I lower the bar they still seem to stumble - I am aware of all our limitations and all our profound frailties - I am aware how everything is in a state of flux - of how we are akin to Sisyphus attempting to roll his huge boulder up that indeterminable mountain - but even allowing for all and every contingency - what are we?

We still let babies starve whilst some have gold taps in their bathrooms of Italian marble - we deliberately make calculated plans to undermine others and we exploit wherever we can - each of us petty, vindictive tiny grains of angry dust - blind to the vastness and the coldness of existence...

Rich/poor - black/white - man/woman - young/old... the numbers add up the same way.

We hide behind a fantastical web woven through time by our more noble sentiments - Michelangelo's visual expression - Bach's strings - Satchmo's joie de vivre - Callas's other worldliness - Shakespeare's words - all these fragments of majesty deceive us into believing in the vision of the grand WE - this proud, beautiful, spiritual collective of worthy individuals - but of course this partial truth is bound up in lies too big to ever really unwrap, concealing the eternal lie.

Small, niggardly, vindictive, self-serving, narcissistic fools - this is our true badge - the one which we live yet refuse to acknowledge. Here is me moralising - the one thing which I

Decrescendo

despise over most other things because implicit in the moral judgments of the moralist is that he is somehow superior to the object of his sermon - no matter how much he may appear to align himself with the source of his scorn, it is still tacitly understood that by doing so he is indeed making the case that this alignment in effect removes him from the equation by virtue of his honesty and self awareness.

And what of me - my excuse is the eternal one - the one taken by the villain since time immemorial - a slight variation on the Nuremberg defence - if I don't exploit then someone else will.

This is what the man who pays a woman for her body says - this is what the thief who steals the unlocked bicycle - the coloniser who takes the birthright of a weaker tribe, the greedy guest who takes the last slice of chocolate cake - the list of suspects is long, almost endless and few names fail to qualify and certainly not you or I.

If you dare be so smug to think that I've maligned you by my accusation then simply take the RED BUTTON test for it is right on foolproof. There is a black box wherein lies a shiny red button.

By pressing the button all and any wish that you desire will be granted... press it and you can be on a paradise island with the partner of your choice for a week and your spouse will NEVER know - this is a 100% guarantee - press it again and as much money as you want will be spirited from a Swiss bank into your personal account and again there is no remote possibility of a legal comeback, none whatsœver. No retribution. Press it again and your enemies will suffer as little or as much misfortune as you desire to heap upon them and as usual, it will never lead back to your door... and so on.

What do you do? Do you press this magical button? Remember no-one will ever know - ever.

A scintilla of philosophy will undoubtedly help you decide - someone once said that everyone has a price and so we must examine this extremely cynical dystopian take on human nature - it is of course easy to sink it but only by ourselves using extreme examples too - I have little doubt that most mothers would not harm a hair on their babies head for all the gold imaginable - that is a given - but outside such extreme poles and back in the land where 99% of human interaction takes place - most have a price for most things.

'I am a proud woman who values her body and mind and I have immense independence - I have huge self respect.

So you won't sleep with me, a total stranger, for twenty dollars?

Of course not - what do you take me for?

A respectable woman who can't be bought by anyone.

Thank you, that's me to the core.

What if I said a hundred dollars?

As I said - I can't be bought by the highest bidder.

Decrescendo

A thousand...

Well I won't deny that the money would come in handy as I've bills to pay and so on but I just couldn't live with myself.

A million dollars.

A million?

I'll make it ten million!

Ten million dollars just to sleep with you once?

Just the once - it's a lot of money but I get off on the belief that human nature is both warped and corrupt - the idea that a respectable lady like yourself is for sale really turns me on.

There's no catch then?

Absolutely not - no tax to pay on it either and I shall confirm the cash transfer into an unmarked Swiss bank account before I even kiss your hand.

Actually you're not quite as repulsive as I imagined you might be.

Thank you for the back handed compliment.

And I could do a lot of good with the money.

Decrescendo

Indeed you could - help your maiden aunt move into a house without damp walls - give uncle Harry that set of encyclopedias he's been after for ages - send your children to a private school and even treat yourself to a mink coat.

A mink coat - Oh I'm not so sure about that - that's far too indulgent.

No, not at all - let yourself go - you deserve it after lying on your back all night with that cynical, misogynistic, exploitative, manipulative, tycoon.

He seems nice - perhaps I'll fall in love with him.

Why not... I hear he adores both babies and puppies.

In fact, although it sounds a bit crazy, I sort of think that I'm a little bit in love with him already.

Not at all - it's easy to understand - he respects your wonderful business acumen and as a tycoon he appreciated your ability to bargain hard and your ruthlessness in successfully closing the deal - he admires your logic in lying on your back to earn ten million in a few hours that it would otherwise have taken at least two hundred years of scrubbing floors to earn.'

You must surely be asking yourself what has put me in this mood of reflection as regards to morality and desire and

all those nuts and bolts of our behaviour - these quasi judg-
ments of all and sundry and here I can only apologise to you
my faithful reader as I seek to inveigle you into becoming my
ever fateful reader also - by the time you read this book, if my
publisher has obeyed my very strict instructions there will be
only 99 copies of this, my life's work, in existence and that's
assuming that none of the putative readers left their copy
aboard the number 21 bus or that no purchaser of it had a
frequently unfed dog and so on - forgive the eternal procras-
tination but as we are approaching a confession of types, I
feel entitled to rabbit on - as I was saying there will be but
99 copies published and why you may ask such an arbitrary
number - surely at least 100 and even then, why so few.

Well as you well know I have had a few strings to my bow
and as well as labouring in the noble profession of psycho-
analyses, where I spent my entire focus on healing and self-
lessly giving every facet of my being to the service of those
less mentally stable than myself - I had another career for
a couple of years and even if I hadn't of informed you, you
would still have easily guessed the profession when I tell you
that after psychiatry it is easily the next most noble calling
- yes my friend the wax that shines all manner of things...
advertising.

Rita sat on the sand and watched the waves - calm and
soothing - early morning dawn - she'd done it so many
times before - always the same and always different, both
at the same time.

She knew things inside her head and she didn't know

things inside her head - same as everyone else except that she couldn't separate what she knew from what she didn't know - they ran into one seamless track - track is as good a word as any to begin to describe it - for no word(s) can even begin to scratch the surface of what memory loss means.

A railway track - an endless railway line - going in many directions - some with station names clearly marked and others with names clearly blurred and others still with no names at all. You couldn't get off the train and whilst it continued to take you places they weren't the places which you wished to go... or were they?... for even if they were, you didn't know it - nothing was affirmed - on the ground you were floating around the clouds and were searching for an anchor but you couldn't use the word anchor for you didn't know that you were searching for it most of the time. Something felt wrong - very wrong but you couldn't name exactly what it was nor could you name it inexactly either. The most articulate thing about you was your inarticulation - this was now the thing that defined you to others and to yourself as well but again you didn't know it. The human mind a vast blackboard full of every kind of data, much trivial, some vital but each day something wiped some piece of it clean at random - if the piece wiped was the piece that contained the information that told you where you left your slippers, then that was no real apparent loss but if it was the piece that told you that you had a mother - well the implication is obvious.

And you tried so hard to stop the train, to reroute, to

Decrescendo

take some control over its destinations but the harder you tried the less control you seemed to have.

You were paranoid but again you didn't know that you were - all was shadow and patterns which you couldn't remotely decipher. You knew confusion though - it still retained a message for you - even in this state you sensed chaos as though it had an organic existence and one only had to draw breath to feel its moist hand on your neck.

There is only loss... each day we live we lose something - each time we open our purse, the pennies get less, each time the moon comes up, the day is lost but this loss is something entirely different - not gradual or seamless - no scale - no slow slipping - quantum leaps - leaps and bites.

Memory - everything is contained in that thing which we call memory - who and what you are and who and what you are not - every facet of your being is printed within those wires implanted inside your brain. These things, the petty and the grave, define every single aspect of the thing you call you and the thing that the wider world calls you as well.

I love the opera.

I'm not sure if I do.

My favourite colour is red.

I can't remember mine - or if in fact I even have one.

Decrescendo

My husband is called Boris.

Am I married?

I have two children.

I have one, no two, no three, no, I don't have any, or do I?

I love roast chicken.

What's chicken.

I've never read history so I don't know much about the Crimean war.

I still remember all the micro details about the Crimean war which I studied long, long ago as I seem to recall the distant past quite well but what use is that to me if I wish to know what day, week, month or year it is right now.

I love walking in the fresh fallen snow.

I used to but I forget that I did so now I think I hate it.

I'm a Catholic.

I'm not sure what I am - I may be an atheist but I forget if there's a God and if there is whether he still remembers me.

Decrescendo

I'll be fifty years of age next week.

I'll be twenty one or forty or one of those ages.

That was such a wonderfully sumptuous filling meal - I'm so stuffed.

I can't remember if I ate or not - maybe I'm hungry or maybe I'm full.

I love beautiful wild, coloured flowers that grow along the mountain.

I do to - their colours and their freedom delight me only I can't express that in words.

And so it goes - on and on - the list is endless - the loss interminable and only going in one direction - you are in a cul-de-sac and the entrance through which you arrived is sealed, invisible for now and for all time. Everything which you were and everything which you were not was contained in that thing which we call memory. Without it you are nothing. Think of all those little problems that you had when your memory functioned perfectly well - now pick a number and then pick another number - now multiply them and add a hundred or a thousand or a million, for it doesn't really matter which, and now double it to infinity - got the picture - this is now a fraction of the extent by which your problems have increased with memory loss.

Yes, you have a saving grace but your saving grace is one that only increases your pain.

You still remain as human - you can be sad or happy - you can laugh and cry - you can touch and be touched but your very humanity only makes the confusion worse - you seek order and explanation but there are none. You still wish to be loved but you know not by whom.

You remain a mixture of soul and flesh - but the inorganic is fuelled by the organic and your tank is leaking, empty, dry. You may still be loved but may not know their name, you cannot know that this love is not guaranteed for they cannot see your soul - it is wandering in places in which they know not how to look - they see a ghost, a shell, a wreck, a vacuum, a ghost ship whose crew have walked or swam or sunk. And you cannot wish that you'd never been born for you have no awareness that you exist in the first place.

The centre did not hold - you fragmented - a billion pieced jigsaw and from hour to hour you lose pieces - some hours it's a few pieces and some hours it's too many to count unless you're a mathematician but you're not a mathematician and even if you were you'd forget that you were. Someone told me that you worked with water and water pipes and even though you are largely made of water this will still not allow you to understand how to perform the simple act of turning on a water tap. If you had of been a mathematician you'd only have forgotten the square root of minus one and could find consolation that you never knew it in the first place. You had

thought that working with your hands contained some
element of nobility - you didn't use those exact word for
you were never one for poetry but you implied it just the
same and now maybe you wonder if the nobility remains..................................

....after everything
else has abandoned you - the stare, the fit limbs, the
strong capable hands, the sceptical mind, the innate independence, the love of planting seeds that you could nurture, the fact that you were beloved - for you there is no
reassurance save this... noble is in the bones and beyond
the bones too, in the sinew and beyond the sinew, in the
man and in the ghost of the woman too - this is all I can
guarantee to you - this is unstolen and unstealable - beyond the grab of memory and all other things and this is
not merely a placebo of clever words fitted cunningly into
place to soothe with artifice for I know how much you'd
hate that - this is the gospel according to what you were.

*Like all the great and profound fields of human endeavour,
advertising is beyond total summation - in its hallowed halls
the art of cliché echœs empty - no convenient label encapsu-
lates the depth, diversity, creativity and above all else, the
immense social influence it has for the good and betterment
of humankind. Like all great sciences (this is not the place
for the debate as to whether it's actually a science or an art
- but suffice to say it's either under the blessed wing of either
Newton or Michelangelo) it has had its mockers, begrudg-
ers, naysayers, doom mongers and misinformed critics - the*

*breadth of advertising's deep interpretation of life was bound
to alienate some and as consumerism increasingly becomes a
religion (rightly or wrongly) then the creative geniuses at its
upper echelons are inevitably going to take on the mantle of
high priest and high priestess.*

*So it was within this noblest of professions that I first
learned to interpret human beings. I worked there part-time
whilst still a medical student. There amongst all those humble, self effacing, honest folk, I learned how to aid and abet
people's needs and especially the desires that the individuals
themselves possessed, yet failed to recognise - as you see by this
it is already starting to equate with psychiatry.*

*We advertising folk are actually quite simple even plain
people - we revel in connecting with the ordinary man or
woman - that is in effect our mission. We take self evident
truths which have been bypassed by people, forgotten truths if
you will, and repackage them in a most appealing way whilst
all the time maintaining the essential, pure essence of the
message - MORE IS MORE - we shy away from the slightly
Zen idea of less being more and therefore it is unlikely that
Buddha would make a good ad man but even as I think of
this I'm aware that he did get his product to market very successfully without the push or should I say pull of advertising.
Mind you I still think that the religion market is still a trifle
undersold and by that I'm simply talking about diversity...
everybody's looking for something...*

*I'd like you to create an ad campaign for my brand new
product a belief system for atheists.*

Decrescendo

Let's begin by calling it a religion for after all that's what it is and already I feel drawn, so yes I'd be very interested in helping you as I strongly believe in such a clever product.

I'm thrilled that you believe so strongly in my product.

Strongly??? I don't believe strongly... I believe passionately.

Mind you, I hadn't figured you for an atheist.

I'm not but you see that's the beauty of your product - it's appealing to theists like me who've become disenfranchised by all those dusty old established religions.

But you don't believe in a deity!

If I may be so bold - you're approaching this from the completely wrong perspective.

I am?

Totally - think of all those lost aloof, lonely, sad alienated atheists - do you really believe that they sleep well on those dark winter nights - do you think that the knowledge that some old dirty bit of fossil is nine million years old really is conducive to any type of well being - mental or emotional or even physical?

Well I'm quite happy myself being a Darwinian.

Decrescendo

Darwin my arse - actually remind me of that phrase later on as it's pure marketing gold - truly inspired - as I was saying, Darwin had the consolation of being the first, the great innovator - he therefore had the buzz, the high, the sense of wonder of positing a credible alternative to genesis - do you really think he'd have bothered his arse believing that broken bone and cracked rib argument if some bearded boffin had unearthed it a century earlier - not a chance - he flourished in the glow of challenging the ancient, embedded tenets belonging to the rest of mankind - and by all accounts he liked travel - all those years on a cruise ship would give a man a lot of time to think - in fact it's somewhat surprising he didn't spin a better tale after so much pondering. So primarily we'd aim our marketing campaign at people like yourself... sad losers living in a single room without a spouse or children.

Do you think you'd have time to regurgitate all that second hand philosophy and science which enabled you to dismiss the quaint but consoling message from Genesis if you'd half a dozen kids running around the house? So in effect we would show all those pathetic losers that they can still hold on to the fig leaf that atheism is and yet have the structure, camraderie and consolation that only an organised religious system can confer.

I must say that I'm so impressed by what I've heard from you so far.

There's a slogan which I had intended to use for an entirely different product but as it seems tailor made for yours, I'm willing to give it to you... DINOSAURS NEIN DANKE.

Are you serious?

As an adman it's my business to always be serious about trivial things - just think of it - in one fell swoop we gain access to the disillusioned believer, those who can't stand animals, the loser atheist who had misgivings anyway over how such large beasts could really become extinct and that's without counting the resurgent West German market...

Thank you for seeing me sir - I realise how busy a successful ad man must be as he struggles with his inner genius.

Not at all - you forget how humble we are too for, ego has no place in our firmament.

I am thinking of starting a business - one which will be solid, respectable, attract a lot of lost souls who are seeking a path to walk and make lots of money and continue to grow after it's been established.

I see... I see - so you're also thinking of starting a new religion then?

Exactly.

It's rare to meet a new start-up client who has such excellent business acumen and such clarity of purpose - I can only

Decrescendo

salute you - in fact I feel I have an idea coming on - I'd hate to strangle my muse, so may I proceed with my inspirational pitch?

By all means.

It'll be based on some bloke or other who was born in the middle of the Greek and Roman civilizations -
This will allow us to borrow heavily from both of these highly desirous and credible ages.
He shall have a pseudo Greco-Roman name - something like Juvenides.

I like the ring of that.

We'll align him as a very minor figure - on the fringes - too proud and independent to follow any of the established masters - yet his noble, isolated being still sure of his purpose - God will of course speak to him but at first he'll have to deny God and even rubbish the idea - naturally later on he'll have a eureka moment - realise that he alone has been chosen by a perfect creator to be entrusted with the sacred mission of spreading the good news to the entire planet - he'll have been lowly born yet from good stock - only his refusal to accept the status quo - the easy way out will have alienated him from his society - he will be a man of few words but what words they'll be - his innate ability to cut to the chase - grasp the essential will endear him to a small yet loyal band of followers - his quotes will be sufficiently simple for the common man to grasp yet also diffuse enough to intrigue the more probing in-

tellect - we'll attribute quasi miraculous ability to him which he'll play down, for his humility is immense - he'll draw on all previous teachings yet acknowledge their incompleteness.

We'll initiate great learned debates about his birth and ultimate demise. We'll put out the rumour that he died when falling from a goat on his ninety third birthday. The sheer frivolity of this story will give it a strange, curious credibility that a more carefully crafted story would lack - people will think it's so simple and unromantic an end... it must be true. There's also the added benefit of using the number ninety three as being suggestive of some deeper mystical meaning.

The goat itself will have a name and have been a runt as a kid and therefore must have been an integral part of some pre-determined fate.

It's all very interesting but it's perhaps a little too elaborate for my modest budget.

Why didn't you say that you were short of change?

I am so sorry for wasting your time for a mere five hundred dollars.

Did you say five hundred... mmmmm... perhaps I can run up something quick for you... how about a man of letters who discovers God when...

Yes, a writer would be ideal.

May I please finish - after all we're only talking five

*hundred bucks - I meant a postman or mail man - he's doing
an early morning mail delivery - about five thirty a.m. on
a snowy winter morning and he's struck by a meteorite... no
that's a trifle too plausible... I've got it... he walks by a snowman and the snowman talks to him revealing profound, sacred stuff which is both idiotic and esoteric at the same time.*

*A snowman? Are you really being serious - isn't it a little
too flippant?*

Flippant! Me? Next you'll accuse me of being glib.
*You must understand how the creative brain of the adman
works - a seemingly ridiculous, mindless idea that appears to
have been whisked out of thin air by the adman is in fact the
result of much internal creative angst and intense searching -
don't let the apparently small amount of clock time in devis-
ing the idea deceive you into thinking that the idea is not the
soul of profundity.*
*So - yes, a snowman, for it fulfils all the criteria which I've
already established - the isolated outsider, the very personi-
fication of the wise, detached observer - his love for humankind has been so vast that he is willing to literally melt in
the rising sun to guide us toward a better way. He represents
both the tangible and as he has no heart he also speaks to our
craving for all things metaphysical and although we call him
a snowman he is in fact a snow person and the very gender-
less nature of him (it only endears itself to us as he) saw fit to
be the first really non-patriarchal religion.*
*And again as in the previous idea it's the very simplicity
of the idea that makes it credible - a simple snowman - no*

castles or kings or apocalyptic visions - the cleanliness of it
all should attract a certain market and as a proselytising tool
- it's perfect for the very young - we may have a difficulty in
selling it south of the equator for obvious reasons, then again
its mystique may attract them even more.

Its plain, quaint, naïve essence makes it virtually foolproof
and it's the fools which we're after, though that's not to say
we won't rein in a few of those so called deep thinkers along
the way.

Professor Young, I really can't believe that you've converted
from agnosticism to FLAKEISM?

My dear boy as well you know all my life I've been the
ultimate sceptic - the one who could dissect and discredit all
those foolish man-made belief systems - at best I found them
as fantasies of wish fulfilment and at worst as contrivances
of deliberate deception. Now in my twilight years, a time I've
spent delving into all aspects of mysticism and other stuff
that's far too complex to explain to a first year student but
suffice to say, whilst appreciating the beauty or the poetry of
some of these systems, my razor like intellect and my learned
scepticism invariably saw their many shortcomings - that
was until I encountered the FLAKEISTS... in them I found
a group of individuals who claimed to have found cosmic
balance and understanding of existence and all its paradoxes
- so naturally I anticipated that their ISM would contain
all kinds of gobbledygook as well as an explanation for every
question, but lo and behold I was shaken to my core to dis-
cover that they had no answer to any question - none at all.

Decrescendo

I thought to myself 'what a breathtakingly fresh thing' ' such profound simplicity' 'such a lack of contrivance'. Almost at once I knew my lifelong quest was at an end for I cannot describe it any other way. Everything just was. An alignment out of apparent nothingness.

Finally, here was a thing beyond the invention of man - a thing so pure and simple that it could only have been devised in the heavens themselves. Each and every snowflake which had fallen since the very first moment represented a human soul and on the last day each snowflake would again reappear and metamorphose into a great snowman - yes, a snowman, who'd have thought that this humble, touching, beloved figure was the epicentre of our entire consciousness - and isn't it just typical that it was literally under my nose during all those days spent playing childish games in each Austrian winter... for me personally, this was the clincher... the Godhead was all around me as all the great masters had so wisely predicted - I could have stayed in my own little garden and communed but with the arrogance of the intellect and the ego, I insisted on engaging in complex searches through abstruse fragments of obscure texts, always seeking to somehow stumble upon a complicated, barely decipherable word or two which would somehow unlock all the questions which humankind has asked since it first gained curiosity but like a sad, demented fool, all my scratchings were in vain... until... I inadvertently discovered the one, true, real purpose of it all - snow...

So my ingenious plan to print only 99 copies of my book will arouse great interest and attention - I will overnight

Decrescendo

*become a sensation - colourful magazines will want to
interview me and elegant ladies will hang on my every
word - well at least that's the theory - and I must confess to
a strange thrill with the idea of my being superior to even
Shakespeare and at the same time my book being so rare -
each copy will of course become priceless and in turn this
will enhance my reputation as a mystery man - an enigmatic
character - as one who shuns all publicity I'm bound to
inadvertently become a media star in time because of my very
anonymity.*

*Yes, I am a trifle uneasy at mentioning the bard's name - I
feel unworthy but find some small consolation in the awareness that all those stage and theatre people who claim to
idolise him would show the man only dishonour if he dared
to cross their paths...*

*I am Claude du something or other and this is my colleague
Lucinda who has studied drama all her life and is really
posh as well. So tell us why you feel qualified to apply for the
post of director for our provincial theatre festival which will
be seen by up to one hundred and seventeen people?*

*I have some little experience in said field - I have put my
quill to many a play in my time.*

Oh how very interesting - give me an example.

*I have written of princes and the ghosts of their dead
fathers - I have described the tragedy of doomed love between
two young lovers and I have drawn portraits of insanely*

jealous kings who fell to manipulation and other kings who would have swapped their kingdoms for a horse.

Very interesting I'm sure but we're more interested in your qualifications - things which prove your ability to stage a small, insignificant, rural theatrical festival.

Claude, if I may be so bold as to ask William about his background and where he obtained his college degree in drama studies?

Alas sweet lady, I have none - time and circumstance seemed to inveigle my entitlement to so do, but I do confess in moments of supreme arrogance, to understand the mien of human machinations as well as any... in my way I think I have added worth to the human canon of knowledge - before me there was no love letter or no addiction or nothing blood-stained nor eventful defeat. Before me there was no employment nor full hearted bloodsucking nor was there water drop or useful, zany exposure. No shooting stars - nothing was motionless or priceless or lonely or stillborn... I gave the world amazement.

That's all well and good but we really seek someone with strong qualifications - you said that you write then?

I have attempted to use ink as the Gods would use blood - to energise all those things within us... both the noble and the ignoble.

Decrescendo

Yes - but have you ever published your work?

No - I can't say that that was ever my desire or perhaps I was simply preoccupied warding of all those slings and arrows.

Well listen old chap... my advice to you is to take your literary output a bit more seriously... shop around... try and have a piece published in some obscure magazine somewhere, even one that no one reads because then you can proudly claim to be a published writer and that carries much weight with professionals like myself - and though I don't wish to discourage you in the least you will do well to remember that the written word is not for everyone and by the way that's a fine pair of gloves which you're sporting.

Thank you kindly sir - my dear father made them for me.

I say Claude, he seemed to take your good advice to heart.

As I always say Lucinda... all's well that ends well.

Decrescendo

CHAPTER 19: FORGET ME NOT

In the coming months pace did what it dœs - gathered. Rita lost her job due to her inability to function in the workplace. She couldn't perform even the simplest of tasks adequately. Her mother understood and apologised but she didn't really know what exactly she was apologising for. Her friends which had been few enough, disappeared completely. They felt confused and awkward. Unnerved. They wondered whether the problem was alcohol or craziness or something. She now had difficulty dressing herself properly. Her brother, noble as always, suggested a lunatic asylum and other such places. Rita wandered outdoors and got lost two streets away from where she lived. Sometimes she recognised Elizabeth but never the mother/child connection.

Rita was wired, energetic, wild. Anger and rage were her tools. Screaming at all and anyone. It was thought best never to leave her alone in the house - especially at night.

Tonight the woman who cleaned floors and had now acquired a name – Maya - was sitting with her as Elizabeth and Kate were going out.

With much trepidation and supreme scepticism, Elizabeth had agreed to accompany Kate to an astrologer - clairvoyant - gypsy - palmist - stargazer - magus - fortune teller - astromancer... take your pick...

Good evening ladies - and actually I'm a soothsayer.

Decrescendo

I'm an educated English woman of considerable age
- I've seen it all - I believe only in what's provable and
real - I tend to need empiric evidence and am wary of
Dr.Feelgood's cure all.

I can only see you as a harmless fool at best and at
worst a charlatan deceiving people at times of their greatest vulnerabilities.

I'm just sixteen and I've seen nothing but I've seen a
lot of it - I'm Irish and so I tend to believe in all things
superstitious - I will not so much give you the benefit of
the doubt as see benefit in your doubt. I come from a
land where we respect all things spectral. Apparitions are
particularly welcome. I seek reasons to believe in spirits
rather than reasons to disbelieve. I represent a trauma-
tised race. Our history is both confused and clear. In the
dark unpopulated parts of my land we prefer to meet a
ghost on a winter's night than an English soldier, for it is
safer to do so - call it wish fulfilment.

I agree... with both of you.

I too am part sceptic and part believer. I am a soothsayer because I find it soothing or comforting to admit that
the empiric world has many paradoxes.

I too have more questions than answers. I do not see
myself as sham or counterfeit but I well understand why
many do so. And although you must cross my palm with
silver, gold is not my primary concern. My profession is
held to ridicule by many who align themselves with far
more dubious creeds and schemes. In the distant past we

had respect. We lit up dark spaces when there was nothing else. Modernity and its obsession with microscope treats us especially unkindly. Other professions whose success rate is equally unproven bask in respectability and admiration whilst we languish somewhere near the freak show. How many of your economists accurately predict a market crash or boom?

How many undiagnosed medical illnesses kill the sick each and every day?

How many of your psychiatric patients are ever truly cured?

Your pharmacy shelves are heavy with pills and potions too many to number but to what avail?

My ability to divine accurately is both flawed and limited but nonetheless it dœs exist - if I correctly tell the cynic true things they will of course accuse coincidence and lucky guess - I earn far less than all those other professions - and I am the witch doctor - the exploiter. I speak to all those who fail to be enraptured by logic and reason. Those for whom rational thought dœsn't quite fit all the patterns and like all audiences, some of them are fools but some of them are not. Some of them refuse to bend to the data gathered by men in white coats - it's not that they don't possess the facility to comprehend their conclusions it's just that after digesting its contents there's still an empty space - an unsatisfied instinct remains which the periodic table for all its beauty dœs not fill - this is the seam which allows me push the door ajar and by the way pseudo science cannot dismantle an atomic bomb but neither dœs it split atoms.

Decrescendo

From your hand your extreme youth is even more apparent than from your fresh face.

You don't belong in this land - and you feel that you also don't belong in some other land.

We can only belong as much as we desire to belong.

You use words far too much. They are your greatest strength and also your greatest weakness. Words can be illusory for they can describe things which they cannot realise.

Words without actions are empty and hollow. Words can deceive far more than deeds.

You wish to be in love. You draw a picture in your mind of the boy whom you wish to love. Then you redraw it... again, again and again. One day he is tall then small, then rich then poor. He is a poet then he is mute. Blonde hair then dark skin. Strong and certain then weak and vulnerable. Love does not work this way. Love is accidentally designed. It happens.

You are compassionate but only on your own terms. You love to love and you love to hate which means that you apply that most precious of emotions to both love and hate.

You were loved as a baby and as a child and wonder how you can ever repay this - you cannot - no-one can... it is an unrepayable debt - it was a gift. You seek something of the eternal but this is only because you sense that you are finite.

Professor Gadree... you don't know me at all... you've been wrong with everything that you've said.

Decrescendo

Well young lady, I can only apologise... mind you your companion is not so sure of my failings... her eyes betray you... would the lady like a reading?

No thank you sir although I must admit that it was entertaining to listen.

Please Elizabeth, go on... not that he's very good... but just for the craic.

I must be mad... but okay.

I must study your hand awhile...

Its youthfulness dœs you credit as well as obviously showing that you've seldom if ever scrubbed floors - but in it I see things so I must warn you that you have neither to confirm or deny anything which I may say and if I offend you in any way I am apologising in advance.

Your life has had more disappointments than most - far more - your face and I guess your lifestyle says enigma and successfully masks it but the palm is far less secretive - it reveals.

At this late stage of your life when you should be putting your feet up - you face your greatest ever trial - I cannot guess as to its mix but I can tell you that it is unsolvable - for it there is no balm. Your hand shows confusion over someone close to you - and guilt, much guilt. You have not directly caused this problem - that much I can say.

And indirectly?

Decrescendo

Who can say - everything is indirect - life's events are akin to a chain reaction – fractal - the street we did not walk down - the book we read - the man we accidentally bumped into in the crowded market - the phone call we let ring and missed - who can say?

There is no blueprint for life and if there was the fine print would be too small for our fragile eyes/senses to read accurately. If Adolf Hitler had been accepted into art college would fifty five million people have perished between 1939 and 1945 - you tell me.

Love confuses you and you wonder if in fact you ever truly felt it... don't worry over the semantics... most of us have loved and in turn been loved in return... in some way or other.

Our problem is not love but rather its aftermath - the tragic realisation that love alters very little - life still exists before, after and during love - this is where our confusion arises - even the holy grail dœsn't mend all those broken things which we may have foolishly imagined that it would. There is no key to unlock those doors and besides even if there was we'd probably spend the remaining time searching for secret passageways - for this is what we are.

God he talked such bunkum... didn't he?

Yeah... he certainly did... he certainly did but the Persians do at least bring charm to the table and someone once told me that they treated their slaves better than the rest of the world treated their free men and women.

Decrescendo

It's a while since I last spoke to you directly and if you had been wondering as to whether something was up, well I can only compliment you on your powerful intuition. Last Thursday during a violent thunderstorm, my doorbell rang repeatedly. I answered it and saw a young girl standing in the torrential rain and to complicate matters even more she had a very young baby in her arms. I brought them in and put them sitting by the warm coal fire and fed the mother well and in turn she gave the baby nature's milk. It transpired that she was homeless, friendless and penniless and she pleaded with me to stay for a while. I agreed. Why, I am not so terribly sure... and in a way the reason is irrelevant as it is now a fact that she resides in my house. Unfortunately for her it is time for my monthly blood supplement and although she is but nineteen and something in me normally recoils at such wanton exploitation of youth... I have to admit that her fair flesh has set me thinking. She is truly alone and lost - only a life of pain and drudgery lies ahead for her. Again this is far from a perfect solution as that would still leave that miserable, skinny baby on my hands. I suppose I could leave it in a basket on an orphanage doorstep. I must give this situation more thought for it is fraught with difficulty.

It is now two weeks since my new 'family' arrived. Last night, to my horror, the girl (whose name I still occasionally forget) got me to hold the baby. At first it was strange and awkward but not quite as unpleasant as I would have imagined it to be. It smiles at me - can you believe that. It is now putting on weight and for all its tininess, feels quite solid. The mother remains detached from the world and from me also but curiously not from this infant. When she picks it up she is transformed in some way. Not in an obvious or an explosive but rather in a quiet yet discernible way. When the baby sucks from her breast or when it lies cradled by her scrawny arms it seems to fit perfectly as if the two bodies were carved by a brilliant sculptor - there is a thing which I can only call a connectedness, which in turn gives this wretched girl a sense of purpose that I would have thought impossible. A thing inside me is telling me that it would be a very wrong thing to separate them.

I must ponder a little bit further.

Six weeks since they've arrived and a further stay seems imminent as also dœs a stay of execution.

She - the mother has been telling me some stories, which sound both harrowing yet scarcely credible.

Her name is Maggie and she is not nineteen as she had first claimed but rather she is almost sixteen. She hails from an island that is allegedly full of saints and scholars but alas the poor child dœsn't appear to have bumped into too many of either. She claims that she was raped and entrapped by some man called Sheehy.

Her widowed father, a most pious man by all accounts was outraged when she told him of the incident. He confronted the said Sheehy, who naturally enough denied all knowledge and suggested he send his whore daughter to church and confession. He informed the police and to be fair a very senior policeman called to Sheehy's house to ask him to account but it seems that the policeman called on a particularly dark,

Decrescendo

moonless night and inadvertently trampled upon Mr.Sheehy's prize orchids - the furore this apparent wanton disregard for Mr.Sheehy's rights and the rights of his property ended up in no action whatsœver being taken against Mr.Sheehy. One wonders why he couldn't have called during the many hours of daylight and so avoided any remote chance of such an occurrence happening - but that's now in the past.

Anyway - a number of months later it transpired that the young girl was indeed pregnant from the incident and the pious father sought advice from a catholic priest who in turn arranged for the girl to go to some type of institution where she and the baby would be well cared for. On arrival, the girl claims that she sensed the place was not as she'd been told and if anything was the opposite.

She tells of a place where young women work from dawn till dusk cleaning dirty linen. All of these women are constantly referred to as 'fallen' women and the highly religious ladies who run the show remind them of their sins every other day. Some of the girls claimed that their babies were stolen from them after giving birth and sent away to some other place. A few older women claim that they've been slaving away in the institution for over twenty years and have also had their baby taken away many years earlier.

I do not know what to make of these stories - they barely seem credible - if it was a gang of pirates stealing babies and using the mothers as slave labour well then perhaps I could believe it - even if it was the last century, one could attribute it to all kinds of ignorance but in the middle of the twentieth century it all sounds a trifle far fetched - somewhat in mitigation the girl herself tells the story in a monotone without

*any apparent embellishment and she also doesn't strike me as
particularly elegant with words.*

After five weeks sir I couldn't stand the place anymore.
Twas so depressin.
Bleak.
Cold.
Sad.
*Everyone cryin' and shufflin'about. The nuns would say
terrible things to ya - an me thinkin' that they were holy
women.*
*Most of the women have terrible sceals to tell - too awful
for words they are sir.*
The nuns call them whores and tell them they're divils too.
*Imagine anyone stealin' a poor wee babby from its own
mother.*
*And the work is never endin' - loads and loads of dirty
laundry - all day every day.*
*One nun told me that it was God's way of punishin' me to
make me do this work an' she added that the dirty linen was
belonging to me social betters anyway - as if I should be glad
about that.*
*At night there's always one or two girls sobbin' - wailin'
almost like banshees.*
*Callin' out baby names like Michæl and Rosaleen - they
seem both crazy and sad.*
*The mother superior will sometimes come into the dorm in
the dark when someone is cryin' an tell her that God always
works things out for the best an will tell her that if she'd
truly cared for her baby then she'd be glad that it had gone to*

a good home an that only a false mother - that was the very phrase that she used - that only a false mother would cry over such a thing an' that she was really only cryin' for her own selfish, sinful, black soul.

And even in that terrible dreary place - I met a nice woman - she was a very young nun with a soft, kind face - she would speak kindly to me and help me with the baby.

She came to me bedside in the middle of the night and woke me up an told me that they were goin' to send me baby to some well off couple somewhere overseas - she thought it would happen in just a few days. I lay awake all the night an' decided that I'd take me baby an run - even though I'd nowhere to run.

I ended up near the docks and told a driver of a truck that I was desperate an that I'd do whatever he wanted if he'd only gave me a lift to wherever he was goin' to - he said okay it's a deal.

He took me all the way to Madrid - imagine - an bought us food on the way an didn't complain when the babby cried. When it was time for me to do the sex with him he said that it was okay an' that I didn't have to - made me promise not to ever do it again till I was married - and eventually I came here to Lisbon an' me aim is to go on to Fatima an say a special prayer to the blessed virgin that this nightmare won't come back again an to thank her for getting' me outta that place safely.........

As you may imagine this story confuses me and I have no accurate way of validating its authenticity. If it were true it would be an appalling vista and then again if it were only half true it would be still a terrible thing. Why would so many people abandon such a helpless little thing and all in the name of God?

And how could a self-confessed bloodsucker like myself see the huge immorality in such a scenario and these educated, compassionate, altruistic people answering a vocation from the highest deity not see the same?

Truly I am going insane - for it would not be possible for an institution founded in the name of a perfect, forgiving, gracious, omnipotent entity to be so devoid of goodness and love.

The girl must be crazy - for a moment she almost had me there.

Kate and Elizabeth and Maya spent their waking and their sleeping hours in the company of Rita. Womanchild. Dispossessed. Forgetter of things. Unretainer. Sometimes she lay in Elizabeth's arms... the forgiver and the forgiven - the forgetter and the forgotten.

Morning time was the hardest and evening time was the most difficult and the nights were the worst.

Dressing - such a simple thing to do - a smart four year old could do it - a well trained monkey perhaps. Dressing - such a complex thing to do - like all those actually complicated things human beings do with all that instinctive dexterity of body and mind take for granted - so many clothes leading to so many permutations - shœs on before socks maybe or shirt worn as jeans or blouse under vest or coat under shirt or jeans on arms or underwear as over wear and then there's shœs which may seem as if they don't go on feet and that's provided you retain enough to remember that you have feet or that you need clothes at all.

Then there's washing and the newly acquired hydrophobia - hopefully before the dressing.

What is soap for and whose body is this anyway and if you try and wash me I'll scream because my social prudery has been learnt at a subconscious level as well and it's not easily undone. If I wish to urinate then I will - I know not what sanitation is and it feels more natural to just go when and where nature intended. We haven't fully descended the stairs yet and Kate or Elizabeth or Maya or whœver will be exhausted and exasperated.

At the bottom of the stairs I see the hall door and I wish to go out - why should I wait for this thing that you call breakfast and even if you permit me to go out in that torrential rain I may not wish to wear a raincoat or hold an umbrella for those tiny drops of water hold no terror for me and in some way they may even momentarily inform me that I'm still alive... even in that fragmented way.

Yes, I'll sit at the breakfast table - at least for now but I may decide to stand again in thirty seconds and of course I may then decide to sit again - who knows - certainly not me.

Okay I'll have that thing which you call scrambled egg but even though I've eaten it with relish for nearly forty years I'll tell you that I've never tasted it before and will surely say that I loathe it. I'm not hungry but that won't stop me from eating double or triple portions and when I've finished I may claim to be really hungry and will almost certainly accuse you of trying to starve me. I can use my spoon and fork for now but any day soon it could happen that I'll forget this action and its purpose and you'll have to spoon feed me the way you used to - funny, I can still remember that. Breakfast's finished and it's only eight a.m for you see I rise early as I sleep poorly for I'm wired or even unwired - things falling apart - disintegration might be a better word - not that words any longer hold value.

It'll be a long, long day being within my orbit - unwanted carer - unthanked carer - unknown carer. I'll run you ragged and then some. I'm unhealthy and I'm healthy. I have superhuman energy. Everything that you do for me will be the wrong thing. Maybe you never truly knew me but even if you did, you certainly don't know me anymore.

The rains stopped now but I no longer feel like walking... then again.

Can I go back to my own house?

Darling this is your own house.

No - I mean my own house - where I live.

But you live here with me.

This house is a nice house but I still want to go to my own.

Decrescendo

But sweetie...

Tell her it's her house... that's it, reorientate her... that's good, tell her who you are... tell her how she has no worries - then tell her it every ninety seconds for the next hour, day, week, month, year and if she's blessed with good physical health perhaps for a decade more or even longer.

Let's watch a film - you know how much you love Laurel and Hardy. You know how you still find them funny - at least for two or three minutes until the wiring fuses again in some other direction. Still, it's almost nine a.m, only another fourteen hours or so to go until bedtime. Well at least she might have a good night. Then again she might not. She wet her bed last night. Perhaps she'll let us put a nappy on her tonight.

This was the way - a cycle of no return. Only death will stop its gallop and when it comes whœver's around her will pop - relief - relief for her - relief for those who tried to care.

The weirdness which you're feeling now in the presence of this person who used to be your daughter will never cease - its strangeness will evolve but it won't ever nearly lose that odd, surreal aura - you will have no points of reference - the world will pass you by because that's what worlds do.

All illnesses are contagious - you don't have to contract it to become affected by it - your daughter's illness isn't one that can pass from person to person but you'll be affected half as much as her as long as you dare care. You too will become a ghost of her twilight zone - you too will lose contact with most of the outside world - your peculiar plague will disturb people - they too will find this memory loss thing too strange to tango with.

Your world will shrink to nothing and then to minus - people will benignly compare her to a child BUT she is further from a child than is imaginable.

She is the very reverse of a child - the child is going in the opposite direction.

The child is moving away from dependency with each passing day whilst she is moving nearer to total dependency with each hour that gœs by. She has none of the delights or the charms of a child because she is not a child. For her there cannot be the comfort of the cradle nor will there be strong arms in which to float off to slumber. There will be no nursery walls of bright colours or blankets of soft baby cotton. No stories where handsome princes come to rescue damsels in distress, nor dreams that turn to magic by a single kiss of lip on lip. For her only the confusion of colour and the roughness caused by unnamed silk.

The only dreams will be ones of nightmare where dark empty castles are haunted by half formed, half living shapes and their endless shadows. And the castles themselves will not have solid well constructed walls nor ramparts nor keeps for that would be to suggest that blueprints for sound structure remained in her unsound mind.

In such a one's presence we can only agree with Lawrence's maxim 'the only tragedy is loss of heart', yet we are tempted to throw in an addendum... 'or loss of mind'.

Decrescendo

Rita's brother the honourable Adolphus was obviously an expert in all matters relating to human behaviour. His opinions were given loud and given often. In fairness to him it must be pointed out that his analyses of what was wrong covered the whole gamut.

'She has a personality disorder'
'She suffers from schizophrenia'
'She is far too narcissistic and attention seeking'
'She must have gotten a bang on the head'
'She enjoys people running around after her'
'She is pathological'
'She's fucking crazy'...
'She could do with one of Portugal's most underrated contributions to medicine... a lobotomy'.

CHAPTER 20: THE LAST SUPPER

Except for that particular one, people usually are unaware that they are attending a last supper. The invitation card rarely mentions such details. Elizabeth, Rita, Kate, Adolphus and his colleague, Roberto and an old school friend of Rita's, Joanna, were all seated the table. The elusive yet proven thing we call ambience or atmosphere was present - just right. Accidental ingredients... unknown recipe. Just one of those evenings when Elizabeth thought they should get together to quaff a glass and break bread - no occasion worthy of a card or a cake. Simply a day in the life. A thing to say we are here and we are now.

Adolphus made a toast and contained within his words were as much sincerity as he could muster. He sounded heartfelt and he sounded genuine for he was heartfelt, he was genuine. Nobody is anything all the time for it is not humanly possible to be so, even if one wanted to be. Nothing or nobody is that consistent. Hitler consented to his mother's Jewish doctor having safe passage even though the physician's treatment of the stricken woman may have been a tad less than ingenious. Stalin too threw the odd 'enemy' to the gulag when it seemed more a racing certainty that he'd have them slaughtered. If we picked a fifty year old man at random, one with a particularly violent, aggressive mindset and we surmised that ten times a week he beat or stabbed people and ranted

and raved and we added up the totality, time wise of his
monstrous behaviour, we might be aghast or surprised to
find that more than forty nine and a half of the fifty years
they had lived, they had not been ranting and screaming
and punching and stabbing and kicking.

So Adolphus talked and toasted, was generous and kind
and inclusive to all at the table. He acknowledged his
mother's trials and tribulations, the generation that lived
through two world wars and a rate of change that was
wicked and unprecedented, their character, their fortitude
and although he spoke in generalisations, for him it was
progress of a kind.

He was warm and even emotional to his friend and
colleague Roberto, who had it turned out been correct a
few months back on the night of his mother's birthday.
There had indeed been a revolution in his homeland. And
although for the tiny handful of people who died in it,
it was bloodless to the rest of the nation the only red-
dish colour which they saw was the colour of carnations
down rifle barrels and of course the colour of freedom
with its infinite palate. No matter how full the powder
keg it still needs a spark to ignite and only the ignition
causes mayhem. But tonight Adolphus had no desire to
dwell on politics yet if he had he'd have surely informed
the onlookers that all those who were now of the impression that Portugal was on its way to potentially becoming
some new Marxist type state would be rudely awakened -
hadn't they heard about Robbespierre?

He toasted Kate too and praised her adaptability, her
loyalty, and how even he on occasion found her a little bit

unique and as he did it occurred to her that this was now officially the first compliment she'd ever received from any male outside of her own family. Joanna the artist also received honourable mention as her paintings now sold exceptionally well. What did it matter that the work was empty and vacuous and shallow... it sold! And with a skill and sensitivity that Elizabeth would never have thought he possessed, he arrived at a place called Rita. These words he chose with uncharacteristic skill and delicacy. Inside his head the words rearranged themselves...

She is this and that and no longer the other but her pulse still beats. She talks a language which I do not understand but her lips still twitch so I suppose she must still make some kind of sense to herself. If a photographer snapped her profile right now, in this light, from this angle, against this backdrop, in that one five hundreth of a second, it would make a wonderful portrait of a handsome, thoughtful, engaging, interesting woman in her prime... the camera never lies.

He talked of her energy and her independent defiance and of her being her own person, of her differentness, how she was spontaneous, her ability to be in the moment - none of the words a lie - all of them being accurate when applied to the current Rita... oh what webs we first do weave...

Dissection of fruit and art aside the meal transcended the sum total of the food on the table - as all good meals should.

One of those all too rare occasions where everyone felt

comfortable. Nothing poisoned the atmosphere. All the mechanics of social interaction forgot their widgets and cogs and all present remained in the moment.

Roberto almost even made a case for empathising with the therapists lot...

'I've been doing this sordid job for nearly fifteen years... I can't begin to describe it... almost no one would believe it and those who did couldn't possibly comprehend it.

You may think that other professions deal with the flotsam and jetsam of society - and I don't doubt others have indeed their share - but it's miniscule, candyfloss, cartoon, compared to what comes through my door.

Every fucked up, misshapen, downtrodden, lost, sad, lonely, abandoned, deceitful, sick, pieces of what we loosely call humanity come to my table to sup - they pay me pieces of silver and then tell me their problems and expect me to wave a magic wand... to undo in a few hours what perhaps took ten or twenty years to come to pass.

Successful, respectable judges and priests who tell me how they can only get a hard on by drooling at naked pictures of small, innocent children - Rich, famous faces who are venerated by the masses and who cry about how nobody truly cares for them - Men who've screwed so many different women in the previous year that they can't remember half their nationalities let alone their names - bored bloody housewives with open cheque books who tell me that all they feel like doing is continually washing and scrubbing the already spotless bathroom and young men devoid of any semblance of charm or personality who whine about how nobody has fallen madly in love with them... Our profession continually has to invent new illnesses whether real or imaginary to give vent to the ever increasing amount of neurotics which we all as a species give birth to... none of my patients want to be told to dust themselves down and to just get on with the job of living - no sir... ladies and gentlemen... that is my lot.'

By some tiny miraculous token, Rita made a new friend. The woman who had never wanted to be a mother and who had never been permitted to fully be a child herself connected with the only child within reach, the little boy next door whose existence she had scarcely before noticed. How little we see and how rarely we observe. We seem to travel through life more as voyeurs than participants and even in the role of voyeur we seem to only notice the things that fall within the range of the lens's narrow focus.

You're a lovely little boy.

I'm a big boy.

Oh, I see.

I'm four.

Are you - four - that's a lot.

Yeah, I'm even more maybe four and a half or some-thing - how many are you?

Decrescendo

I'm... I'm not sure... I suppose that I must be a lot... maybe twenty one or so.

That's a big lot... my mama is twenty one as well... do you like our cat?

No... when they bark it scares me.

You're funny... I like you.

I like you too.

Do you have babies?

I don't think so... but maybe I do and they're asleep or something.

Do I have to play quietly in case they wake up?

I don't think they'll waken - I think that they sleep all the time.

That's funny that they don't wake up never.

It's better like that because the only time a baby is truly safe is when it's asleep - didn't you know that?

Do you want to play cowboys and Indians with me?

How do I play that?

Decrescendo

I hide with my gun and then you come into the room I say 'put your hands up injun'!

What bad things have I done?

You're an Indian silly.

But Indians wear such beautiful clothes and did you know that at one time they used to town the whole wide west?

They did? Well then we'll both be cowboys, here I'll give you my other gun.
Now you try and shoot me... bang, bang,bang.

She was dead.
Kate discovered Elizabeth's body.
Even though she did not quite know what dead was - she still knew that she was dead. She will age no more.
Dead - as progression of decay, it hung limp. It had a sound and the sound was mute.
Too inevitable a thing to send chills to all its heir's as they waited in their turn. Snap past the point of break where there had already been stretch.
The body lay there, crumpled for the moment and still and quiet for all time. She was tempted to think that the inanimate things around the room suggested the merest hint of life as if to mock. What sparked their derision she could not say... life... death?
The frailty of all things living - only life can cease.

Decrescendo

She remembered how she had felt on a particular day
as she had walked out of the gallery in London at closing time. The sense of melancholy that had enshrouded
her, the sadness at leaving... the sensations, the colour
and the beauty. When the door closed behind her as the
last footsteps faded, what had been animated then blew
inanimate. Alone again. Life into death - metamorphose
in reverse. A notion had passed through her head of putting a Van Gogh into a cab and driving slowly around
the streets of London and attempting to observe things
through the eyes of a dead artist and wondered too if
even a dead Vincent might still see more than she herself
could.

The absurdity of the metaphor didn't deter her as she
liked all metaphors - she liked how they could be instantly assembled and just as quickly disassembled. Something
from nothing - nothing out of something.

Colour was life and death was colourless.

Colour moved - death didn't.

Dead bodies, she thought, were strange objects - scary
but curious. They were profoundly important and yet they
had no value whatsœver and this valueless state simply
increased as decomposition set it. Increased in valueless-
ness?

They could go no further down any given road - they
could retain no position on paths already travelled.

Just before entombment or cremation there would be
this weird ritual whereby the body was elevated to a sacred plain - its lumpen congealment of listless nerve ends
took some sacrosanct place in all our symbolic thoughts

and our practical prayers too.

Nothing lasts forever but sometimes it would be nice to receive a slightly bigger slice of the cake - just a wee bit more - another century or two or at least a few decades or failing that even a measly year or two more - how could such a vast bank of time as eternity dish out such incredibly meagre portions of such a desired commodity - eternity was mean and petty - even grudging - what grand design could possibly be discomfited by a few more paltry crumbs of time.

At the graveside amongst the small crowd Kate alone cried and cried and cried. Irreplaceable. So this was what the thing called love was. This was what was meant by loss. All those silly things which were meant to convey the rites of passage from childhood to adulthood were trivial and wrong - there was only one gateway of entrance and it was the understanding that this thing called death was a living thing after experiencing it closely, nothing could ever be quite the same again.

She had not known that she possessed so many tears - wet tears, wild tears, blinding tears. She cried for Elizabeth, she cried for herself, she cried for her lovely brother and she cried for the whole world.

Flowers and black clothed people - serenity, dignity and through it all she thought how beautiful the graveyard called Prazeres looked - this would be a place to bury a pœt.

This was the place where reality and unreality met in a head on collision that emitted no sound - save the sound of a single girl's tears.

Decrescendo

Surreal wave lending spurious credence to the claim that death was simply a stage, a passage, a transferrance to some unspecified plateau - one where harmony and perfection lived hand in hand - a place where infinite wrongs done unto countless people would somehow be undone, rectified, mended. The logistics of this were of course beyond her comprehension - the permutations of who did what to who and why were entangled beyond measure - only a mind with celestial bent could hope to engage its weave - how would this God or any other determine each and every micro deed accurately, fairly and even more importantly... to the total satisfaction of each and every plaintiff - would this almighty being take full account of the dehumanising effects of social conditioning - of impulses genetically spawned - what of those who flirted with evil all their lives and then on stony deathbeds proposed a marriage of contrition and found a halo to fit - was each human soul redeemed by the very essence of being flesh and blood and therefore would all human movement both physical and mental since life began be entered into some huge mathematical equation unsolvable to an infinity of Einsteins yet miraculously completed in some instant of arithmetic divinity - no winners - no losers - just a sisterhood and brotherhood of participants.

No what was - no what might have been - simply what is.

Negativity no more - a holy glow to shine under, above and beyond... rest for ALL those confused souls - avenging angels put gently to sleep for all time yet to come.

And she thought of reincarnation - that's what we'd need - a chance to go around the course again but only if the memory of past remained - reminders of why and why not.

Kate sat in her room reading aloud but she couldn't concentrate although she badly wanted to finish the Lisbon vampire - it was a little strange that Elizabeth who had read so many novels should recommend this one above all others. But she kept arriving back at the point of loss. She wanted so badly to write a letter to her mother as she had things to ask her but she wasn't at all sure what those things were. She loved her mother so much and was confused over the love she had felt for this other woman. She sought to put the two loves into some type of context but was unable to do so.

Out of respect for her mother she couldn't possibly equate the two loves but she wasn't sure as to why this was so. If she told anyone that she loved this dead old lady as much as she loved her mother she knew that they would instinctively think of how she mustn't love her mother so much but she knew that this wasn't so and besides she didn't think of Elizabeth in mother terms at all. Why did everything have to be measured - what was our obsession with quantity - and why was more always better?

Her thoughts wandered back to the evening when Elizabeth had talked to her about love and about how she didn't believe in what people referred to as unconditional love.

She had called it a most ridiculous concept - positively bizarre, she had said.

Decrescendo

As things unfolded she would stay in Lisbon eight
more years - looking after Rita - at Adolphus's request
- he too seemed more than a little changed - he told
her that his world would never be the same again - and
wondered why he had never guessed this before - he
told Kate of some theory or other he had about happiness and how it occurred to him that it could only be
retrospective - and he admitted that this was of course
an unusual paradox as we tend to only associate it with
the now but how he felt this was wrong and that the
past was our oasis - it was constant and unchanging and
that when we revisited it we achieved a profound sense
of comfort because it was a sanctuary - a place where
nothing strange could happen - a map whose boundaries were already carved in stone for all time - and even
the bad things that may have occurred didn't perplex
or upset us quite so much because the very fact that
we were in the now meant that we had navigated past
travails successfully.

Rita remained as shadow but even shadows are in a
certain sense alive... as long as they still move.

There would be tears too when Rita died - tears of
sadness for a half lived life that was itself only half lived
but also tears of relief and the realisation that there
are indeed worse things than death and a knowing that
there are many ways to be buried alive.

She now knew too that although she had come from
only one place - she was no longer of any place - that
there are only spaces and the people who inhabit them
and even then they only inhabit them by accident or

chance and no matter how high we build the stone wall it still comes tumbling down.

I am still troubled... something about the girl strikes me - I can't exactly define it - but I have seen my share of liars and my share of lunatics and she dœsn't seem of either to me.

Her story is only dramatic when interpreted by others who naturally enough are upset by the alleged events but when she herself tells it, she dœs so without drama - in a very matter of fact way - stripped of all pœtry and within her tale there is a type of balance - it reminds me of how prisoners on arrival at Aushwitz would be processed in such a routine way - almost ordinary - being given absolutely no indication of the total horror and hell that awaited them.

Which reminds me of a story that I read the other day - the writer of the piece wondered about what the statute of limitations should be for minor war criminals - well I'll tell him what - if a proven war criminal was blowing out the candles on his one hundredth birthday cake in the nursing home - I'd force the entire cake down the bastard's throat in one swift go - candles and all - one, two... ninety nine... a hundred.

This is my complete opinion on the subject.

Maggie will be sixteen tomorrow - and baby Kate will be baptised at her mother's insistence of course - they have been six months with me now and I can easily say that they've been the happiest months of my life - corny but so. Something within me has changed. And before you ask... no... I am not in love with this young girl. But perhaps I do love her. I am aware of the problems of love and loving. Love is unquantifi-⊠

*able. Love has no scale. Love has no ceiling. Love may be
carved from granite or else it can be sculpted from fairy dust.
It is all things and also all the opposite things too.*

*It can enslave and liberate us both at the same time. It
can be organic and it can also be metaphysical and these
are simply the tiniest example of what it is or can be for
its book is never finished - so it must never be closed. I am
slowly convincing her that she was not bad and did not do
a bad thing - a baby's birth can never be a bad thing - its
timing and circumstance may be less then perfect but this is
no reflection on the baby and nor is it any indictment on the
one who carries it.*

*We may use rules and protocols in two distinctive ways -
one is to use them to punish people and the other is to fa-
cilitate or empower people - and how we choose to use them
is the mark of who and what we are. Who is so wise to
always know who should be judged and when they should
be so judged. Who on earth would ever possess the necessary
humility and perfection to put any other being under the
microscope of moral scrutiny. All those anti-clerical feelings which I thought long since laid to rest are resurfacing
with each passing day. Perhaps I too should seek atonement
for my sins - but atonement from who? A peasant girl who
eighteen months previously was scrubbing floors some place
or other has acted as a catalyst within me - he who thought
he had aspects of existence all figured out - such delusion.
Such arrogance. She has things which I shall never possess.
Things which I could not find in books. I see now that there
is no inevitable connect between age and wisdom - none.
Age simply permits us to mask our stupidity. The wrinkled*

*brow allows us to feign sagacity and comprehension. Life
is unwinnable but age allows us to reduce our world to the
size of our own personal limitations and fears. That old
bearded man in the corner with the seer like countenance is
as much a fraud as the young poseur at the next table. Each
in control of the 'his world' which he inhabits and its planet
where he personally sets the boundaries. He can include and
exclude what he feels to be important, threatening, beautiful, etc... Each a King over all he surveys. Each wary over
the other's dynasty. The young pretender wearing a cloak of
ignorance with pride and the older one defending the ancient
regime with all its inequities.*

*Good evening my young friend and may I join your table as
the place seems pretty crowded.*

*Yes, indeed pops - this place is becoming too popular for my
liking - losing its feel.*

Have you been coming here long?

*Over six months - since I've been twenty one - but it's
changed so much since those days - and you?*

*Some fifty odd years I guess - since I was your age - it used
to be a wonderful place in those days.*

I'll just light up this Gitane if you don't mind.

Well I must confess that I find cigarettes a trifle repulsive but as I'm about to have a pipe of tobacco just now, I can hardly object.

I find pipe tobacco a little too drab myself - old fashioned, if you will whereas this slim, elegant Gitane which has been sealed to retain maximum freshness seems to offer me so much more.

Each to his own - personally speaking I find the long, languid puffs from the pipe help me think a little more deeply about important issues pertaining to the human condition - it takes a little more effort of course than the cigarette but its usefulness as a contemplative aide makes it all worthwhile.

My cigarette reflects some part of my personality and its very independence mirrors my own very unique individualism - adds to my sophistication somewhat.

What's that book that you're reading - I'm an avid lifelong reader myself - all the classics naturally enough - Shakespeare, Dickens, Shaw, Proust, Pœ, Flaubert and of course the Russians and not forgetting Dante, Sophocles, Milton and all those obvious ones.

I suppose I respect all those ancient writers you mention but they've really had their day - nowadays one is looking to capture the zeitgeist.

Ah you speak German then?

Decrescendo

No.

And the book which you're reading is?

Lord of the rings.

By?

Oh pardon my manners - I thought you'd probably have read it for it's a few years old now - it's by a chap called Tolkien.

Did you say Tolstoy?

No - T O L K I E N... it deals with the peace being shattered by a war.

That is Tolstoy.

No not Tolstoy - whomever he may be - I suppose he writes in some archaic style that was perhaps useful when we were a less sophisticated people.

You seem to enjoy usage of the very word sophisticated.

Well observed old timer - I do indeed - it seems to fit perfectly my cool, modern outlook - my lack of simplicity - I'm sure I read some place that it also implies wisdom.

That it dœs... it surely has a Greek etymology... don't you

Decrescendo

think ?

Now that you mention it... it dœs indeed... great people those Greeks - that they were - hugely influenced by the Romans of course.

So you appear to think - this Tolkien that you're reading - I suppose he draws characters full of all the diverse aspects of human nature?

In a way... yes... and in another way he's beyond all that endless human drama with its repetitive insight into the lives of all those nobodies - he paints a bigger canvas as it were.

So you prefer writers who go past the trivia of the ordinary individual's little microcosm?

I do - I find I need to reach for the stars.

Perhaps that's why the Greeks leave you so cold - they're simply inferior imitations of the Romans.

That must be it... yes... may I ask you good sir what's your profession?

Didn't you just hear the waiter call me engineer?

Pardon... I did indeed - so many engineers in such a small city - what dœs an engineer do then?

Decrescendo

What does an engineer do?? Why, engineer stuff of course.

An ancestor of mine was an engineer - it was a while back mind you - worked on a project in Egypt for the pharaoh - building a huge stone triangle.

That must have taken considerable ingenuity.

Well actually they took a simple short cut - they just built a huge square cube and cut it in half - got two for the price of one as it were.

Remarkable - still nothing surprises me about my fellow engineers and may I be so bold as to ask you your own area of study or particular interest?

Well you too may have heard the waiter address me as doctor just now?

Indeed I did sir.

So naturally I do a lot of doctoring stuff.

That's remarkable as I coincidentally had a relative a doctor some time back. In fact you may be familiar with his work as he was to the forefront as a pioneer - Frankenstein was his name.

It seems to ring a bell - if memory serves correct, his ideas were well before their time and were quite misunderstood.

Decrescendo

Yes they were - he suffered the fate of all true geniuses.

I also recall a film about his life in which the ignorant rabble with their half baked reactionary response to the great doctor attacked and mocked him and his assistant... a Dr. Igor Watson.

I can't confess to ever seeing it as I'm not a fan of popular culture but it sounds about right.

I understand your reluctance to embrace this cinema fad as I too have my reservations and am most circumspect about my viewing - usually only bothering with films in a language I scarcely comprehend that have poor storylines and vague meaning and a bit of irrelevant symbolism chucked in.

Indeed you speak my language - what's the world coming to when photography is considered an art form - how hard can it be to click a button on a camera - after all couldn't a monkey accidentally take a photograph that would win a competition amongst all these elite photographers?

Or if the camera was placed in an exact spot a banana falling from a tree could achieve the exact effect?

Exactly.

In the end my difficult decision was like many such decisions, incredibly easy. I have sent mother and child away to a better life. No this is not some dark allusion to the fact that they are floating in the river Tejo - I may be a little evil but I am not bitter and twisted. I have returned them to Ireland - not South but North. An old friend of mine from my medical days has a widowed son in law in Belfast - a place called the Falls road, I think. By all accounts he is a bright, decent man of about twenty years of age - not terribly hard working but apparently with a heart of gold.

He has a small house and was affected by the young girl's plight and has promised room and board to mother and baby for as long as they wish it - he writes poetry which may be a good thing for only the romantic soul seeks to rearrange all those badly misplaced blocks... the ones badly laid end to end since before the world was made.

THE END.

There is a thing called home but it is far more transient than we sometimes acknowledge it to be - home is indeed where the heart is.

THE END

Gerry Brennan is a Dublin born poet who has lived in Lisbon, Portugal for the past number of years. In this, his first novel, he is attempting to break away from the traditional prose novel and instead infuse his work with poetry, dramatic dialogue as well as prose, whilst still maintaining a narrative.

Pski's Porch Publishing was formed July 2012, to make books for people who like people who like books. We hope to have some small successes.

www.pskisporch.com.

Pski's Porch

323 East Avenue
Lockport, NY 14094
www.pskisporch.com